Why Me?

By

Mary C Hughes

The moral right of Mary C Hughes is to be identified as the author of this work and has been asserted by her in accordance with the Copyright, Designs and Patents Act of 1988.

All rights are reserved, and no part of this book may be produced or utilized in any format, or by any means, electronic or mechanical, including photocopying, recording or by any information storage or retrieval system, without prior permission in writing from the author (publisher).

Copyright © 2024 Mary C Hughes

All rights reserved.

ISBN: 9798391647386

DEDICATION

I dedicate this book to Amy and Owen, who have inspired me since the day they were born. They are both intelligent and beautiful inside and out. May you always dream big and follow your heart.

Cover Illustration by

Elroy P Hughes

Chapter 1

Evelyn was feeling extremely lucky this evening. Every time she thought about it, her heart skipped a beat and sent her head into a spin with excitement. The jackpot was over £800, a small fortune to most of us mere mortals. It must have been well over two years, if not more, since it was this high. Tonight is going to be her night for sure, she could sense it in every fibre of her body. There was no other way of explaining this feeling she had. She could not find any words to describe it truly, it is a knowing that is as clear as if she had seen it in a crystal ball. Normally, when the jackpot was this high, the hall would be bursting to the brim! More often than not, there would not be enough seats, leaving any late comers sitting on the floor or standing up for the entirety of the evening. With the jackpot this big you would see faces that you wouldn't have seen since the last time there was a large pay-out. Every Tom, Dick and Harry comes out of the woodwork when the pot is ripe for the taking, especially this close to Christmas as everyone is looking for a few extra bob. Oh, there is nothing worse than when one of these yolks wins. The good old regulars would be extremely angry, cursing them to the high heavens and back again as they fired their book to the ground, nearly dancing on it in temper. It is a wonder how they ever managed to get out of the door with all the hex's the old regulars placed on them. We often wondered how they

Why Me?

made it out of the hall at all - if looks could kill then certainly they would drop dead on the spot. The evil glare would be seen as soon as they released the words 'bingo' out of their mouth. You could nearly hear a pin drop as the regulars pray to the Virgin Mary for it to be a false alarm. They always look so smug going out with the winnings in their pocket - it is as if they were laughing at the rest of us saying look at me, see you need not come and freeze your butts off week after week wasting your money. They have some neck turning up, more like a death wish if you ask me anything. Evelyn might be brazen, but she wouldn't have the guts to turn up for one or two nights of the year only to disappear until the next jackpot.

Hopefully, there wouldn't be too many people there tonight, as it is only the complete nutters like us that would venture out on the worse night in living history. The Irish weather service had advised against all unnecessary travel, so we were surprised that the bingo hadn't been cancelled. Evelyn would go mad if she got there only to find the place closed. Both Evelyn and Marion laughed at their craziness, Evelyn's bump wobbled so much that her sides began to hurt. She felt as if she would throw up at any minute if she didn't stop laughing. "It will be worth it when I win the jackpot", she screamed, "I can feel it in every fibre of my body she said to Marion." To which Marion responded, "As long as it's not your waters you are feeling we will be all right, but can you please stop with all that touchy feely crap" and she roared with laughter.

"Ha Bloody ha, Mar, have you ever thought of being a

Why Me?

comedian?"

"Sweet Jesus", shouted Marion, as she tried to keep control of the car. "These roads are a death trap. They are a joke on a normal day, they are not for the faint-hearted that's for sure, but tonight, in this weather they take on a life of their own. I have no idea how they can even call it a road, as it must have been built for the ass and cart. One thing for sure, they were not meant for cars." She ranted on, "The locals had launched so many campaigns to the council over the years to improve the roads about you could see by the state of them the efforts had fallen on deaf ears time after time." "They will more than likely wait until someone gets killed on them before they do anything - it seems to be the only way anything ever gets done around here. It's not unusual for a tourist to come a cropper on them." During the summer, the farmers had a full-time job pulling them out of the ditch. Even the locals are known for saying the rosary as they grip the wheel as they prepare for the dangerous bends ahead, praying that there would be no cars coming in the other direction especially a tourist who would not realise that the road is a two-way system. One slight touch of the wheel in the wrong direction, you could end up in the sea. Throughout the summer months the roads are full of tourists cycling and walking as for the drivers they are themselves unaware of the dangers as they are enthralled by the view, more than half of them forgetting that we drive on the left hand-side in this country. There has been many a night when even a local farmer has fallen off their bike on the way home from the pub in the early hours. With a skin full of drink without a care in the world and then they would find themselves spending the night clinging to the edge of the ditch not only to stop themselves from falling into the sea but also for any bit of warmth they could get as the relentless winds that rolled in from the wild Atlantic would take your breath away. It is just as well their bellies were full of the marvellous stuff in the first place, it is this that keeps them alive. No-one has a clue how they make it home as often as they do, it is only the good Lord himself that knows how they could cycle the bike in the first place never mind be able to stay on it as they can hardly walk out of the pub, one would wonder how they would make it home on any night of the week on a good road never mind these poor excuses for a road. It must have something to do with their wives saying the rosary for their safe arrival.

"Never mind them", Marion laughed, "So long as we are not the ones that end up in the ditch we will do well. The roads were far worse than I had imagined, both of the lads already thought we were touched in the head most of the time but tonight they were just short of signing us into the Nuthouse, we will have to make it up to them tomorrow if we are ever to live this down."

"Sweet Jesus, Evelyn, that's if we get there in one piece, the road is lethal; it is like an ice rink. You do realise that I have never driven on icy roads before, right now I wished I hadn't chosen tonight to start." Never in living memory has there been so much frost and snow at this early stage of the winter. The forecast has promised that it would only get worse from here on.

Evelyn was thinking to herself, part of her was regretting coming out in the first place when she could be at home nice and cosy by the fire, not that she would dream of saying it out loud in case mad Marion decided to lynch her as it was she who had insisted that it would be grand, that the roads where not as bad as everyone was saying but, now she's not too sure it was the right decision. "What can we do about it, there is no going back now as we are nearly there, in for a penny in for a pound. With the extra cash on offer tonight it will make the trip worth it, in the end."

Marion shot an evil look in Evelyn's direction - on second thoughts, I better keep my thoughts to myself she thought, or she will have my guts for garters. She has been ranting like a lunatic since we left her house, yet she had not once stopped the car or suggested that we should turn back, she is worse than a broken record. At this stage she was beginning to give me a headache. Listening to her you would think I had a gun to her head and I was making her do it, you don't have to be psychic to know what will come out of her mouth next. She can be a right pain in the arse at times thinking she always knows best and loves nothing more than to be able to shift the blame for anything and everything that did not go her way to anyone available, she has been that way for as long as I can remember. Nothing is ever her fault; she had perfected the act of being the martyr to a T, somebody give that woman an Oscar please.

Why Me?

"Marion, you know that the jackpot would go a long way towards Christmas. It would also be great to get a few bits for the house and the baby, the last few months have been manic, it has been like I was caught in a whirlwind. I have barely had time to catch my breath with having all the major stresses in life or so they say, in the last four months a wedding, new house, a baby on the way. Who knows what is going to be the next thing?"

Marion snottily replied, "Who are you trying to kid that you need the money, there are more deserving people out there than you. Besides, if you had done things in the right order, you could have it made it a lot easier on yourself and everyone else, and it would have saved us all a lot of grief. I'm sure your mother blames me for all of this, as if I was the one that lead you down a dark alley and held you down. You are very lucky that it worked out the way it did. Only for the priest did your mother a favour in the first place by allowing the wedding to go ahead as soon as it did, you certainly would have been shipped off to England or worse to the Nun's in the back of beyond never to be seen or heard of again."

That's Marion for you, always having to get the sly remarks in, to make herself out to be holier than holy. Her life is perfect she always does the right thing, she acts as if she is lady of the manor, Lording over the rest of us. Good God, the woman has no faults. Three kids later yet apparently, she never had sex, three amazing babies by Immaculate Conception, not one but three. You would think the church would have her canonized by now, maybe they will any day now! Sweet Marion butter would not melt in her mouth. She drives me insane at times, sometimes I wonder why I even bother putting up with her nonsense, as she is so up herself and moody. I have always known that she was two-faced. She loves to be involved in everyone else life, thrives on the drama. Nothing made her happier than when she had a story to tell about someone, it did not matter too much if it was true or not. We have been friends since our first day in school and to this day I wonder why or how we ever became friends in the first place, never mind that we still are today. I guess one major advantage is she has a car, that must be it, it's all because of the car for what other reason would I stick around and put up with all her crap. Laughing to herself, Evie had never thought of that before she was half afraid that Marion might be able read her thoughts. Now, if she could do that it would be the end of her for sure. Evie thought that maybe she should learn to drive and then she will have her freedom to go wherever and whenever she liked and the very best part would be that there would be no-one watching every move she made, running home to spill the beans and making up extra legs to the stories. If I learned to drive and got a car that could be a perfect solution after the baby is born. Me on the open road with the wind in my hair, sounds like a brilliant plan. Probably one of my best ones yet.

The sound of Marion's whining voice was piercing through Evie's skull, here she goes again on and on, one of these days I'm afraid that I will lose the head with her and tell her what I really think, but then World War III would break out in a small village in the West of Ireland. Evie repeated her mantra, "smile, it will be worth it in the long run, and try to ignore her stupid comments."

Marion's voice penetrates through the air with the notes of disapproval. "Well, put it this way: there is not much more you could do at this moment in time, is there now, especially in your condition. You have never been someone that does things by half have you? You didn't get the name, full steam ahead Evie, for nothing".

'I don't know what you are talking about, Marion. There was no one more surprised by the last few months than myself and sure my bump is still tiny. Thankfully, it's just about showing if you look closely.'

'You're very lucky at this stage I could barely move never mind see my toes.'

'Cheers Marion, that has cheered me up no end. I can always count on you to cheer me up. NOT! to be honest I feel like a beached whale, I'm bursting out of my clothes, it feels like what was fitting me in the morning is too tight by lunchtime and by the evening there is no hope at all. I can't imagine what I will look like in four months from now, I guess even more of a whale than I am now, I bet.'

'You don't know it yet! But these are the good days, it is all downhill from here. Soon, you will not be able to find a comfortable position to sleep and you can forget about painting your toes for a while. You don't understand how much your life will change once that bundle of joy is born, no idea at all. There will be times when you will think you have lost all of your marbles, there will be so many changes they don't tell you about in those daft baby books, the hidden secrets of pregnancy and life there afterwards. I'm convinced that they were all written by a man with no clue to what happens to our bodies or our minds for that matter. There's no mention of the extra body hair, the moods swings, the fact that your bladder is never the same again as for your boobs, they will be forever lopsided I could go on and on but I don't want to frighten you too much. You'll find out for yourself soon enough and just so you know it, the first one is the easiest despite what everyone say. Life will never be the same again, so enjoy these days for as long as you can.'

'Are you having a laugh or what? How could these days be called the good times, there is nothing like morning sickness to give you the feel-good factor, and whoever called it morning sickness should be taken out and shot, as it should be called anytime any place sickness? I bet it was a man again with his sad attempt to have a joke at our expense. I would like to see how they would cope with it.'

'I take it, that you are still not feeling any better?'

'No, it is worse now than what it was in the beginning. I have tried the entire book of old wives' tales, and nothing works. Everyone said that it would only last for the first three months. What a load of dribble. There are days when I think I'm losing my mind I see more of the toilet bowl than anyone else; I have even started talking to it as if it is human. Can you believe it the other day I was waiting for the fecking thing to answer me can you believe that? The only thing that seems to take the edge of it is a drop of Poteen.'

'Evelyn, you shouldn't be drinking in your condition, I thought you had promised Eddie you would stop especially while you are pregnant, it is bad enough that you are smoking like a chimney, but drinking and to make it worse Poteen, that stuff is lethal. Are you completely off your head? Does Eddie Know?'

'No! he does not, what Eddie doesn't know will not hurt him, and you better not open your big gob either - just because you have never touched a drop in your life, it doesn't make you the next Holy Mary for once can you please stop judging me.'

'Keep your head on. I will not get in the middle of the two of you again. You are both big enough to sort yourselves out, I still think that you should not have got married in the first place, for one do you not think he is too old for you and second you were on the rebound, and that's always a disastrous way to start a new relationship. Who knows, if you had waited a little longer, you might have gotten back with Stephen. His mother would have gotten over herself, eventually? Why a grown man would listen to his mother the way he does is more than a bit weird if you ask me. Does he have to ask for her permission every time he goes outside the door? It wouldn't surprise me if he had to ask for permission to go to the toilet.?'

'AHH, shut up, Marion, would you stop giving him a hard

time? He is a lovely, lovely guy, but you are right, he listens to his mother way too much.' I guess she is the way she is because she had to rear him by herself you know only too well that his father was one of the fishermen who drowned when he was only young, and it was weeks before they found his body in a way, she was one of the lucky ones as many off the other men were never found, never getting the chance to be laid to rest. Their families left clinging to a false sense of hope that one day they would be found. It must be hard not to have the closure a funeral offers. It couldn't have been easy for her, she was only a young woman herself at the time, with no family around to help her. She surprised everyone by not going back to her home place.'

'I know all of that Evie, but still think about it. Any normal man in his right mind would have grown a pair by now and told her where to go. You know, I don't think I have ever seen him with anyone other than you. Even in school you two were joined together at the hip,'

'Would you give over and sing a new tune… You are just like a broken record you know better than anyone that it was long over with Stephen before we had even started as he was such a mummy's boy it never could go anywhere but the moron I was I thought I could get him to cut those aprons strings. There is no woman on earth or in heaven for that matter that could put up with his mother; she will never find anyone that would be good enough for her beloved Stephen.'

'Deep down, Evie, would always feel that Stephen Campbell was the one who got away. She will always wonder what if?'

'Now Evie, I know you have told me it was over more than once but just because everyone else believes you, it does not make it true, because I know that you have been spending a lot of time with him on the quiet. I just hope you know what you are doing, believe me - you are playing with fire. If you have any sense in that mad head of yours you will put an end to it and concentrate on your marriage. Let's be honest you have to think of the baby now it is no longer all about you. It's time for you grow up and think about someone other than yourself for a change. Once this little one is born, life will never be the same, everything changes in ways that seem alien at the minute.'

'Can you please just watch the road and keep your nose out of my personal life?'

'All right, keep your knickers on I'm just trying to help, I'm on your side, not everyone is out to give you a hard time. You might want to remove that chip on your shoulder before it knocks you over, I would love to know why you have that chip in the first place. You've not had it any harder than the rest of us, but I want you to know that I'm here for you if you need me to be as usual, no strings attached.'

'Sometimes Marion, I think you're here more for the drama than anything else as your life is so perfect and boring.'

Why Me?

'Stop Quacking like a duck, and get over yourself, Evelyn.'

It seems like two lifetimes had passed by the time we arrived outside the hall. Thankfully in one piece! We were delighted to see that the lights were on and the hall door was open. We both gave a sigh of relief as we stepped out of the car.

'God only knows what the roads are going to be like on the way home,' said Evie.

'Stop that, so let's be happy we got here. We can worry about the roads later I need some time to recover after nearly being traumatized by all that driving.'

We hopped out of the car just a little too quickly, I was trying as hard as I could to stay in an upright position. I said, 'You are right Marion, we will cross that bridge later there's no point of worrying about it before we have to, sure we can take our time as there will be no rush.'

Christ - it was so cold; the wind could cut the nose of your face. We walked towards the hall, holding on to the rail with both hands as our legs were both going in two different directions. The more we tried to straighten ourselves, the more we slipped and slided around the place. We had tears in our eyes with the laughter, for sure, we looked like two loons let out of the asylum for the night. Once inside the hall, we were struck by how quiet the place was. By Jesus it was even cold in here, it's hard to tell if it is colder inside or out. There were a few heaters plugged in around the hall, so the big question now is do we sit in our normal seats or move to beside the heaters, in the vain hope, that we will warm up our icy bones and avoid pneumonia. Now everyone knows the serious bingo players believe that moving seats could cause you bad luck and in addition to that and maybe a worse end result it can really upset the rest of the regular crowd. Generally, the regulars are very territorial when it comes to their seats, and no one wants an angry hall. It can be a nightmare for any unknown person trying to find a spot, especially if they are by themselves. It is not unheard of, for them to be asked to move several times before they find a safe seat, it was much easier if they are already friends with one of the women, then no one seemed to mind an extra seat been added to the row.

We decided that the jackpot was too high to risk jinxing ourselves; so instead, we would battle the cold and stay in our normal seats. Looking around the room there were only about twenty people here - a lot less than I had expected. A few more might turn up yet.

Evie, turned to Marion and said, 'I hope they don't cancel after the journey we had to get here. Everyone that is here is just a short walk from the hall so it would not have been much of a hardship to them to get here, I would say that any sane person would have stayed at home in front of a nice warm fire. By the end of the night, we will be lucky to leave this place without ending up on our deathbeds. 'You can see the headlines now, two lunatics found frozen to death in a bingo hall on the coldest night in history.

There is an indistinct murmur in the hall, Jesus I cannot feel my feet, or my fingers and we have only been here for ten minutes. 'How will we be able to mark the numbers if we can't even hold the marker in the first place? Marion said.'

It was almost eight and there was no sign of it starting yet. 'I wonder what is happening asked Marion?'

'Hang on, I will find Dee and check with her, as she is the only member of the committee here at the minute.'

Before I had a chance to get up, Dee came in and told us that Jack would be here shortly with some extra gas heaters, which should help heat the place up nicely. He will be here in no time at all, she tried to reassure us.

One of the old dears at the top of the hall shouted back to Dee, 'Be a love and ask him to stop in the pub and bring us hot whiskey as well?' She roared with laughter. Here, here echoed the rest of the room.

'Now, that's not a terrible idea at all,' Evie said as she leaped from her chair. I'm just going next door for a quick one. Do you want anything, some Tayto, chocolate?

'Evelyn, seriously! Drinking it is not good for the baby.'

'Well, in this case, it is for medicinal purposes, besides one will not do any harm' and with that she turned on her heels and was heading for the door before Marion had a chance to start on another one of her lectures. Not for the first time recently, she was doing Evie's head in.

Evie, just couldn't listen to another word about what is

good for the baby, what about what is good for her, does anyone ever ask. No, they don't, it is as if she is not even here at all? No one ever asked if she wanted this baby in the first place, they just took it for granted that it is something she did want, like she had any other choice in the matter. She knew Eddie was so excited, you should have seen the look on his face when she told him he would be a dad in a few months. It was like all of his Christmases had come at once. For a big stack of a man, he was overcome with emotion. He threw himself on the floor and asked me to marry him as soon as he had stopped blabbing like a baby; he made a right idiot out of himself. She had no other option but to say yes, did she, trapped I would call it. It put her on the spot and once she had said yes everything else moved so fast, she couldn't have stopped it, even if she wanted to. So, she plonked a smile on her face and told everyone she was over the moon to be marrying the finest man in Ireland, which is true, as there is not one person in the county that would disagree with that statement. If, only she lived in England she could have gone to someone that would make sure she would come back without child and no-one would have to be any the wiser.

Every single woman in the town had their nose put out of joint Connemara's most eligible bachelor was off the market! They thought that Evie had not heard their comments - when her back was turned, 'saying that she was not good enough for him and he was marrying below his station.'

Evie's only saving grace is that Eddie is a wonderful man, a gentle giant with a heart of gold. It helped that she had him wrapped around her finger before he was told about the new addition, but, ever since she told him about the baby he was treating her like a princess.

Ireland was not the place to be if you are an unmarried mother. We all know what happens to those poor women, some of them have never been seen since the day they left, more often than not they were hauled off in the middle of the night under the cloak of darkness so no one could see them. You would swear that they were after killing someone, with the way they were treated by the people who should have protected them. Those poor women must have been terrified, being dragged from their beds in the middle of the night not knowing where they were being taken too or ignorant to the fact that their lives were about to change forever. There's plenty of talk around the village about fallen women, never a word about the men, it is as if they got pregnant by themselves. The priest armed with the Gardai would arrive often late at night and that was the end of the story, no more questions asked or answered.

What Evie didn't understand was, if the church believed that Jesus was conceived by the Immaculate Conception, and they were waiting on the return of their saviour how come they never asked themselves, were any of these women carrying their next saviour. How do they know it was not another Immaculate Conception? If she happened to be brave enough, she would love to ask the parish priest for his opinion but he has the fear of God in everyone, including Evelyn, and that is no easy task. She had never feared anyone in her life, not even the teachers when they would wave the cane in front of her nose, banging it on the desk to instill some more fear before they would let it land across her knees.

Instead, the good old church just shipped them off to God knows where, out of sight, out of mind. Any of the women that had been lucky enough to come back many years later were not the same somehow, the light had gone out of their eyes, they were the closest thing you could get to the walking dead, most of them were like an empty shell the lights are on but nobody's home! None of these poor girls knew where their babies had gone, some had been adopted overseas or sent to other homes. Many of these poor unfortunate mothers had been told that the babies had died, there is no way of knowing if this was true or not as there was no funeral or grave, no birth or death certificate nothing to say that these poor souls ever existed. Many of them were just taken without the mother ever laying eyes on them, never to be spoken about again and if the women asked questions, they would be beaten to within an inch of their lives. They sent my poor aunt off to some laundry in the back of beyond; she was gone for fifteen years and no one would even mention her name. For years we were told she had gone off to England to look after some distant aunt, not one word about a baby. It was only after Evelyn told her she was pregnant that she took her to one side and told her she had given birth to a baby boy many years ago in one of those places they never allowed her to hold him or give him a name; he was taken from her as soon as he was born, all she had to remember him by was his cries as he gasped for his first breath, she begged and pleaded with them to let her hold him or at least if she could see him, to no avail her cries falling on deaf ears. They had left her alone in a room for days with barely enough food to feed a pigeon, as soon as they let her out she was sent back to the laundry working 10 hours a day. They were heartless and cruel beyond belief. To this day it still haunts her even in her dreams. She does not know what happened to him and there is no way to find out. If Evelyn hadn't told her she was pregnant, she would have never opened up and told her anything about where she was for those years and the pain that she suffered every day since, she did not understand why they had taken him or why they wouldn't tell her anything, even after all this time she still wonders where he is and every time, she sees a stranger around his age she wonders could he be her son. On his birthday every year she would light a candle and wish him a happy birthday and pray that he was okay. The shame she feels keeps her up at night - she should have been able to protect her baby, but she had fallen from grace in the eyes of the church, she had no right over her body or her baby.

Not knowing anything sounds good to Evelyn at this moment in time. She could have been tempted to sign herself in a heartbeat if it wasn't for how, they treated these poor girls they were nothing more than slaves to the church that need to pay for their sins, but still in holy Ireland this is all hidden from the world, once you went in you might never get out of the place. Her aunt said there were so many women, that had been put in there in their early twenties and are still there in their late sixties, many of these women only came out in a box and many of them are buried in a grave somewhere, many of them unmarked, long forgotten about by all that knew them. She said that those places were filled with nothing other than pain and misery, that is the truth of what goes on in there, it would make peoples stomachs churn. It is safe to say that she scared the living daylights out of Evelyn, her advice was to walk down the aisle with Eddie, as she would never find a better man than him and above all to keep her mouth shut the fewer people that knew the better.

Evelyn's aunt tells her as often as she can to count her blessings and to be happy, that she's one of the lucky ones, but lucky is far from how she feels. Maybe it is just the hormones that has her head all in a muddle and she will feel better once the baby arrives. She prays day and night that she would just wake up and this would have been a terrible nightmare then she could get out of this place as fast as her legs could take her. Sometimes she thinks it would be a wonderful idea to say hello to the bottom of the lake. It is such a shame she's a coward we all know that is another sin in the eyes of the church. If she did go through it, then she would burn in hell for all of eternity for that as well. Another charming thought dammed if she does and dammed if she doesn't.

Chapter 2

Well, there is nothing like a whiskey to make you feel better, it makes all of your problems smaller. Sitting here at the bar seems to be the only place that gives Evelyn a bit of peace these days, her mind can switch off, as the whiskey touches her lips it is like liquid gold as it slides down her throat taking Evelyn to her happy place. As she takes her first mouthful, she orders a 'hot one' for the road. Sure, no-one will be any the wiser in for a penny in for a pound. By the time she had returned to the hall, she was feeling a lot better: she had lost the doom and gloom that followed her around all day. If only this numb feeling could last forever. The numbers in the hall had increased, there must be at least fifty people now, much better than the twenty from earlier less chance of it been cancelled. Still, her chance of winning was good.

'Evelyn, roared Marion about time, what the heck took you so long, I thought you had forgotten your way back,'

'Me never, how can I win the jackpot if I'm not here,'

'Funny, don't give up your day job, Evie.'

'Would you just sit down, shut up and take your book, they are about to start.'

'Marion, do you know what your problem is?'

'No, I don't, but I suppose you and your amazing talents

are about to tell me. Go on then enlighten me, the suspense is killing me. You are a killjoy, and you take life far too seriously, you need to loosen up, live a little. You only live once as the saying goes 'We are here for a short time.'

'Right, that's expert advice coming from you where everything is a joke,'.

With that, one of the old biddies in front of us turned around and tells us to shut up. Well, I guess that is us being told.

Silence fell in the room as the balls whizzed around the big glass drum. Then we are off to the start with a big fat hen, number 12. The night moved on like any other night. Thanks to the coldness in here Evelyn has a pain in her back; and her arse is so numb she can barely move, her head hurts like mad, she could really kill another whiskey right now.

Mrs Crabby roared bingo from the front of the room. The line had gone ladies and gents we are now playing for the goal post. It would be worth £20. so let's start the ball rolling. Marion was next to shout bingo and then we were on to a full house.

By the third game, the pain in Evelyn's back was non-stop, no matter which way she turned it made no difference. She was looking like she had ants in her pants. I have to say winning the next game had put a smile on her face, nevertheless she was looking forward to the break after the next game. At least then she can get up and walk around it might give some relief from the stabbing pain in her back and you'd never know she might just be able to warm up a bit, even with the heater beside her, she was not feeling any warmer. At least we will be able to get a cuppa, and that might go some way toward warming up our icy bones. If we are not careful, we will all have pneumonia tomorrow at this rate: the extra heaters had made little difference. On and on the night went, Evelyn thought it would never end each number they called was like a hammer going off in her head, just after the break we were halfway through the game when she couldn't help herself, and she let out a scream as the pain hit an all-time high.

'Evelyn, Are you ok?'

'Yes, I'm fine just a pain in my back, it must be from the cold in this place not to mention that this seat has my arse broken it took me off guard that's all.'

'Do you think we should leave and get you checked over by the doctor, you're not looking so great?'

'I'm fine, stop fussing, anyway I came here to win the jackpot and I'm not leaving here without the cash.'

'If you are sure, but I don't like the look of you, you are as white as a sheet. I know it is far from your due date but if the pain does not go or gets worse, I think you should see a doctor tonight there would be no harm in giving him a call when we get back into town. Better to be safe.'

'Would you give me a break, you are such a worrywart. I

have another 12 weeks if not longer to go. If it is anything at all, it will only be Braxton Hicks, the doctor said that they can start from now,'

'It's a little early to be getting them, Evie'

'Sure, it was only the other day we were laughing about the time you had made a fool of yourself traipsing into Galway thinking you were having the baby. You'd would think after having two already you would have known the difference.'

'Stop, Evelyn, please don't remind me I was totally mortified, anyway, I was further along than you. Thankfully, the nurses were brilliant. They did everything they could to make me feel better; the best part was I got a break from the mad ones at home with breakfast, lunch and dinner handed to me, tea on tap, what more could a woman ask for? There is nothing better than having your dinner handed up to you even if it is hospital food, just knowing that you didn't have to make it yourself or having to worry about the washing up afterwards makes it taste so much nicer. I know it is kind of sad, nevertheless it's a luxury,'

'Just you wait in a few months from now you will feel the same and that is with just one baby never mind three of them to drive you around the twist.'

'All I can say is that if you didn't know what was happening, there is no hope for me, at all.'

'We better be quiet, we are getting daggers from Mrs Byrne, and the old fella in the corner looks like he is about to explode,'

We were laughing so much Evelyn's belly was wobbling like mad. The baby was getting a good old shaking, 'if we don't stop, I will wet myself. I'm not sure what hurts more my belly or my back at this stage.'

'Can you imagine us been thrown out of a bingo hall for causing a commotion. We should not be finding anything funny but suddenly, it was now hilarious indeed.

'The lads would disown us for sure.'

'Stranger things have happened when we are together, trouble just seems to find us. I cannot imagine why that is. Can you Marion?'

'Shush, what was that last number?'

'49' the old lady in front of us growled, in the hope that we would be quiet.

'That is great, now I only need all the ducks number 22 for the house. Well, that is the only number left to be called in the twenties,' said Marion.

Number 88 two fat ladies was shortly followed by a loud Bingo from old Pete.

'Well feck that anyway I was sure that was mine, I had been waiting for ages for 22 to be called. Actually, looking back at my book I noticed they have not called 22 since the second game, I wonder if they have taken the bloody number out of play.'

'Now, Evelyn don't be such a sore loser, you have already won a few games and a box of biscuits on the raffle, it is not a nice trait to be getting greedy just try to be nice and leave some games for the rest of us didn't your mother ever tell you to be nice to others and share?' Said Mrs Kelly.

'I suppose you're right; I can wait for the jackpot.'

'You and this jackpot you are doing my head in, I will have grey hair before the end of the night.'

'Just you wait and see, I will treat you to fish and chips on the way home out of my winnings, just because I'm such a gracious friend.'

'You're on, you may as well push the boat out and add a coke to it seeing as you are such moneybags tonight.'

Thankfully, we were on the last game, the big one that everyone had been waiting for, the one we have all risked our lives coming out in this weather for.

'Eyes down, no talking. We cannot afford to take any chances. Right, we are off. Good luck everyone called Dee.'

The line has gone, four corners have gone, now it is getting all too real, Evelyn could wet herself with the excitement.

'Marion, I kid you not, but I need just one number, legs eleven.'

Why Me?

'For the love of God would you give over how could you be down to one number already?'

'Honestly, I am, Jesus the excitement is sending me over the edge, I can barely breathe. My heart is racing like mad it is making my head spin, I need to go to the toilet but now is not the right time. I will just have to cross my legs and hope for the best. If I have to, I will wet my knickers. 'This is mine for sure; said Evelyn.'

'Oh Jesus, oh Jesus Evelyn, I think you're waters have broken.'

'Yeah, yeah whatever, just admit it, the jackpot is mine you don't have a chance, you have still six numbers to get.'

'Can you just stop for a minute and have a look at the floor, and you will see for yourself,'.

'Stop, maybe I have peed myself, I needed the toilet after all,'.

'For feck' sake can you please be serious for one bloody minute, you daft mare.'

Marion is on her feet in hysterics, 'Ah for fuck's sake, would you just listen for once in your life, stop acting the idiot and look at the floor for yourself.'

Silence fell in the hall before I had a chance to look, I let out a roar, as the pain in my back was unbearable.

'Evelyn, I think you are in labour; the baby is coming.

Someone please call an ambulance quickly and let them know we are on our way.'

'Don't be stupid, Marion, you are always overreacting.'

'Mother of God, would you cop the hell on and listen to me for once in your life,'.

'We need to get you out of here before this baby comes before you end up making a holy show of yourself. Eddie and your mother will have my guts for garters if you have the baby here.

You are lucky this is your first, as it normally takes longer for the baby to come. Fingers crossed you will definitely make it to the hospital, if we take you into town and get an ambulance to Galway.'

'Why is this happening to me now? Why Me? I ask you.'

'I'm not leaving here without the jackpot, Barbara. Can you just get on with calling the numbers! There is nothing to see here but a false alarm.'

'Are you completely off your head, Evie this baby is coming whether you like it or not, you can't just tell baby to wait that you're not ready, please try again tomorrow my calendar is free. Can someone please call an ambulance for this crazy bitch?

Maybe if they tell her the baby is coming, she might believe them.'

Why Me?

'There is no way this can be the baby; it is far too early.'

'Evie, your goose is cooked, excuse the pun.'

'Please, can we get back to the game? We may as well keep playing while we wait for the ambulance.' It was with great reluctance, Barbara started the machine, we did not have to wait too long as within a few minutes, we could hear Bingo through the hall much to everyone's relief.

Evelyn lost it she was like a volcano that had exploded she just picked her book up and slammed it onto the floor in temper, if she could, she would have danced on it, if she wasn't in so much pain.

'Well, are you happy now? We can go now, what a waste of time it was coming out here tonight and to think I had myself convinced that I would win the jackpot. What kind of moron am I? It is a bed in the mental hospital in Ballinasloe for me, not the maternity ward,' moaned Evelyn.

'Unbelievable. I cannot believe that old biddy won, what the fuck she will do with that money is beyond me. Sure, she has one foot in the grave, has no-one ever told her she cannot take it with her. It is so unfair that someone who does not need the cash would win.'

We were just walking out the door, or should I say crawling and howling; the pain was becoming so bad that Evelyn had to grip the wall; I guess the excitement of the game had her distracted from the pain. She had just stopped walking so she could catch her breath when we heard Barbara call.

Why Me?

'A false alarm, everyone, please take your seats.'

Once again forgetting about the pain, Evelyn turned on her heels and wobbled back inside as fast as she could, picking her book up from the floor.

Marion was just about to blow a gasket; 'you are going to give me heart failure at this rate. For the Love of God Evie, you need to get to the hospital now. This is not a joke, and you don't have time to mess about, if you are not careful you will have the baby here. I hate to be the one to remind you that this baby is very early so having it here will not go well for you or the baby.'

'That will give the old dears something to talk about over their nightly cocoa, replied Evelyn.'

'Evie, seriously will you just grow up this is no laughing matter, if something happens to you or the baby Eddie will feed my guts to the pigs for their dinner. You know this will end up being all my fault as usual, and I have no line of defence this time as I was the one who drove you out here to the middle of nowhere against both of the lads wishes.'

'For your information, I can look after myself perfectly fine, and the sooner Eddie gets his head around that the better, I could manage before I said the famous I do, and that has not changed by putting a ring on my finger. I didn't turn into a weeping violet just because I've gotten married. Besides, he knew what he was getting into from the beginning. I was never going to become a yes sir no sir type of girl, so he will just have to get used to it.

If he goes off on one of his rants, just tell him there was nothing you could do as we were waiting too long for the ambulance to arrive, and while we were waiting for the ambulance like good responsible women we are, there was no harm in marking our books just in case. Sure, we are women after all, we can multi-task unlike them. When I have the jackpot in my pocket that will draw the smoke out of his pipe, there is no way he can complain about that.'

'Evie, listen to yourself for a minute. Can you hear how ridiculous you sound, it is not as if you guys are short of money. Why are you so obsessed with the jackpot? I think this pregnancy has turned your brain to squash. Maybe when they admit you to the maternity ward, they will need to send you to the psych ward to see if there is anything between your ears.'

To say the hall fell into an uncomfortable silence when we took our seats and picked up our books was an understatement. You could hear a pin drop; even the auld ones at the top of the hall could be heard in their low whisper saying that they always knew that I was demented and she is showing it more and more every day, she must have been dropped on her head as a baby as she was never right all the others in the family were mild-mannered. She on the other hand is a different story, as for that one she has always been as wild as a March Hare God help her poor mother.

Mrs Hagan came over and kindly offered to mark my book for me, as she has had twelve kids herself, she could tell it was time for me to go as this was not a false alarm, that the baby was coming regardless of the fact it was not due for weeks yet. Her entire body moved in all directions as she laughed as she said that the baby had not got the memo of when it was to arrive. That this little one is on a mission and there is no stopping it once it starts, and then she said that she didn't want to worry me, but as the baby is so early it is not a good thing, you need to be in the hospital.

'Mrs Hagan, thank you very much for your very kind to offer and I appreciate your advice but sure I'm waiting on the ambulance there is nothing else I can do until they get here but for me to mark my book it might help keep my mind off the pain.'

She turned around to Barbara and shouted, 'You better hurry up with this game or we will have a lot more than we bargained on. My days of delivering babies are long over thanks be to God and I don't want to be here when this little mite arrives.' With that, the hall erupted into a nervous laugh.

It was a welcome sound to hear the machine whirl into action. Number after number, and Evelyn was still waiting. Not that she can say anything to anyone here, as she would not get an ounce of sympathy from them, but her head was lifting off her neck. It was getting harder to see, sometimes she could not see the numbers properly it was as if the place was covered in fog. She could just about hear the noise of the ambulance siren outside when Tim and Roger came bursting through the door at the same time, she though she heard legs eleven being called but she was not sure. She just about managed to shout Bingo it was more of a howl than anything else with that the whole hall started to clap and sigh with relief I'm unsure if someone else had the game before her, but they were afraid to call it just in case she gave birth there and then.

Chapter 3

Luck was on our side as we made it to the hospital in one piece but Evelyn was fading in and out of consciousness more often than the paramedics would have liked. 'There was no way she could do this any longer,' said Roger. They took her to the express lane, straight into the labour ward where there was a hive of activity. Doctors and nurses were talking so loudly Evelyn thought her head would explode into a million pieces, before she could say a thing, they hooked her up to even more machines. There were so many of them she lost count.

'Please, can I have the epidural? Evelyn begged. Everyone raves about how good it is.'

'Sorry my dear, but it's too late for that this baby is on its way now you will have to make do with gas and air,'.

They asked so many questions it sounded like mumble jumble; they may as well have been talking in a foreign language. No matter how hard she tried to answer, she just couldn't get her words to leave her brain. She heard Roger and Tim, telling them they believed that I was in labour for several hours, waters had broken at least two-and-a-half hour ago, the contractions were strong and although they were eight minutes apart, they had been erratic for the last 20 minutes. Saying that she had lost consciousness frequently and at times was very confused on the way in. 'Had I!' Evelyn couldn't remember very much at all.

Why Me?

They spoke in medical jargon and she did not understand what they were saying and she did not care, she just needed the drugs everyone talked about. With that, the boys waved and said "Goodbye, Evelyn; 'we wish you all the best and be sure we will see you and your little one in a few weeks when you're home.' Tim jokily suggested that if it was a boy I should call it after him. "Right, we are out of here" said Roger, "before this fella gets carried away altogether."

From the bottom of the bed, this young doctor who looked like he should still be in school shouted. 'I think there is a problem; the baby is getting tired, and it is possibly stuck, we will have to help it out, as this is your first baby. We need to avoid a C-section at all costs, pass me the forceps nurse, I will see if we can help this little one out as its heart rate is beginning to show signs of distress and I'm not sure how much more mum or baby can take, mum's blood pressure is rising to a risky level."

Evelyn nearly fainted when he held up the tool for helping baby out 'what the hell are you going to do with that thing? Now, is not the time to make a salad,'.

The midwife laughed uncontrollably. 'There is nothing wrong with your sense of humour, love, which is a splendid thing in these situations.'

The tension in the room was so electric you could cut it with a knife, everyone was on high alert for the safe arrival of the baby. I could hear them saying that they were getting the incubator ready, saying the baby's chance of survival was less than 50%, that they had never delivered a baby this

Why Me?

early before they had only read about it in the medical journals.

The doctor spoke for the first time in ages, and said Congratulations, you have a baby girl. The room was silent. You could hear a pin drop as they worked on her to get her to take her first breath. They shouted to me, "she needs oxygen" as they rushed out of the room; Evelyn did not have time to see her, never mind hold her. I'm not sure how I feel about that she thought but right now all she wanted to do was go to sleep and for them to leave her alone, after they cleaned her up and moved her into a bed. They rolled her out of the delivery ward and into a side room. Evelyn was so tired she just wanted to sleep and pretend this was not happening the last thing she remembers was the doctor giving her an injection telling her to rest. Evelyn had been caught in a whirlwind for the last few months, she welcomed dreamland as she drifted off to the land of nod. She could just about see two of the doctors approaching her to tell her baby girl was 3lbs 13oz, which was a good weight for a baby that was born so early. She was no bigger than a ruler. They spoke so slowly and quietly she was unsure of what they were saying, as her eyes were becoming heavier and heavier, she was slightly annoyed that they kept talking to her, how stupid are they; do they not realise I'm too tired and I need to sleep. I would feel better after I had some sleep.

Sometime in the middle of the night she woke suddenly, as it dawned on her that none of them had said if she was dead or alive or had they? She just couldn't remember; she was just so tired she couldn't keep her eyes open. The harder she tried to keep her eyes open and to listen to what they were saying, the more distant their voices were becoming as she was drifting off into a world of her own. She tried to speak but the words coming out of her mouth no longer sounded like her voice or even words for that matter.

She had so many emotions rolling around inside of her, she did not know which way was up or which way was down; she was afraid to ask, terrified as she did not know what would have been the best. From the minute she found out she was pregnant, she wanted nothing more than for it to disappear. She foolishly had prayed day and night for God to answer her and for it not to be so. Now that she was here not knowing, either way, she felt unsure of what she wanted, what would be best. Does this make her an awful person, a terrible mother, is it a sign she will be a failure? How did she get herself into these situations, she must be jinxed? God help this poor child; she will need all the help she can get with a mother like me. If this is what she has been reduced to God help us both? Did she want this baby, or would it be better if she does not make it? In many ways, if she did not, it would make her life easier. She would not have to face the responsibility that was ahead of her, She knew she was unprepared to be a wife let alone a mother or whatever that means in the first place.

It would buy her a lot of sympathy from Eddie, she could play the heartbroken mother for as long as she could it would give her time to sort herself out. Stop, stop for goodness' sake what kind of person am I? When did I turn into this selfish person? It must be the drugs. It had never entered my head until now how poor Eddie would take the news, she knew for sure it would devastate him. Evelyn thought if she closed her eyes, the doctors might leave, and then she could try to get her head around all this mess. With that, she gently closed her eyes and prayed they would leave me alone and then just maybe this will all have been a nightmare, and when she wakes up, it will be just her, carefree and single. Everything will be much better when she's fully rested. She doesn't function well without plenty of sleep.

With that, they took the hint and left the room, saying they would check in on me later. 'You need to rest for now, as you have been through so much it will take your body some time to recover, said the doctor. Finally, we agreed on something. Thankfully, I was finally left alone with only the sound of the machines beeping; it was soothing in a funny kind of way. Before she knew it, she had drifted back to sleep into a world where she was travelling around the world, first stop New York where she would find a job in one of those fancy shops that you see on the telly she would be dressed in fabulous style from head to toe. She'd be the bell of the ball and she would return to Clifden for her holidays every second year or two and parade around the place like a queen bee wearing the latest fashion with a handsome, rich man on her arm. She would show them she was no fool. Then they would not be able to look down their nose at her anymore. Evelyn would be just as good as the rest of them if not better.

Why Me?

Something woke her early in the morning. It sounded sort of like Eddie. Hang on it was Eddie's booming voice that he wants to see his wife, he did not care about the hospital visiting times or who needs their rest. At first, she was unsure of what all the fuss was about or where she was; she had forgotten all about the nightmare of last night. It took all of her strength but she eventually opened her eyes when Eddie gently placed a kiss on my forehead.

'Evelyn, I'm so sorry, my darling, I couldn't get here last night. The Guards had the roads closed off because of an accident just after Maam Cross. Old Seamus and his wife took pity on me and insisted that I spend the night with them rather than going back home. I'm so sorry, my darling, I was not here for you. Please forgive me. How are you this morning? What happened? Where is the baby? He had so many questions that I couldn't answer that the tears rolled from my eyes. Shush, don't cry, my girl.

Nurse, can you tell me what has happened, and where is our baby? I don't know if it's a boy or a girl?'

"It's a Girl, 3lbs 13oz, a tiny little thing, Mr Woods", the Nurse replied, I will fetch a doctor for you both you and he will tell you everything you need to know, I have just come on duty and I'm not yet up to speed on everything that happened last night.,"

Evelyn couldn't look Eddie in the eye, she couldn't tell him she had no clue if there was a baby anymore. A voice in her head told her it would be best to close her eyes and stay silent for now. She did not want to see the hurt in his face if she had not made it through the night, Evelyn just couldn't deal with his grief. He was over the moon when he found out he would be a dad; not once did he see any obstacles; he jumped for joy for days, saying it was a dream come true. That we should get married straight away. He repeated he was the happiest man in Ireland. Evelyn knew she was lucky, as most men would have run a mile with the mention of the dreaded four-letter word "BABY". She felt ashamed of herself. Once again she was asking herself what kind of cruel person was she? Surely, she did not really want her own flesh and blood to be dead - am I a monster? There is no excuse for her to be so self-centered in attitude. She would have to adjust to the simple fact the world did not revolve around her, not that it ever did, and now it never will. They both sat in silence waiting for the doctor, neither one of us sure of what to say next.

Finally, the two doctors that were there last night walked into the room. 'Good morning Mr and Mrs Wood's, as you know your daughter was born very early and her birth weight is low, your daughter has had a tough night of it, but she is a fighter and she is determined to be here, currently, she is in an incubator and is relying on oxygen to breathe. We are by no means in the clear yet but we are hopeful. She is still very much on the critical list; we think it is a good idea to get the priest to visit her and to get her baptised just in case she does not make it. At this stage, we can't be sure what complications she might have as it is far too soon, if she makes it through the next 72 hours it will be of huge benefit and then she will have a fantastic chance. We have to advise you that your little girl is very sick and maybe this will be so for the rest of her life, it is extremely rare for her to have survived the birth in the first place as her body is not fully developed, and as you know she currently needs oxygen to help her breathe, without it, it can lead to brain damage we can't say anything for sure at this stage, we do know that her lungs are not fully developed so we are giving her steroids to help her. She is in an incubator which helps regulate her body temperature. She is also very jaundiced, so has a UV lamp on her. For now we are monitoring her closely as there are lots of challenges ahead. There are a lot of monitors and tubes attached to her which can be overwhelming when you first see them. But, you will need to prepare yourself for the event that she might not make it and if she does she could have some very serious side effects, such as Physical development, she may never walk, sit up or be able to feed herself she may not have any control of her body, learning difficulties are strong possibilities such as not been able to read or write or to master that basic skills to take care of herself, communication problems she may not talk or have hearing difficulties, not to mention behavioural issues that follow with any of the conditions mentioned, she will always be a high risk for all kinds infections, problems with her heart, kidneys lungs and breathing for the rest of her life. There is no actual way of knowing what the full effects of being born so early are at this stage and we may not know until she reaches four or five years. Do you both understand the risks that face your little girl if she survives? We need you both to know we are doing everything we can for your little girl. We know all of this is overwhelming, no new parents

Why Me?

should have to face this situation.

Now that we have given you as much information as we can at this stage, we must ask if she stops breathing do you want us to intervene? Many parents when faced with your situation often request a DNR.'

'We do not know what a DNR is? so how can we say Yes or No!'

'DNR is short for Do Not Resuscitate, which will allow your baby to pass away. We will make sure she will be in no pain so she can fall asleep peacefully.' Eddie was fit to be tied.

'What kind of fucking question is that to ask us? Are you really asking if we want to let our baby die? With everything you have said, it sounds like you have already given up on her? shouted Eddie'

'I can assure you both that we have not given up on her and nor will we. We will give her the best care we can to give the best chance of a good outcome, but sometimes nature has a way of taking matters into its own hands and there's not a lot we can do if that is the case.'

'Eddie, please calm down, pleaded Evelyn. We need to talk about this, I think it might be the best for her if the situation arrives. What happens if she is a vegetable for the rest of her life? We can't provide the care they are talking about for her, she would have to go to one of those awful places where they are just left lying there day in day out

Why Me?

being prodded and poked being used as a guinea pig I can't do that to her. We will have to think about it before we make any decisions. It is not something we can rush into without weighing up all of our options.'

'What if, what if she is a normal beautiful little girl, just like I always imagined? You heard them; they don't know anything, there is no way of them knowing anything that the future will hold.'

'I know Eddie, but we have to think that it could be possible, you can't just dig your head in the sand and say it will be all right.,'

'You cannot be serious, Evie, are you seriously thinking about letting her die? What the hell is wrong with you? I want to see my daughter now. Fuck the rest of ye. I will not give you permission to let her die, not today or any other day over my dead body will they ever turn those machines off. We will take her anyway she is and pray for her to be best that she can be.'

'Mr Woods, we don't think it is a good idea for you to see her just yet, as we said earlier, she is still in a critical condition.'

'Are you fucking deaf or something I want to see my daughter now, and there is no man on earth that will stop me, do you hear me? You lot are just a bunch of murderers, the lot of you I thought you took an oath to save lives. You even have brainwashed my wife to think like the rest of you lot.'

Why Me?

'Now, Mr Woods, you are being unreasonable. We never said we wanted to kill your daughter, but it is our duty to advise you of all your options in a case as complex as this: there are no guarantees either way. We need to prepare you for the worst case and pray for the best, being a parent to a baby born this early is tough, it can be heart wrenching with each new day and sometime every hour you can face heartbreaking decisions. I promise we will never lie to you or mislead you. We will give you all the facts as we become aware of them. The next few days will not be easy for anyone. If you guys are a believer in God, I would suggest that you pray to him as there is only so much, we can do.'

'Would ye just get the hell out of my way or I will end up decking someone?'

'If you don't calm down, we will have to call the guards to have you removed from the hospital, as you are causing a scene and upsetting not only your wife but many of the other ladies as well?'

'Call whoever you like, but I want to see my daughter and there are not enough guards in the country to stop me. I'm not a violent man but I swear I will not be responsible for my actions if you don't bring me to see her now.'

Evelyn, was shaking in the bed; she had never once heard Eddie raise his voice, soft and gentle Eddie. He is not taking this very well. He will never be able to cope if anything happens to her.

With that, Eddie stormed out of the room like a madman

in search of the baby unit. One of the midwives followed him down the corridor 'Mr Woods let me take you, but first please have a cup of tea and calm yourself you are no good to anyone in this state especially to your daughter She will be able to pick up on your stress and that will do her no good at all.' Eddie followed the midwife with a sense of relief.

'Finally, someone talking some sense.' Eddie mutter under his breath.'

'Mr Woods, you never gave the doctors a chance to tell you that it is wonderful news that your baby girl has survived the night. She is fighting with all of her strength to stay alive. The best thing you could do for both your wife and daughter is to pray and to stay stronger for them both. I have seen many miracles happen in this place and your baby girl is on the edge of the two worlds I would not give up on your daughter just yet. I would even go as far as saying that if I was a betting woman, I would put my money on her. She may be small with odds stacked against her but don't be fooled, she is going to be a tough cookie. Every hour she is here, her survival rates increase. Only time will tell how well she is going to be. Try to not let all the medical jargons get into your head. Take each day as it comes and stay positive. The doctors have got to be upfront and honest about what is going on and they are afraid to get your hopes up just in case things don't work out the way we would like them too. The best thing is to prepare for the worse and pray for the best."

Mr Woods, in cases such as your daughter's we recommend she be christened as soon as possible. The priest will be in later today I can ask him to call to see yourself and your wife so you can make the arrangements.'

'Oh, yes, that might be a wonderful idea. I will talk to Evie,'.

'Drink your tea and calm yourself and then I will take you to see her. It might be a good idea to go back to your wife first and go to the Special care unit together as I understand she did not get to see her last night.'

'Why the hell not?'

'There was no time as your wife blood pressure was too high as soon as the baby was delivered, Evie was heavily sedated to help her sleep It was important to reduce her blood pressure as quickly as possible or you could have had both your ladies in intensive care or worse. I assure you we will do everything in our power to help your little girl. So, your job is to keep a cool head for both their sakes, they both need you now more than ever. The chances are your little girl will be here for a long time but as long as your wife continues to improve, they will discharge her in a few days. She will have to be well cared for, as this was not an easy birth for her, physically or emotionally. It is not natural for a woman to go home without her baby, so she will need to nurtured.'

Chapter 4

Eddie took a large swig of the scalding tea. For a man who never drinks during the day, he thought a slug of whiskey would be good just about now. Maybe he should carry a hip flask for such occasions. It looks like there might be many more days like today. Then made his way back to his wife, making a promise to himself that he will keep the head no matter what. He should have been more sensitive to her feelings. As he approached her bed with a tear rolling down his face, his hat twisted in his hands and his head slightly bowed, he fell to her side and apologised for his outburst begging her to forgive him and promising he would never act like that again. He said he did not know what had come over him. 'I'm sorry Evie' he had tears in eyes and there was a pain in his face I had never seen before. After that, they went hand in hand as the nurse push the wheelchair towards the baby unit. We were like any new parents; we were both anxious and excited to see our daughter for the first time. Eddie was so excited, I could feel a little bit rubbed off on me maybe this will be ok after all, maybe this will be the making of me, maybe I can be happy for the first time in months, the heavy cloud had lifted from my heart and I could see a future, not the one I planned but a future and who knows this might just work after all. It felt like an age since we left the ward and arrived at the baby unit. I swear you could hear our knees knocking together. When we arrived at the incubator, we were both stunned into silence, there before our eyes was the smallest baby we had ever seen. The doctors were not joking, there were so many tubes and wires making all sorts of noises. She was so small you could barely see her, her skin all wrinkled and reddish purple that looked so thin you could almost see through it. There was not an ounce of fat on this little creature. The only word I could use to describe the sight in front of me was an Alien from outer space. She is exactly like what I imagined an alien would look like. The nurse explained what all the tubes and machines were for, one was for breathing, one for feeding, one to administer the drugs as they were needed. The lamps were for jaundice and to regulate her body temperature, the truth to be told we could no longer hear her; we were so focused on the dot in the cot with a nappy that was so big she nearly disappeared into it. We were speechless. We had never seen anything so small and fragile as the tears flowed from our eyes, and once they started there was no stopping them. We were both at a loss this was our little girl fighting for her life. We were useless to her now all we could do was watch and pray that she would make it to prove the doctors wrong.

The nurse continued to talk, but we were not listening to a single word she was saying. Finally, Evie found her voice and asked if she could hold her, to which the nurse says not yet as she is too small to be taken out of the incubator and the risk of infection was very high, however, you can open the little window on the side and put your hand inside. It will be good for the baby to feel your touch you should also talk to her, she will be able to recognise your voices.

'Have you got a name for her yet?'

Why Me?

'We looked at each and said we never got around to it; we were sure we had loads of time to choose, until now we couldn't agree.'

Eddie suggested Molly Rose after our grandmothers before I had a chance to object the nurse said that was a lovely name.

'Welcome to the world, little Miss Molly Rose'

She opened the two windows on either side. Eddie and I put our hand inside and we're overcome with love for this little girl. Our hands looked like giant hands in comparison. To our surprise, she wrapped her tiny fingers around our giant one. There was nothing that could have prepared me for how this feels. Eddie spoke with a croak in his voice that this little lady of ours would one day be a force to be reckoned with. His eyes were glistening with pride as he spoke. Our hearts were full of hope.

'She is a fighter, Evie,' he said. She wants to be here with us. She is our little girl.'

Eddie, 'do you think she looks kind of like an alien?'

'Well, Evie, it could only be you that would think like that, but now you mention it you might not be wrong. Despite that, she is the prettiest alien I have ever seen if she is.'

We stood there in our own little time warp, digesting the last twelve hours, how much our lives had changed in such a short space of time. I think we are both trying to adjust to the reality of our new life, whatever happens next. For now, at least I can safely say that I'm thrilled.

Eddie broke the silence first with a 'Thank you, Evelyn, for making me the happiest man alive, I promise my girls will never want for anything, I will work day and night if I have to make sure I can look after you both always, ye will want for nothing.'

'Would you stop Eddie with all that mushy stuff, people will think you have gone soft in the head? You know where they will end up putting you.'

'Let them think what they like. What do I care now I have the two most beautiful girls in my life? Sure they would only be jealous? I cannot wait to take you both home and show ye off to the whole town.'

The nurse was fixing her feeding tube just before adding more mixture to the bag when she said to Eddie and I 'that we will need to take each day as it comes, as it will be a long time before she is ready to go home. We need to get her to breathe on her own before we can do anything else.' It nearly killed Eddie altogether when she came over with the needles to take her bloods, 'for the love of God, what are ye doing to her, sure there is not enough blood in her for herself never mind for you lot the needle is nearly as big as she is.' The nurse offered him a chair as he looked as if he would keel over the nurse laughed and said, 'you be surprised at how much she could spare.'

'Eddie, I think you will be an amazing dad to our little girl, not like half the amadan in the town that doesn't know which end of the baby is up.'

Eddie gave a hearty laugh and replied, 'that was a backhanded compliment if he had ever heard one. Thank you, my darling wife. You too will be a wonderful mother. This little girl is one lucky lady.'

Later that afternoon we had our beautiful daughter christened just in case the worst was to happen. It was only the two of us and the doctor and the nurses. It saddens our hearts that we had no family to surround us. There was no big celebration, no wetting the baby's head. The stillness was very sobering. But we placed all our trust in God to make her strong. About two hours later they told Evelyn she needs to go back to bed for a rest and that the doctors will be doing their rounds soon and she will need to be checked over, you still need your rest 'as for you Dad, it is time for you to go home and let these two ladies get some beauty sleep.'

'All right, Evie lets head back to the ward as this man knows where he is not wanted.'

'Goodbye Nurse, thank you for all your help.'

'Goodbye Mr & Mrs Woods.'

Eddie came to the hospital every day to visit his little princess and me, of course. He was half the man he was when it was time for him to leave each evening. At times it was frustrating watching him Ooh and Ahh over her, the love he had for was impossible not to notice, it was like someone had put a spell on him and the once macho man was like a bowl of jelly around Molly Rose. The way he looked at her was just like watching someone who was in La la land, he was besotted with her. I just wished I felt the same, there are times when I'm over the moon and so in love with her and there are the times when I want to roar and shout at the unfairness of it all. I had expected that it would bore me senseless being stuck in here day in day out but strangely it was not too bad having your meals handed to you three times a day and the tea on tap. Marion was right on that front. The doctors and nurses couldn't have been any nicer if they tried.

Molly Rose continued to improve a little bit every day. There were many setbacks too, each hour things changed often one step forward and two steps back. Progress was slower than I expected, but they insisted that this was normal. They were growing more confident each day that she was doing much better than they had expected. All I could do was just smile and say that's great news. The doctors were delighted with her progress, but I couldn't see any difference from the day before. The nurse would call me when she needed to be fed or if her nappy needed to be changed. I'm not sure why, as I was so nervous to use the tube to feed her, as it was the easiest thing of all to do as for changing her nappy my God, I feared I would break her she was still so small and delicate her skin was so soft and thin, you could see her veins so clearly. Every hour things

Why Me?

changed one minute all was well and the next we were being told she was not doing too good. If they tell me one more time that all we could do now is pray, I will throttle them I'm half afraid to tell them I don't believe in God. If he had existed, I wouldn't be standing here now would I, my head was in overdrive. I did not understand who I was or what I wanted anymore. I was on autopilot. Thank God that they cannot read my mind.

At the end of day four, the doctors said that they would discharge me the following morning. As expected Molly Rose would have to stay for longer and at this stage, they were unsure how long that could be; they did not expect she would be discharged until she was closer to her due date at the earliest she would need to be able to drink from the bottle and put on more weight, not to mention all the other medical issues. I was unsure how I felt about going home, especially without the baby. I guess I was secretly happy and heartbroken at the same time, as I would have another ten weeks without her to myself. They recommend that I came to visit her as often as possible, as there was no replacement for Mum. They suggested no less than every second day as they understood it would be difficult to get to transport in everyday they said I was lucky that she was my first and I didn't have a brood at home to look after.

Tomorrow I will tell Eddie every third or fourth day would be ok as I'm not sure I can spend my days sitting in the baby care unit listening to all the lovey dovey nonsense mothers who are under the illusion that their baby is the most beautiful baby in the world all that blah blah blah.

Why Me?

They go on and on they literally wreck my head. I would love to tell them they all looked the same at this stage and yes all babies poop, yours is not special. Can you imagine having a conversation with someone over your baby poop and burping habits, Christ shoot me NOW if this is what I have to look forward to? I just don't see myself as the type of mum who spends her day talking about 'my baby does this' and 'my baby does that' part of me was jealous as Molly-Rose was not doing any of that, she was still struggling to breathe and she is very slow in gaining weight.

All the other mums in there were in love with Eddie. Listening to them telling me how lucky I was to have a husband like him, sure isn't he a magnificent man to be in here every day to be with his girls. Imagine him coming all the way in here after a hard day's work, that their husbands live so close and yet they barely come near the place and when they do, they are out the door at the first opportunity down to the nearest pub for a few jars before going home. While the cat's away, the mice will play.

Did it ever enter their heads that he might be the lucky one to have me in his life, how do they know I am not the most amazing wife and housekeeper ever to walk on this planet? I can't believe even in here I'm surrounded by people I have never met before and they still judge me, it feels as if they are looking down their noses at me. Everywhere I go it seems I fail everyone expectation's. Can anyone tell me what right do they have to look down their nose at me?

Why can't I just fit in, be accepted for who I am?

Why Me?

I failed as a daughter, sister, friend, in fairness I know that this is more how I feel rather than what anyone has ever said to me. I'm clueless as to why I feel this way but I have for as long as I can remember, always second guess myself and feeling that I never reach the same standards as everyone else. Mam was always telling me off for it as a child, "Stop comparing yourself to everyone and be your self" was her advice. It will not be long before Eddie sees I'm a fraud as a wife and on the road to failure as a mother as well! It would be much better for society as a whole if I would just disappear. Maybe that is what I should do: I have thought about it often enough. I could never have done it in the past as I didn't have enough money to get me out of this hellhole but now, I have more than enough to get to as far as England at least, the big question is what would I do once I got there, also I couldn't leave Molly-Rose I love her that much, I'm sure of. Why am I kidding myself I would have the courage to go in the first place. I guess I will have to continue to smile and play happy family? To be good old Evie, always free to be the butt of other people's jokes. I have always felt second best I'm not sure why or where it came from. It was drilled into me for as long as I can remember to be quiet and to suck it up to follow the words of my parents. My sisters will want to have total control and once Molly Rose comes home, I will be downgraded to third place if I'm lucky. To be fair to my parents, I can never remember them say anything like that to me. They have always been very kind and patient, even when I rebelled. I have always been fighting mostly with myself, I now realise it is more of an internal battle I have

Why Me?

going on. There was always a lot of love in our home, plenty of hugs and kisses to go around. My sisters were a different story they were ten years older than me and as a result, they thought they were the boss and that I should do everything they said, they were as nice as pie in front of mam and dad, it was a different story when they were not around, they would tease me about how mam and dad always went the extra mile for me, how I got away with so much more than they did at my age, in fairness my brothers were not like them at all, they were always in good humour and brought me sweet or ribbons for my hair on payday. It was not unusual for them to slip money into my pockets when I was going anywhere.

Thankfully, I no longer have to live with the girls so I should give thanks for small mercies.

One enjoyable thing about going home is I will be able to have some peace and quiet, not to mention a quick visit to the pub when I feel like it. I would not have the baby unit calling all hours of the day and night asking me to come down to feed her or whatever else they thought was a good idea or whatever they got into their heads. One thing for sure, I was no nurse and now I'm sure I never will be. I wouldn't be surprised if they were calling me just for the sake of it. Every time I closed my eyes, I would hear my name being called to go down to the baby unit. I could imagine them saying get Evelyn to come down as she has nothing else to be doing. My head is all over the place, I worry about myself at times like this; I know they are only trying to be helpful. What good am I to her, I'm not the

Why Me?

one with the nursing degree? I just sit there like a plank, not sure of what to say and no clue what to do. Talk about making me feel like a complete waste of space. Sadly, I don't appear to be bonding with her as the nurse has said that is not surprising given the fact she was so early and that we have not been together the way other mothers are. They reassured me that will all change as soon I hold her in my arms, everything else will fade away. Please God, they are right. See, I still call her rather than Molly Rose or one of the pet names the other mothers call their pride and joy. What could be wrong with me? Am I right in the head or what? I wonder if this is normal, as no one has ever said that they felt like this when their baby was born. All they ever talked about is how much they fell in love with their little bubble as soon as they clapped eyes on them. I swear, If I hear them say ah don't worry love, you get the hang of it in no time, or she will not be that small for long, so enjoy it. I'm sure that they are talking about me when my back is turned. Sweet Jesus, get me out of here quick or I will be in the nut house.

What I wouldn't give right now to have a shot of whiskey, it would just about make this place bearable. I wish we had the phone in the house and then I could tell Eddie the good news, then he might be able to get in a bit earlier than normal. The sooner I get out the better, being in here for the last week has been tougher than I could have ever dreamed of. If I could get a goodnight sleep, I'm sure I would feel a lot better. I hated that I had to call the local shop to get them to pass on the message to Eddie. You could be sure that before Eddie ever gets the message, half the old Biddys in the town would have the story dissected and would have got legs and grown. No such thing as a private message in these parts.

Chapter 5

Eddie should be in tomorrow after work sooner if he can get a lift in. The blasted Honda 50 is only fit for the scrap heap. It is nearly as old as he is. It had belonged to his father, he cherishes it, and on the odd occasion it would come out of the shed you would think he was driving a Harley Davidson, telling anyone that was listening he felt like he was King of the Road him and his Honda. He believes that Christy Moore wrote the song My Little Honda 50 especially for him. Maybe now he might consider getting a car for his precious Molly-Rose, up until now he would not hear any talk about a car, if you didn't know him you would think he was a madman he was always on his high nelly for short journeys day or night rain or shine or the Honda for the longer ones. He looked like a fool at the best of times. Any time I said this to him he would only laugh and say that the others were only jealous of his fine body. Why would you be wasting money on petrol when you had two good legs and reliable wheels, he didn't like the hemmed in feeling you get from the car. For the rest of us, it makes us feel safe and secure, not Eddie!

Hopefully, his brother Jack will be the one that's driving that way I can be sure I get out of here quickly as he won't want to be hanging around for too long and knowing Jack we will have to stop off at the pub along the way. Either way, I will get up early and be ready to go home. With the help of God, old Joe will have given him the message as he is going a bit doddery these days. He is still as sharp as a new pencil when it comes to the money side of the business, but there are signs that he does not function on all cylinders, he drives the girls in the shop batty as they spend more time going around after him putting things back in the right places than they do taking care of the customers.

Eddie will be delighted that I will be going home with him tomorrow and so am I for sure he will pamper me no end, especially as Molly will still be here for another nine/ten weeks if not longer. We will have to take each day as it comes. The doctors so far have been very happy with her progress as she continues to get stronger every day, she is slowly putting on weight but is still the smallest baby in there by a long shot, she still needs to be topped up with oxygen on a regular basis as her lungs are still weak. She has not yet developed the ability to suck, so feeding is still done through a tube. The risk of infection is still very high, and it is far too early for them to tell if there is any brain damage or if there will be any long-term difficulties. The good news is she is starting to regulate her temperature and her blood sugars are stable. She no longer looks like an alien from outer space, and I have yet to hear her cry, I wonder if that is a good sign or not. I guess I should start to ask a few more questions, but in truth, I'm afraid of the answers. God only knows how I will cope when she is released from the hospital. I was dreading looking after a baby and now having no one to help, especially with her extra needs. Now more than ever I'm terrified and surer than ever that I was never meant to be anyone's mother. It must be someone's idea of a sick joke. What the hell am I going to do. There is so much more to get my head around. I hope she will sleep as much as she does now when we take her home. I presume I will have to cross that bridge when I get there. I hope that when that day arrives I will be ready, I will be stronger and somehow we will muddle through it together. I know I'm lucky to have Eddie by my side, as he will do everything he can for both of us. We will want for nothing. He is one of a kind and a true gent. There are not too many ladies that can say that now is there. Too many of them have inept men who believe a woman's place is to be barefooted and chained to the bed or the kitchen sink that their only role is to breed like rabbits and to look after the kids not forgetting to feed their hungry bellies and boost their egos.

Looking on the bright side, I will have a chance to get the house ready and to buy what I need for the nursery and all the other bits before she comes home. I pray I will be able to show her I love her more than life itself, more than I could have ever imagined. Is it possible that I will love motherhood and will take to it like a duck to the water after all, I guess I can live in hope?

Eddie was totally unaware of how Evie was feeling. He was the happiest man in Ireland. His natural good humour was better than normal he had that extra bounce in his step. His life was better than he could have ever planned. It is funny how life turned out not as exactly as he had planned, but life is good. His plan was to marry his childhood sweetheart Ruth and had popped the question in May 1961, they were both over the moon as he slipped the ring on her finger. They spend the rest of the night talking about when they would get married, where they would build their house, how many children they hoped for. Life couldn't have been any better for Eddie than it was then. It was agreed that they would get married in October, as neither of them had seen the point in a long engagement. Sure, they had known each other all their lives and had been courting since they were thirteen. Nobody would be surprised with their news it was to be expected most people were shocked that they had not tied the knot before now. If truth be told, Eddie had no idea what had taken him so long to pop the question other than now they were 29 years old they no longer needed anyone's permission or blessing, Ruth's mother the old Mrs O'Dea was as contrary as hen's teeth she was never happy, she always has to be giving out about something or someone. The trouble she caused when Ruth's older siblings, when they said they were getting married, was uncalled for: it was ridiculous. She was like a baby that had her toys taken away. The priest used to bless himself when he would see her heading his way. She was full of woes; she was widowed when the kids were nearly all reared, but that did not stop her from playing the poor me card she would often be heard saying she raised her thirteen kids on her own. Ruth was the youngest of her bunch as she was only seven when her father fell from the tractor and passed away a few days later. It didn't help that her favourite son was drowned later that year in a fishing accident. Thankfully, Eddie was in her good books she had a bit of a soft spot for him possibly it was because he never arrived at the house to collect Ruth without a little something for her whether it was a small bottle of poteen or a pack of sweet Afton cigarettes. It did not hurt that he could charm the old dear ever since he was a nipper. The best part about Eddie was he never really tried to charm her or anyone. It just happened that way. He was sincere in everything he did. When people would say she was the meanest women that ever put a foot in a shoe, he would gentle laugh and tell them they should not talk bad about anyone, no good ever came from it. That was Eddie's way. kind and gentle to a fault.

It was late September when Eddie saw Ruth standing by the bus stop; it surprised him to see her there and thought that one of the family must be home from the states on holiday. Strange that neither she nor her mother never mentioned it last night. Perhaps one of the girls has surprised them with a visit to help them with the wedding planning. Ruth was planning to go to Dublin to find the wedding dress of her dreams. He called out to her, but she ignored him, it was as if she didn't hear him. He was shocked when she stepped onto the bus with her head nearly hidden in her coat, without saying a word or looking in his direction. Before he could get across the road, the doors of the bus closed and drove off down the road. He could have sworn that she looked him in the eye as she waved, he could see her mouth move it look like she was saying I'm sorry, but I have to go. Her big brown eyes were covered in tears. Eddie cursed the fact that he didn't have a car to follow the bus. He fell to the ground in disbelief what did this mean, what had happened in the last few hours, last night they had spoken to the priest to make the final arrangements for the wedding. There was no hint that anything was amiss. She was happy, as they left arm in arm and went to the pub for a pint they stayed until closing time, then he walked her home. She was the happiest that he had ever seen her, they both were. He was wrecking his head with what could have happened in less than twelve hours to make her get on a bus without saying a word to him. He had an overwhelming feeling of dread. This was bad, really bad. Every bone in his body said so.

Mrs O'Dea, the old trout, seemed to be happy for them to get married. She offered no objection. Her only complaint was, what that it had taken me so long to ask the question. She was looking forward to having a decent son-in-law as she saw it, it would be good to have a dependable man around the house.

Eddie sat on the ground as he was afraid, he would fall as the power had left his legs. He was feeling so weak he was sure he was going to pass out. He was trying to work out what was happening. He could feel it in his heart that his world had just fallen apart, that much he knew. The skies opened and torrential rain fell, hitting his skin like bullets. Each drop was like a nail was being hammered into him, even this was no match for the pain in his heart or the mental anguish the rattle around in Eddie's head. He was not sure how long he sat there. His heart split in two, his mind in tatters. He was broken, unable to move. Jack was shocked to see Eddie sitting in the middle of the street like a drowned rat. Jack was worried, as he didn't seem to be able to get through to him. He eventually had to lift him off the ground and carry him like a baby and put him into the

Why Me?

car. He was totally silent all the way home. There was no way he could get a word from him, and anything that came from his mouth was total gibberish.

Eddie had not improved by the time they arrived home. Jack had to get their father to come and help get him out of the car. Once he was in the house, they had to strip the wet clothes from his body, as Eddie was motionless. The light was on but there was nobody home, they drip fed a hot whiskey into him, it was useless. There was nothing else they could do but put him to bed and hope that when he got up, he could make some sense. Later that evening, Mother suggested that Jack went over to Ruth to see if she could make any sense out of his behaviour.

Jack returned to say that Mrs O'Dea nearly scalded him with a pot of boiling water as she told him that Ruth had gotten some sense had left. She didn't know where she was going, only that she would not be coming back anytime soon. Oh, and by the way, I or my lot were not welcome at her door.

They all agreed that they were in shock, as that couldn't be the case. The old woman must have finally gone mad altogether. They would have to wait to hear what Eddie had to say. But if Ruth was really gone, they feared the worst. What had happened, and why had she left? This didn't make any sense at all.

There was no doubt in their minds that the old trout herself had played a part in whatever had happened. They were terrified at what Eddie would do. How would he recover?

Why Me?

His mother must have said the rosary ten times over that night. She pleaded with the good Lord to protect her beloved son. Lord, hold him in your arms and give him some comfort and strength to deal with this ordeal. She feared he would never be the better of this.

It took Eddie a long time to accept that she was gone and was not coming back. He had not a clue as to why she left. To say he was heartbroken was an understatement. He was half the man he once was. The light in his eyes had gone out, his smile no longer looked the same. After a few months of Eddie moping around the place it was more than anyone could stand. In the end, Jack thought it might be a good thing if they went to London to work for a bit. He told Eddie it would do him the world of good to get away from here for a while to start fresh somewhere he had no memories of Ruth.

A month later himself, Jack and his younger brother Pete left the lovely Clifden for the big lights of London. The boys worked hard on the building sites; they found the work hard, but the pay was mighty. The boys stayed in London for the next five years, Eddie's heart never left Clifden, and longed to return to his home by the sea. He missed the sea and the wide-open fields most of all, here in London the place was so closed in, when he first arrived here he loved the noise of the place it was a distraction from the torment in his mind, now he prayed for the peace and quiet of home. He was getting tired of the building sites, it just didn't seem to give him the same joy it once did. Then one evening an old fella in the pub asked him if he could give him a hand a few nights a week in the bakery as he was finding it hard to lift the heavy trays. Eddie found it hard to say no to anyone that asked him for help and turned up the following evening. The months passed and Eddie found that he had started to look forward to going into the bakery, he loved the smell of the bread baking and it was a blessing to be there after a tough day on the building sites, especially when the weather was so cold and wet, slowly he spent more and more time there than on the building sites, learning the craft of baking. For a while, it took the pain away and his yearning to go home. Pete surprised them when he got married out of the blue to an English girl and moved to Cornwall to settle down to a quieter life. In wasn't long afterwards all of Jack's playing the field with a different lady every night was beginning to catch up with him. Jack had announced that he was going back to Ireland due to the fact there were too many unhappy women on his case and not to mention one or two of their husbands. The last thing he needed was to get into a scrap with one of them. He was afraid that he might have gotten one of them pregnant, and it was best he went before someone trapped him. There was no way he was going to be getting married anytime soon, never mind having a kid running around the place.

It was around the same time that old baker died and left the business to Eddie in his will, he said he was the closest he had to a son. Eddie was knocked for six as he did not know what shocked him more: his sudden death or him leaving everything to him. Eddie sold the business and left London with Jack, returning home to where his heart had always been.

Chapter 6

Evie was going home today and much to her amazement; she was overcome with emotions, leaving little Molly Rose behind. She felt a mixture of guilt and pain that was so unfamiliar that it left her blindsided as she walked out of the hospital she wanted nothing more than her own bed and the comfort of her own home, but she was angry that Molly Rose was not coming home with them. So much so when Jack pulled up outside the pub in Oughterard she no longer wanted to go inside, she just wanted to get home as quickly as possible. Before she had a chance to say anything Jack was out of the car in a flash and in no time at all, he was standing at the bar ordering his second drink, he can knock them back in a blink of an eye.

'Eddie said he would go and get him. He hasn't got a brain in his head. He will be oblivious to how tired you are, never mind, how hard this is for you.'

'No, it's ok Eddie. I just need a minute. You go ahead and I will follow you in. Can you order a gin and tonic for me?'

'Are you sure, Evie?'

'Yes, I'm fine. Stop fussing, now go and order me that drink, for goodness' sake,'

Once inside, I knew for sure I didn't belong here. My drinking days were over. I nursed my G&T for the first time in my life, the taste of it was turning my stomach so much I thought I would puke.

Eventually, Eddie persuaded Jack it was time to go.

Jack fell around the place laughing, saying that he would have lost his house if he had put a bet on me wanting to go home. True enough, it was a first for me.

'Jack, I think you have the wrong impression of my Evie. She not as fond of the drink as you are. So shut up and drive. You might want to try to give it up yourself, you might even find a woman for yourself if you were not half cut the whole time,'

'Eddie the saint, would you ever shut up, you would think that you were holier than the man upstairs since that little girl has been born.'

'What can I say, I'm a changed man. No more nights down in the pub boozing for me.'

'You might want to give it a try for yourself one of these days, Jack.'

'Not for me, dear brother, there is no woman on this earth that will make me give up me sup of porter, many have tried and failed.'

The journey home took forever. I prayed to a God I no longer believed in that Jack would not stop at any other pubs until we got to Clifden and then he could stay in one all night if he wanted to. For once, God answered my prayers, and Jack bypasses each one along the way.

Why Me?

When we arrived at the house, the fire was on, Eddie had asked the next-door neighbour to put it on and to make sure it didn't go out, as he wanted the house to be just right for when I got home. Not only had she put the fire on but had a lovely beef and Guinness casserole on the hob, there was an abundance of pies and cakes on the table, there was more on the table than in the shop.

Eddie laughed and said, 'that everyone on the street had been in with dinners and desserts since I went into the hospital, I think they have forgotten that I'm a modern man and I can make my own bread and cakes for a living.'

'I guess they are just trying to be helpful and in fairness, you have not been here long enough to eat anything, never mind to cook it.'

'Too true, Evie. But there is enough food here to feed a small army. So, I hope you are hungry,'

'It's good to know that you didn't have a chance to miss my fine cooking, my dear husband,' laughed Evie.

'Never mind your cooking. It was you I missed that bed was awful big without you been sprawled across it and pulling the covers off me.'

'Now, let's get some of this food into you. We need to build up your strength after everything you have been through. I can't imagine that the food in the hospital was up to much. Afterwards, I will wash up so you can have an early night.'

Why Me?

'Eddie, do you think Molly will be ok? It is just a bit strange coming home and her still in the hospital.'

Eddie wrapped his arms around his wife. 'I have no doubt at all she will be fine, she is a tough little cookie'. Evie, broke down and cried into his chest before she knew it she had blurted out that she was afraid that she would be a terrible mother, that she was not ready and then all of this had happened so fast. She hadn't any time to get my head around it. Sure, I had just gotten used to being pregnant. All of this was my fault, the pregnancy and the early arrival of Molly.

Eddie was taken back to see the tears streaming down her face Evie, was not known to show her emotions. He guessed that it might have something to do with the hormones 'Shush my love; you have done everything just fine. None of this has been your fault you heard the doctors they said that sometimes babies come early no one really knows why. It's just the luck of the draw.'

'What if she is not all right, what if she has problems breathing or if her brain has not developed, what if she never talks or walks?'

'Stop that now, we cannot think about the what if's? There is no point worrying about something that might never happen.'

'But what if it does, I don't think I can cope with it? It's ok for you! You will be the most amazing dad. I could see that from the first time you set eyes on her.'

'Evie, we will cross each bridge if it comes our way together, you will be great just you wait and see.'

'Eddie, do you really think that she will be ok or are you just saying that to make me feel better?'

'Yes, I do. Now, no more of that talk. Let's eat.'

Both of them ate their dinner in silence, both exhausted. Eddie made sure Evie went to bed as soon as she put her spoon down as he was washing the dishes. He realised he had never seen her so fragile or talk so openly about her thoughts or feeling. He knew it would have taken a lot for Evie to open up the way she did and made a promise to himself and to anyone that was listening in heaven that he would do everything in his power to mind and care for his girls.

He just wished that everyone would be easier on Evie, as she was not as tough as she pretended to be. If only everyone could see the Evie, the way he did?

Evie woke late the following morning after sleeping like a log. She was amazed when she looked at the clock to see it was after 11:00 am the house was so quiet there was not a sound to be heard. There was no rattling of trays no alarms beeping and no crying babies she stretched out in the big bed wondering what she would do today she was not ready to go outside as she was not in the humour to talk to every Tom, Dick and Harriet that felt they had the right to bombard her with questions, sure half the town did not know she was pregnant in the first place, can you just imagine what they are thinking. For now, she would take it easy and put them to the back of her mind. Evie had just put the kettle on when Eddie came in from the yard, his arms full of turf.

'Good morning sleeping beauty, how did you sleep?

I thought that you would never wake up. You must have been exhausted, I'm not sure how you got any sleep in that place with the Nurses in and out all hours of the day. As for the cleaning staff it seemed like they has a mop permanently in their hands.'

Sit down and I will make you a nice fry for breakfast. You must be starving we need to get your strength back. No better way than with good food and plenty of rest.'

'I will be as fat as a fool if you keep feeding me like this. You know I was looking forward to being able to see my toes; I had kinda hoped that I wouldn't have lost them forever.'

Evie sat by the warm fire and curled up on the chair. God, it was good to be home at last: Home Sweet Home. With a deep breath, she knew she was very lucky all around.

'I never heard you getting up this morning, Eddie. What time did you come downstairs?'

'That's me, as quiet as a mouse. I didn't want to wake you! I not sure, it must have been around six you know me I loved getting up to the sound of the birds.'

'Eddie, after we have eaten, can you call the hospital to see how Molly Rose is doing today. It feels strange not to be able to go down to see her and for the nurses not coming in to give me an update on she was during the night.'

'Don't you worry, I have been up to the phone box earlier to call before you got up; I thought you might have been anxious. So no need to worry. She has had a good night's sleep like her mother. I gave the nurse the number for the Garda station and they said they would call if there was an emergency.'

'Thanks, Eddie. I am finding being away from her a lot harder than I thought I would.

Do you think we should go to see her later?'

'The nurse thinks it would be best for you to rest for a day or two before going in to see her. They said that they had called Dr O'Connor to come and check on you later today, after his clinic.'

'Why? I feel fine.'

'They said that it is routine with all new mums, especially in your case and when the baby has to stay in the hospital for longer.'

'They are fussing over nothing; I hope you told them that. Having Dr O'Connor traipsing in here every day is not my idea of fun. He could easily do my head in. He is a superb doctor and a lovely guy, but I would prefer to be left on my own. Besides, he is very old-fashioned. I know where he is if I need him.'

'Let him come for today, and then we can play it by ear. Now, eat your food before it goes cold. I can't have them saying I not looking after you properly. Eat up, girl.'

It was later that evening, when a boyish-looking man that we had not seen before called to say he was the locum in place of Dr O'Connor. Dr O'Connor was on holidays for a few weeks. If you were to ask I would say he was barely out of his school shorts, never mind a fully qualified doctor he introduced himself as Dr Dunne. He was new to the area and was still finding his feet. He checked me over and sat with me for almost an hour. I'm sure it was because he had no idea of what he was doing. The sooner Dr O'Connor comes back, the better. When he was leaving, he said he would call again next week but to call to surgery if I need anything in the meantime.

I had asked when Dr O'Connor would be back and was surprised to hear he would not be back before the end of the month. It was unheard of for him to take so much time off. Normally it would be a day here or there to play a round of golf. I must ask Marion if she knows anything about it.

Why Me?

It amazed me how tired I was as soon as I had finished my cup of tea; I had a bath before going back to bed. I could hear the neighbours downstairs dropping in more food and asking after me, each one saying, 'Now if you or Evelyn need anything, we are just next door.' I was glad Eddie had not gone to work today as he shields me from having to deal with them. The idea of having to smile and make small talk was overwhelming.

I was delighted to see Marion later that evening. She was so refreshing. We laughed and cried at the same time apparently I had nearly given half the hall a heart attack when I went into labour, 'Imagine Evie, you could have had the lot of them in the bed beside when you were in labour.'

'That would be a sight I would pay to see,' Marion roared with laughter. Here are your winnings before I forget.'

'Thanks Marion, I can go shopping next time I'm in Galway.

Marion, I have missed you during the week. I could have done with you in that place.'

'Now stop that maudlin, Evie. We would have been arrested if we were together. I would have gone in but when I rang, the hospital they said that I would not have been allowed to see you as you need your rest in between being down with the baby.'

'The no visitors rule was a pain. We only found out about it when we asked when our mother could meet the baby.

There was no way they would let them into the special care unit. Neither one of them was thrilled with the news but, my mother went berserk when Eddie told her. She even called the hospital to complain.

Marion, all joking aside, I'm terrified she is so small and they are not sure if she will make it or not.'

The tears strode down my face as I spoke. I realised not for the first time that I loved my daughter and want her to be in my life. I vowed then that I would be the best mother I could be, even if it is terrifying me half to death. I felt so strong and in control. I told myself that I could do this. Nobody warns you that becoming a mother is as scary as hell. It was such a relief to know that it was normal to feel like this.

'Marion, what do you know about Dr O'Connor taking such a long holiday? Where had he gone, too? There must be something big going on. It has taken so much time off from the surgery?

'Did you not hear that his son was getting married in Spain and Mrs O'Connor said that she would get some sun on her old bones before it was too late? She said that she might never get himself outside the N59 again so she was going to take full advantage of the opportunity as she has waited long enough to get away.'

Over the next few days, I got into a routine. I was feeling human again and looking forward to life. I found myself looking forward to the trips to Galway, to see Molly Rose,

Why Me?

after a long day in the hospital it was a joy to visit the shops, or just to meander around the street. It was impossible to buy clothes for her as everything would smother her even the newborn clothes were too big. Thankfully, my mother had knitted some small cardigans for her and Marion had taken some baby clothes and made them smaller: she was a dab hand on the sewing machine. Just after Christmas Molly Rose was taken out of the incubator and put into a regular cot, but still in the ICU. She was now gaining weight, and her facial feature looked less like an alien. The doctors were thrilled with her progress, each day they became more confident that she would be just fine; we were all hoping for a full recovery, but only time will tell. When she started to take her feeds from the bottle with no difficulty and they would like to see her reach at least 4lbs before thinking about sending her home. Once again, they warned us to be patient and that there were no guarantees. It was still in the hands of the Gods.

Finally, the day came when they said we could take her home on the 23rd of February, all going well. I couldn't wait to get home to tell Eddie. My entire body was shaking with the pure joy she was going to be ok. Thank you, God. I got this and now the hormones were more settled I was looking forward to being a Mum; the nurses had reassured me that everything I was feeling was completely normal, especially after such a traumatic birth and that most women feel the same only the brave ones admit it. I have to say hearing this raised my confidence no end, it put me in such a good mood I could take on the world and his mother.

Chapter 7

The day had finally arrived; She woke up super earlier to put the last touches on the baby's room. Eddie had outdone himself. The crib was beautiful. He had hand carved some of it from a tree that had fallen down in the garden. He had spent hours and hours crafting the old tree to create the most amazing crib ever; he carved in pictures of baby animals, there was not another one like it in the country. He could easily make a few more of them, and he would be able to sell them for a fortune. In the corner of the room, he had also made a lovely rocking chair for her to sit in when she was feeding her, the room looked better than she had ever imagined. She had often told him he was wasting his talents in the bakery, he was ever so gifted with his hands and a piece of wood.

Evelyn was so excited that she found it hard to eat breakfast. Jack is going to collect them after work. 'I'm not sure how I will last till four o'clock' Evelyn said. The time was moving so slowly, each minute felt like an hour. She rang the hospital at ten to make sure that there had been no changes to the arrangements; and was relieved when they said she could definitely go home today. Eddie was going to pop into the shop for a few hours as he was getting restless waiting in the house. He was like a child on Christmas morning. While I was uptown, She decided to pop Into Maggie's for a quick brandy, just to calm her nerves, She had not had a drink in weeks, and one would steady the

Why Me?

ship, so to speak, should have known better! one would never normally have been enough, so she had to have three more before heading home for a quick nap as the brandy had gone to straight to her head never before in her life had four brandy's made her tipsy, 'I must be out of practice' she thought to herself.

Jack arrived early just after two o'clock, come on, my girl let's go and get this little one. I can't wait to see her and bringing her home is the icing on the cake.

The three of us hit the road to collect our little princess. Of course, Jack had to stop in Recess, Maam Cross, Oughterard, for his tipple. By the time we left the last pub in Oughterard, he must have had at least five pints and a few whiskeys. In his words, he just had to wet the baby's head.

Let's just say Jack has had a few mishaps while driving and on more than one occasion he has wrapped the car around a tree or ended up in a ditch with or without a drink in him he was a terrible driver. The roads would be a lot safer if he was not on them. Why did I think today he would be any better.

We were about five miles outside Oughterard when a small mini overtook him. He was furious and when he realised it was being driven by a nun, he lost it all together. Jack started to shout at the car as if they could hear him. He roared in anger at how their small banger could overtake his fine beast of a car. He had himself convinced that they could hear him and that they were ignoring him. The more

Why Me?

Eddie told him to calm down and to take it easy the more fuel it added to the fire, it just drove him around the bend altogether and he pushed hard on the accelerator and overtook the nuns, without paying attention to the oncoming traffic, No one had a chance to shout stop before he hit the back of the nuns car sending our car to the other side of the road hitting the side of the wall, next thing we knew the car was travelling along the road on its roof until it finally came to a stop after hitting a tree. I'm not sure how long we were hanging there upside down, but the first thing I heard was Eddie roaring at Jack, and Jack fecking and blinding those Nuns; look at what they have done - they had put a curse on us, his fine car was ruined. I was speechless how in the name of god could he blame the nuns; he was the one driving like an idiot. Now, the nuns and another passer-by were trying to pull open the doors, trying to help us get out. We sat there on the side of the road covered in blood, our clothes completely ruined. I was sure Eddie would kill Jack; I had never seen him in such a rage before, and he was scaring the crap out of me. It was a godsend that we could move at all. One nun tried to clean the blood from my head and offered the lads cloths to hold over the cuts in an to attempt to stop the bleeding, the older nun had said one of the local farmers had left to call an ambulance, to which Eddie had said that there was no need as we were going to the hospital to pick up our daughter. One of the other drivers offered to give us a lift, which we

jumped at. The three of us were a sight for sore eyes by the time we arrived at the hospital. The nurses did not know what to say to us as they cleaned our heads and bandaged our cuts. It was clear that they were appalled at the thoughts of letting a little baby home with us. After a lot of nodding and talking the doctor informed us he couldn't allow her to go home with three adults who were under the influence of alcohol - I tried to object, but they stood their ground and told us to come back tomorrow when we had sobered up. Eddie was uncontrollable as he had only had one pint. Now, I wished I could say the same, but that would have been a lie. Once again, I told myself that I would have to cut back on the drink; It had been weeks since I had, had a drink and I hadn't really missed it. Why in the name of all that is holy did I choose today to start. I should have known something like this would happen.

We booked into a B&B close to the hospital with our heads bandaged and our spirits low, we were so ashamed of ourselves, I guess we were lucky that we had no broken bones or worse, I was not sure which hurt more, my head or my ego. Jack was a pain in the arse, as he couldn't see how badly this reflected on us as parents. He just laughed as he said this will be a cool story to tell her when she is older. I lost it with him I couldn't believe that he could find any of this mess funny, 'Do you not realise that you were nearly responsible for making that poor child an orphan' Eddie was roaring at him.

Take it easy you two, there was no harm done was there. You're both still alive, unlike my car. It is a complete write off.

With that Eddie told Jack to get a taxi home and he booted Jack out telling him he could find his own way home. Jack roared with laughter and said, 'I will see you two tomorrow when ye have had a chance to cool the jets.'

It was well after nine by the time Jack got home and sure enough, the entire village knew about the accident before he had a chance to turn the key in the door. That's life in a small town for you, everyone knows your business almost as soon as you do.

Chapter 8

It was over a week later when Molly Rose was discharged from the hospital, as the doctors wanted to be sure we were ready to take on the role of being parents to a preemie baby. This time we got the bus in and a taxi home, Jack stayed at home, he said he would have the fires on for us as we didn't want Molly coming home to a cold house. The last thing we need was her catching pneumonia, before we were allowed to take her home we had to meet with social workers as a result of the incident the week before. They told us that they will be calling to see us and as their visit will not be announced, we would have to be on our best behaviour.

Molly-Rose was a wonderful baby, she slept far more than she was awake, life was simple feed, change and sleep. We were very lucky as she slept through the night from the first night home. We would have to wake her for her bottle.

The weather was still freezing, so I did not want to take her out in case she would catch a cold. True to their word, the social worker arrived on a regular basis for the first six months. After that they were never to be seen again, thank God. As they had no idea of personal space or the idea of what was off limits. They would be just short of asking you what you had for breakfast. They were a right pain in the arse.

Why Me?

As Molly-Rose continued to grow she was developing just like any other full-term baby would, the only difficulty that she had was she was very prone to chest infections and would need to go the local hospital regularly to be put on a nebuliser, other than that she was totally healthy.

The same Locum Dr Dunne called to see us when Dr O Connor was away for the next year. Each time he called, he was even more handsome than before. I would prefer if it was old O'Connor as he asked fewer questions. Sometimes I think Dr Dunne could see inside my head he kept going on and on about the baby blues and how normal it was. No matter how many times I said I was fine, he would give me a look that said I know you're not telling the truth. On one occasion he left prescription on the table for me, as it was better to prevent the baby blues than cure it, he was saying. I was in a fit of rage and as soon as he walked out the door I threw the paper in the fire. He has a neck that one, in his posh clothes and fancy accent, who did he think he was he would be more suited to a tv screen. I'm sure he was looking down his nose at me. There goes that voice inside my head again if only I could get it to be quiet. Imagine he had the neck to suggest that I join some stupid group that was running from the surgery. For the love of God who does he thinks he is, with all his fancy ideas. They may have worked in the big city, but here in the back of beyond, it will never take off. In the future, I will only see old O'Connor he is old school and does not talk about feeling and baby blues or joining these daft groups, he's more of the opinion just get on with it, he must be losing the plot altogether if he is on board with this new age nonsense. I'm very surprised that a young man would have such notions.

Little did I know that these years were among the happiest I would ever have. I knew I was blessed with Molly-Rose as she was such a calm baby. I was in doubt that she had won me over. By the time Molly-Rose was four, she was stubborn as a mule. She had her own mind and was determined to get her own way. The battles between us happened on a regular basis. She was still the apple of her father's eye she couldn't do any wrong he was the good cop and me as the ogre. She always gravitated toward her dad as soon as he walked into the room she runs into his arms like an angel fallen from the skies. She adored him when he was around. She would not look in my direction - the little witch. If he was going to the bog, she would want to go. If he was in the bakery, she would be by his side. It was like he had a shadow, a mini-me. Maybe it was because she knew I didn't want her in the beginning, maybe she heard me praying for the pregnancy to end. Who knows, but there is one thing for sure: our relationship will never be the same as her and her dad. I could feel the resentment building and building day by day. All Eddie talked about was Molly this, Molly that, it was just short of driving me crazy. Of course, she loved the attention but could she not see I have been trying my best. Can she not see how hard I'm trying and how much I love her?

A year and a half later I found myself pregnant again this time, I knew there was nothing I could do but accept what was happening. Nine months later, I gave birth to two healthy boys. After the boys were born I found life very hard. They demand attention twenty-four seven. Sleep was something they knew nothing about. Just as one would close his eyes the other one would start crying and I would be back to square one again it was as if I was on a roundabout, it was not long before I started to slip back into my old habits, three kids one husband and no time for myself. As you can imagine, I couldn't get out very often without the three of them hanging out of me, but that didn't stop me

I would buy a nag or two of whiskey when I was doing the shopping and hide it in the house just for those times when I would be at my wit's end. No one knew what I was up to. Or did they? My sanity came from an old woman who lived in the next street. She liked to have a drink and was known by the whole town as having a problem with the bottle. She was barred from every pub in the town, so now she has to buy her naggins from the shop and would happily spend her days in a drunken slumber, she didn't have a care in the world. Without thinking, I said to her to pop in anytime to see Molly-Rose, and without much delay, she did most days with her bottle of Old Navy Rum. At first, I refused to drink with her but it didn't take too much to persuade me to have a drop, after all, it would be very rude of me to let her drink alone. Little did I know that this would turn out to be my downfall. I would supply the ham and mustard sandwich and tea, she would bring the rum. She would drink it neat which I couldn't stomach, I would have to add some lemonade. She provided me with much needed adult company I was missing, since the boys were born, she never judges and always supported my woes, she was a kind-hearted old woman but sadly the drink got the better of her; she was unlike others in the town, she never spoke badly about anyone and always had something nice to say. Her way of disapproving was, when she said let God be their judge. She would often tell me stories of old, I was surprised when she said that she was married as I have never seen or heard of a husband, she laughed when she recalled how he ran off with her best friend to England. They were married less than a year before he announced he was off. "Thankfully, we had no children. In the beginning, people felt sorry for me. But I'm relieved he left as he had a bad streak in him, I pray and thank the good Lord every night for a lucky escape." For the first few years, he used to send me a few pounds every month. Guilt money, I used to call it, but when they started having kids, he stopped the giro. I was lucky that I never gave up work like so many other women did at the time I worked in the hospital until I had to retire about ten years ago. I was no longer able to lift the patients in and out of the bed. I have had a good life, Evelyn. There is no need for anyone to feel sorry for me. I know I'm the talk of the town as they think I'm a witch, as I never go near a doctor I make all my own potions just like the old folk used too. Sure, my own sisters tried to sign me into the nuthouse on more than one occasion. I collect the nettle and dandelion and many other herbs and blend them together, and they cure every ailment going. I don't believe in doctors and all their drugs, half the time they are too busy to listen to the patients, so the quick answer to everything is a tablet; they used to go mad when I would put the potion in the tea for the patients in the hospital,

Why Me?

eventually they left me to my ways as the patients were happy and in the end I was doing no harm. So if you ever need anything, you let me know."

She was the one who came to see how Molly-rose was when she has her chest infection, with her bottle of nettle juice and her batch of tea she would rub Vicks on Molly's chest and cover it with brown paper that I was not to remove, for it to work you had to leave the brown paper on until it fell off by itself, onion on the sole of her feet and sure enough when the paper fell off the chest infection would be gone in no time. She had many weird and wonderful concoctions. It was hard to keep up with her.

Molly-Rose found a bottle of Gin one evening and brought it down to her dad to ask him to take the top off as she wanted her special drink, I nearly died on the spot. As far as Eddie and everyone else knew I was off the drink. Eddie wanted to know what was this and why was it in the house, I lied of course and told him it was for my father, lucky for me he accepted my explanation but it was still close. Thankfully, he didn't ask any more questions as he knew my father liked an occasional drop. After that, I was much more careful about where to hide my stash.

I found myself pregnant again this time I had another boy, not long afterwards there was another one. Then a miscarriage, followed by a stillbirth. Jesus Christ, I must be the most fertile woman in Ireland at this stage. All Eddie had to do was look at me and I seemed to be pregnant. Still, after all these kids, you'd think I would get some sense, If I had my life to live over, I would never have one, never mind six of the little ungrateful brats running around the place. They just end up sucking the life out of you. So much so that you wake up one morning and you no longer recognise yourself, you're a stranger in your own body. In fact, I would never get married. I would spend my life travelling the world, never staying anywhere for too long and not get stuck in the rut. I should have taken my chance and done a runner, in the beginning, had the baby in a barn and left her in a box at the church door if I had any sense.

If my head was not fried before all this crap it is certainly fried now as I no longer know where I'm going or what I'm doing. I fall between feeling sorry for myself and being angry all the time. I'm not sure which is worse, all I do know is that I'm not in control of anything I have this sinking feeling day and night. I'm not too proud to say I pray at night that I will not wake up in the morning or if I did this life was only a nightmare. With the morning light comes the realisation that it is all real and that there is no escape.

Late one evening Molly-Rose was barely breathing, so we had to call Dr O' Connor. We both paced the floor as we were waiting for him to arrive. We had never seen her like this before. I was startled when I opened the door and standing there was a young lady dressed to the nine, I initially thought she was at the wrong place until she spoke and said Dr O'Connor was out on a call and was not due back for hours as he was with a patient who was coming close to the end of their life.

Why Me?

I swore after the last new one that came that I would never have anything to do with anyone other than Dr O'Connor himself. But Molly was in such a state, I had no choice in the matter.

When the Doctor arrived Eddie welcomed her in and quickly brought her up to see Molly, who was in an awful condition I have to admit she has frightened the living daylights out of me I was frozen in time, it was if we were transported back in time to when she was born. The Dr was wonderful with Molly and stayed by her side until her breath has eased off. It was hard to believe she was a doctor at all as she looked far too glamorous and very young if I had met her in town and I was told she was the new Doctor I would have said it was a joke. It was only then she asked if any of the other children were sick. When we said no, she asked if it was ok to check them quickly while she was here. She promised that she would not disturb them from their sleep. Fair play to her, she checked them out in super quick time and not one of them stirred she gave them a clean bill of health.

Amelia Reid left the Wood's house with a heavy heart, as she was sure that mum was not bonding with the little girl in the way that would be expected. She seemed to react slightly different to Molly than the other children there was something in her tone when she spoke about them maybe Amelia was imagining it but she made a mental note to talk to Dr O'Connor when he gets back from his rounds, as he knows the family much better and he might be able to put her mind at rest. He will know more about the history of the family.

Amelia was sure as anything that the mother was not coping with the role of motherhood, that there was something amiss. It may well be down to the fact she was worn out with so many young kids the baby in the crib couldn't have been more than six months old.

Amelia felt that she might have offended her when she asked her to come along to the new support group she had set for mothers to have a cup of tea and chat. I'm sure she can't see the benefit of getting out of the house and meeting with women in a similar situation. It is such a shame that there is such a stigma attached to new mums that might not be coping if they would just open up and talk about how they are feeling it is half the battle. Motherhood is hard and there are no shortcuts or quick fixes, but it is easier when you have a good network of support.

On the bright side, little Molly-rose was the cutest little girl I have ever seen. She will be a character it would not surprise me if she turns out to be quiet a feisty one. It was a little worrying at how small she was for her age; she looked no more the five years. The fact she was nearly eight took me by surprise.

Evie called Marion the following day to find out more about the strange Dr Reid. Marion always knew who everyone was and what was their story and she just loved the chance to gossip, she was on every committee in the town just so she would be in the loop, she was only short of playing golf as she wanted to rub shoulder with high and might of the town.

Marion was around in record time, as she had not yet seen Dr Reid, and she wanted to know all about what she looked like, etc.

Marion finally took a breath and said, "Well, surely you must have heard all about her and know who her mother and what her story is?"

"No. If I did I wouldn't have called you to find out.

Would you now get on with it and Tell me?"

"She is from London and is engaged to O'Brien's son from Ballyconneely. But that is not the interesting bit.

Do you remember all the talk about Maeve Lynch who went missing all those years ago? It was before our time, but our parents used to talk about how strange it all was?

Well, she is Maeve's daughter.

Only nowadays she is better known as Elizabeth Reid. She changed her name when she ran away."

"You're kidding."

"I kid you not."

"She moved here a few months ago, not long afterwards she got engaged".

Maeve has done a complete makeover on the old house and according to the neighbours she has done an amazing job.

Chapter 9

Eddie was no fool. He knew Evie was struggling, but he was at a loss on how to help her. Every day she seemed to slip further and further away from him. She was so angry all the time he could do nothing right. If he was at home, she was giving out he was under her feet if he was out of the house she was giving out; he was never there to help her. There was just no pleasing the woman. He knew she was torturing herself but didn't know why or how to stop it. No matter what he tried, it didn't make any difference. He either didn't do enough or did too much. There was no pleasing her these days.

The only time I would see a smile on her face would be for a few hours on a Saturday night in the pub, dolled up to the nine's. Sitting on the high stool at the bar she was at her happiest she came to life for the evening. We would often wobble home arm in arm and she was like my old Evie, the girl I fell in love with all those years ago. Sadly, by the time Sunday morning came, she would return to an angry and bitter woman. I knew she loved me. I just wish I knew how to help her. So that everyone could see the woman I knew was still inside; instead of what was underneath and the bitterness and spiteful words that flew from her mouth like venom. I know having the kids has not been easy on her, she has not had an easy time of it and for some reason, herself and Molly just rub each other up the wrong way. Molly would just have to walk into the room and Evie

Why Me?

would tear strips off her for no reason at all. I was clueless as to what I could do to help them get along better.

I know for a fact that Molly-Rose feels the hostility her mother has towards her, she more than the others was always trying to escape from the house from the moment she could walk she wanted out. She would jump at every chance she had to come to the bakery or the bog. She would be in having tea with the neighbours or running errands, anything to get out of the way.

Her mother would say that she was just lazy, and it was her way of getting out of doing any work around the place. In fact, she is too lazy to catch a cold, and that's no lie.

Molly-Rose was growing up fast, still so much smaller than any of her friends. Her brothers and sister are twice her size and she looked so delicate you would be fooled into thinking she would break in two if she fell. But after each fall she would bounce back up brush herself off and carry on as if nothing had happened. I have never seen a tear fall from her eyes, so much like her mother on that front. To the world, they see her as tough as old boots, but I see the soft side of her, a young girl who just wants her mother's love. At times, it frightens me that she has built a wall around her and no one will be able to get through to her. She has so much to deal with; it is hard for her to be just a little girl.

She was wise beyond her years and knew that her mother had a dislike for her more so than her other siblings, just like me she did not understand why. Molly-rose loved her brothers and sister and enjoyed minding them for her. It was like having a real-life doll to play with. All her friends played make-believe with their dolls, she didn't have to. One of the many things she didn't like was that if they did something wrong her mother would take the belt to her as it was always her fault, she should have stopped them. She is older, so she should have known better. Her mother seemed to think she was older than her years. Eddie had grey hairs asking Evie to go easy on her. The more he tried to protect her, the harder Evie became. He knew a father was not meant to have favorites but he couldn't help loving her a bit more than the others. It may be because she had to fight so hard to be here.

There was one evening both her parents had gone out to awake in a neighbour's house, James found a bottle of what he thought was lemonade and he drank some of it, just bad luck it was not lemonade but turpentine or something of the sorts. By the time my parents came home, there was an ambulance outside the door waiting for them to arrive. The doctor said he was ready to be taken to the hospital. She didn't hear the Doctor saying that he was lucky that I had acted as quickly as I did or he would be in serious trouble.

Only for her father was there, Evie would have killed her on the spot for sure. She had the perfect excuse; She had nearly killed her brother. Any normal person wouldn't have left a child looking after five other kids, but her mother felt it was her duty to mind them. What else would she be doing, it was not the first time they had left her alone to mind her siblings and I doubt it will be the last time?

Why Me?

Molly-Rose loved going to school when all her friends complained about having to go, she loved it because it was a place where she didn't have to mind anyone and there was no mopping or cleaning to be done. She cried and cried to start school early, so finally, her mother brought her up to the school and told the teacher that she was four when in fact she was only three and a half. When the teacher found out they sent her home telling her to come back next year, but she would turn up day after day so eventually, the school gave up sending her home and allowed her to stay, she loved to read, her head was always stuck in a book she was always daydreaming which drove her mother insane. As she firmly believed that school was a waste of time, it was ok to spend six hours a day there because that way she didn't have to look at her miserable face. In Evie's mind school was no place for her child, she should just get out and work to earn a crust as soon as you are able to - no matter how young you were there was always something you could be doing. When Molly-Rose was doing her homework, she would often be shouted at to put the books away as there was proper work to be done. The words "you can't teach a dunce anything" would echo around the house. It wouldn't be unheard of for the books to be torn or end up in the fire. Molly-Rose would have to make up excuses for the teacher as to why her books would be missing or why she had no homework done again. She hated the way the other kids would laugh at her when this happened, they all thought she was play acting.

Why Me?

I knew long before I had the words to express it that my mother hated me and that she was a very angry woman. I also knew that she drank a lot on the quiet. She didn't want Dad to know. It was not unusual for me to come home from school to find her passed out in the chair, the babies crying with the hunger and their nappies would be filthy, changing nappies was my least favourite thing to do afterwards I would scurry around the place changing and feeding the younger ones and putting the dinner on before Dad got home. I loved my Dad and could never understand why he would put up with the nastiness which he was subjected to on a daily basis. I would often beg him to leave her as I could see how unhappy he was.

He would just smile and say he loved her so much and that she was trying her best. That no one was perfect. If he only knew the truth about what went on when he was not around, would that help him make his mind up? Sometimes I wonder if he wore rose-tinted glasses. Maybe it is true that love is blind.

I continued to suffer from severe asthma attacks and chest infections. Every single cold or flu that was going, I would get it. Out of all the kids, I was the one that was always sick, but underneath, I was as tough as old boots, often refusing to say anything as I didn't want to draw any attention to myself. These attacks no longer phased me, they were just part of my daily life. I was choosing to be happy-go-lucky.

I would spend so much time in and out of the hospital that I was well known by all the staff. Dr O'Connor would love to see me coming, he would always have a bar of chocolate or a pack of crisps in his desk for me. He would hook me up to the nebuliser and then I would be off on my way back to class, as happy as can be munching on my treats.

I must have been about 8 or 9 when I was sent to the dentist for a checkup by myself, which was not that unusual, but by Jesus, and for the love of all that is holy, the man nearly killed me. There was my first life used up. I sat up in the chair. Nothing strange about that, I hear you say. Little did I know he was as drunk as a skunk, much more than normal. To be honest, I couldn't tell the difference between the drunk man and the sober one as I don't think I had ever seen him without a drink on him. He was well known to have a drink even when he was working. He started off injected my gums with an anesthesia; he stuck the needle into my mouth I almost jumped off the chair as I could feel everything, then he gave me another one and another one so much so I couldn't talk I couldn't move; I was just about able to keep my eyes opened and after sitting there for nearly an hour he was losing his cool and shouted – "right, that's it! It is time for that tooth to come out". I nearly passed out with the pain of it, I never had a tooth pulled before but I was sure it shouldn't feel like this. One side of the mouth was numb and the other side pumping blood, my head was in a spin and I was only short of vomiting on top of him, the room was spinning so fast I was afraid I would fall of the chair, there was no way I could scrape myself off the chair never mind stand up. Not only was I high on drugs, but weak with the pain. After several attempts to move, he realised that he was going to

Why Me?

have to do something to help me. So he very kindly helped me off the chair and carried me to his car and drove me home it was the luck of God's that we made it to the house without crashing into a wall.

Of course, my mother was like 'she is grand, don't be worrying about her, she is just a drama queen. Thanks for dropping her off. It was very good of you, she could have walked.' With that, she sent him on his way, no questions asked. I was barely conscious, unable to stand or talk, but still, I was given the task of peeling the spuds for dinner. No rest for the wicked and I guess I must be very wicked indeed. There was no way to coordinate any part of my body, never mind peel spuds I couldn't even see them in the first place. I crawled up the stairs on my hands and knees and fell into bed.

When my father came home from work he was outraged at the state I was in, there was blood all over the pillow and he went to call the doctor. It was the lovely Dr Reid that came and she was furious at the condition I was in and demanded to know how this had happened. I couldn't speak, so my mother told them that I had been to the dentist, and she knew no more than that.

'Did she come home in this state?'

'How did she get here?'

"The dentist dropped her home afterwards."

Why Me?

"In this state? Did he say anything at all?"

"No. Nothing."

After taking a quick look at my mouth. She turned to my parents and told them, 'I had been given an overdose of anesthesia and by the looks of it on the opposite side of where the tooth had been taken out.'

To say she was hopping mad was an understatement. I will have to report this to the health board. She filled out some forms and asked for parental signautures.

She left, saying she would call to see me tomorrow morning before she started her surgery. If there were any changes during the night, they were to call immediately.

She left strict instructions that I was to stay in bed to get plenty of fluids into me, and I was not to go to school in the morning.

It was the first time I had seen her since the night of an asthma attack and which was a year ago and once again I was struck by her kindness.

Little did I know it this would be the start of a beautiful friendship.

Chapter 10

Many people would say I had a hard life, but for me it was normal. I was no different from anyone else as far as I was concerned. I learned early in life to stay out of my mother's way, I could sense for the longest of time that my mother didn't care for me very much. I could see that she was always a bit meaner to me, even when she was trying to be nice. To everyone else who knew me, they loved me. They said I had the cute factor in buckets loads; I was just the right amount of cheeky and always helpful to the older folk who lived in the street. I would be the first one to help them with their shopping or run to the shop for their cigarettes when they ran out of them. I was a quiet child and rather shy as I didn't have much confidence, but I had the temper of the devil himself. My friends knew that I was no pushover despite my size, and if they pushed me too far, I would have no problem in landing them a right hook, regardless of their size. Once in a full temper, I had knocked out one of the school bullies. He was a fine stack of a fellow, but he was no match for me when my temper took over. To my friends I was loyal, but to my enemies, they feared me. They would mock me in their groups safety in numbers, I guess, when they were together I was no match for them. I was patient and would wait my time till they would be by themselves, it would be then I would let rip. After a while, they got the message and finally left me alone.

Why Me?

I wished that would work with my mother as she never let's go. If I hear one more time that I have ruined her life or it was a sad day, the day she gave birth to me. Or the best ever is that she should have drowned herself when she found out she was pregnant in the first place. Her voice would boom into my head: "if I had my life to live over, I would never have any kids." On and on she would go like a broken record. She prayed for no kids, I just pray for silence or that she would lose her voice, whichever would come quicker.

As I grew, so did the arguments. I know I shouldn't have answered back, but I couldn't help it. The words would fly out of my mouth before I had a chance to stop them as if they had a mind of their own. It was always easier when I would stay at my grandparent's house where I would be spoilt rotten, and I never spoke about my mother. I would often wonder if they knew what was going on or not, but one thing for sure, I was not going to be the one to say anything. That would be all I need for World War Three to kick off. I just enjoyed the freedom and peace while I was there.

I was lucky that Dr Reid came to see me that evening after the saga with the dentist. She has been a rock, my grounding force. I'm not sure how it happened, but I ended up helping her a few times a week, tidying files and to dust around the office and she would help me with my homework, we would talk about all sorts of things like friends or boys, about what I want to do when I finished school. If I had a foul day at school, I would tell her, and she would always say the right thing to make me feel good. When I doubted my abilities to sit a test, she would help me study. Yet, I never told her about my relationship with my mother or the fights we would have. The most I ever told her was that I didn't see eye to eye with my mother and how I felt that I would never grow up quick enough to get out of this place. She made me believe in myself and that I could do anything I wanted. She became the support that a mother should provide for a daughter. I found myself in her office most evening after surgery, she would have the biscuits ready for me when I arrived in. She was a kind lady with a warm heart, I would often wish that she was my mother. When she had children of her own, they would be very lucky that would be for sure.

I loved watching her and Dermot together. You could tell that they loved each other so much. I prayed that one day I would find a love like this.

Over the years I became an honorary member of their family and would often go out to their house for dinner.

I was over the moon when she invited me to her wedding; she was having a small intimate affair out in her mother's house in Ballyconnelly. There would be no church or priest, just a guy from Cork to sign, seal and deliver their declaration of love. This sounded so cool to me, as I had never been to a wedding before, never mind one like this! Most people around here had never heard that you could get married like this. I was so excited I could hardly contain myself as the days drew closer.

Why Me?

The day itself was nothing short of spectacular, it could have been straight out of a movie scene. I was completely enthralled. Even to my untrained eye, you could see that everything was perfect. Her mother had handmade her dress and her sister was her bridesmaid.

I was looking forward to meeting her mother and sister as I loved the way she spoke about them both. Both of them were even more charming and kind than she had said. I fell in love with the complete family; I wished that they were my family. It also made me realise that my own family were very dysfunctional.

I would love to have this type of relationship with my mum and younger sisters when I get older. Amelia said that she was blessed with her life on more than one occasion. Now I could see why.

Just as I had expected, my relationship with my mother had deteriorated even further, not that I could have thought it was possible. She kept comparing me to everyone else's amazing child. She was never short of her old words and how much of a disappointment I was to her. I had stopped trying to please her a long time ago as I knew that I would never be able to, no matter what I did or didn't do. She and Dad barely spoke to each other these days. He was always in the firing line for something. The level of violence had escalated, and it was not unusual for her to fire plates across the room or take a knife to his throat. There were many demons battling inside of her. She was drinking more and more these days I was never sure of what mood she would be in when I would come through the door so I always aired on the side of caution better to be safe than sorry. She could be a sweet as pie and the next minute like a raving lunatic.

I found myself trying to stay out of the house more than I already did if I was there it only seemed to make matter worse for everyone. It was as if all she had to do was take a look at me and it would send her off the deep end. After school, if I was not working, I would go to the bakery and sit by the ovens as Dad baked the bread. It was not unheard of for him to have to work late into the night during the busiest times of the year, or if a member of staff called in sick. Yet to the outside world he was still the cheerful man he once was, I knew how much he was hurting inside, I could see the pain in his eyes. When he smiled, it never quite reached his eyes. Despite this, he would never say a bad word about my mother.

At times like this, I couldn't understand him. I loved him with all of my heart but couldn't get my head around this no matter how hard I tried. He repeats his love for her, and that she was doing the best she can that she had a good heart underneath. She loves you Molly-Rose she just doesn't know how to show it, in many ways you are both very similar.

This drove me insane altogether, as I was nothing like her and I swear if I ever have kids of my own - not that I ever plan to but I will love them with all of my heart and will never treat them the way she treats me. That is not loving someone, that is not how I would want to love my children.

'Shush, Molly- moo don't be so quick to judge.'

I was adjusting to life without Amelia since she moved to Cananda; it was much harder than I expected. Life was boring without her. I would write to her every two weeks and would have a letter from her as well. She would often send me gifts, like a chain, a bracelet or a new top which she would send to the bakery otherwise I might not get anything. I would be sixteen in a few weeks, and I had started to go out with the girls. We loved going to Discos, and soon we got tired of seeing the same old faces in Clifden House every week. So, Sadhbh suggested that we go to Westport as she had heard that there was a great nightlife, and the best part would be that we wouldn't know anyone there and no stories to follow us home.

I was not working the following weekend, so the four of us headed off on the bus to Westport. We had booked a B&B for the night, which was very exciting since it was the first time away from home for myself and Aoife. Sadhbh and Niamh had been there before on a shopping trip with their parents, so they knew where to go. Fair play to Sadhbh, she had researched the best pubs and bars, leaving nothing to chance. The night was a success; we danced all night in the Cattle (Castle) Court as it was known locally our feet were so sore we almost had to crawl to the chipper for curry chips as no night would be complete without them. The

Why Me?

craic was mighty in the chipper it was as if the whole town had gathered for the unofficial after party. The night was so successful that we agreed to come back again soon. For me, it was like a new dawning - that there was life outside my four walls. For the first time in a long time, I could see a light at the end of the tunnel.

Early the following morning, we went down to breakfast high on last night's excitement. Afterwards, we headed for the bus stop only to find out that the bus didn't run on a Sunday. We were jolted off cloud nine and back to reality at the thoughts of trying to get home our parents would kill us if we were not back in time for dinner.

'What in the blazes are we going to do now?' I asked the group.

But we were all at a loss. We sat at the bus stop like idiots for what felt like an age. What kind of stupid are we, why didn't we check to see if there was a bus going back?

We all agreed we got carried away with the excitement of getting out of the town that it never entered our heads. When finally, I said we would have to thumb a lift and what other choice had we. We asked in the local shop for directions to Clifden, as we had no clue of how to get home. There was an old farmer in the shop and said he would give us a lift out the road. The four of us prayed to God he was not a mass murderer as we jumped into the car. He told us he would only be going about twelve miles out the road - where he would drop us off just before he would turn for Liscarney. He told us to keep straight on the road

Why Me?

and we needed to be heading in the direction of Leenan.

We all thanked him in unison, as if we knew where that was. Standing on the side of the road in the middle of nowhere in the freezing cold was not the best plan we ever had. We must have been there at least an hour and not one car had passed us. The cold got the better of us and we agreed that we should start walking and fingers crossed a car would come along before too long. We must have been walking for an hour or more before a car finally stopped. I know it was still early in the morning, but the driver looked as if he had not been to bed the night before as his eyes were nearly falling out of his head; We figured he was on his way home from a party. He couldn't have been much older than 18. So, we hopped into the car, grateful to be out of the cold for now at least. He said he was only going as far as Louisburgh but would take us to Leenan as it was unlikely there would be many cars on the road this early on a Sunday. If we were lucky, we might catch someone from Mass going our way. As soon as we sat in the car, we nearly had a heart attack as the floor in the back of the car was full of rust you could see the road through it. The car itself made all sorts of loud, strange noises. Now I was no expert when it came to cars, but this one didn't seem quite right. It was not too long afterwards it started to rain, and we were relieved that we are no longer on the side of the road, well that was until he hands Aoife a piece of rope and told her to pull on it as the wipers were broken. I thought Niamh would lose her life there and then. She nearly fainted altogether - as he drove on both sides of the road. Sadhbh was completely silent. Something that never happens. She was swearing under her breath that we would be better off walking. I reminded her that we were lucky as there were no other cars on the road and not to mention he was very easy on the eye.

Thank God Aoife was in the front as she chatted to him as if nothing was wrong, as if he was perfectly sober and the car was not Zig zagging across the road.

He would laugh his head off after he narrowly avoided the sheep that were minding their own business as they munched away on the grass. He was asking us we if fancied lamb for dinner and he was not joking, at this rate he could very well end up with one of them in the boot before he gets home, apparently it wouldn't be the first time to happen.

By the time we arrived at Leenane we were all as white as ghosts, we nearly fell out of the car - we were afraid if we didn't get out quick, he would continue driving. He apologised that he couldn't take us any further as he was afraid the guards might be on the road and he gave a deep belly laugh, he said "I'm not sure if you girls have noticed but I'm a bit worse for wear; I went to a house party after the disco, jasus; the craic was mighty shame ye weren't there. Well, any other day of the week I would have no problem driving you fine ladies all the way, but not today. I have already had a warning from them."

He said he would come up to Clifden with a few friends on Saturday night and would meet us in Clifden House.

Why Me?

We all said yes, that would be great, and hopped out of the car before he decided to risk the drive to Clifden after all. After we watched him drive off, we prayed that he would make it home in one piece and the sheep would stay out of his way. We laughed at the idea that he would come to Clifden at the weekend, sure he will not recognise us - I'm convinced, he was driving with his eyes closed. Well, I guess we will have to wait and see what next weekend brings at the rate we were going, we could still be here waiting on a lift.

'Not Funny, Molly.'

Just our luck that the pub and shop were closed.

At least there was a bus stop across the road, so we could take some shelter here until the rain stops. There are worse places to be stuck girls. Look around the view is breathtaking, it is stunning.

'Tell me, Molly, are we in Galway or Mayo at the moment? '

Well, here is a bit of history for you girls as you never listen in class. We are currently on the border of Galway and Mayo at the head of Killary Harbour; it is a Fjord, not a lake of which there are only three in the whole of Ireland, those mountains over there are called the Maamtrasna and Maamturk. No, I don't know which is which, but I do know that the area has been inhabited since prehistoric times. It is surrounded by ancient tombs and the potato ridges climbing the mountains.

Also, did you know this is where they filmed the movie 'The Field'? People travel from all over the world to visit here, and that was even before they filmed the movie.

Jesus Moll, you are like a history encyclopedia you could easily get a job as a tour guide. How you, can keep all that information in your head is beyond me?

'I just love Irish history, Aoife, but don't ask me about world history as I can never remember it.'

Eventually, the rain stopped, and we agreed that we should start walking again as sitting here would get us nowhere. Not one car had passed since we got here, if we wanted to get home at some stage today there was nothing else, we could do.

We were only two miles out the road when, believe it or not the heavens opened, the rain was relentless and the sound of thunder began to mumble at first, and then it roared like an angry lion. I loved the sound of thunder, but the girls screamed like babies at each bang, clinging to each other in fear. We must have walked for another four or five miles until we arrived outside the church of Our Lady of the Wayside. We were drenched to the skin our clothes were literally a ton weight the water was falling off our clothes as if they had just come out of the washing machine. We were miserable, wet, cold, and hungry, not a good combination. As we walked around the corner, there was a church on the right-hand side of the road.

Sadhbh burst into life and said, 'let see if it is open.'

Why Me?

Yes, yes, it was open. We went inside, relieved to be out of the rain. Niamh touched the radiator and bonus it was hot. We took off our coats, socks, and shoes, placed our socks and coats on the radiators and our shoes underneath, hoping that they would dry before anyone came in. We routed through our bags to see if any of our clothes were still dry. Sadly, they were nearly as wet as what we had on. The ones that were dry were not suitable to be worn in a church. We huddled up to the heaters and feasted on chocolate and Lucozade, relieved to be inside. We were exhausted before long we fell asleep only to be woken by the noise of shoes banging on the tiled floor. To say we were embarrassed to be seen in such a state would be an understatement. We looked a sight with our clothes on the radiators; we were mortified. Half afraid to open our eyes, we were stunned to see a priest looking down at us with an enormous grin on his face. We frantically tried to explain, but our words came out in a mumble jumble. We sounded like we were lunatic's that had escaped from the asylum. Lucky for us he found it funny, and in a weird way he rambled on about how the Bible refers to a similar incident, I was not sure what he was trying to say.

As we apologised, he said, sure isn't that what the church was for. To provide a sanctuary for those who need it. I would not mind, but not one of us had been inside a church since we made our confirmation. Best we keep that information to ourselves. We packed our bits and piece into our bags at rapid speed and put on our half dry socks and shoes. When he asked us - where were we from? We were afraid to say in case he would have our local priest on our doorstep before we even got home. My mother would surely kill me if that was the case, there would be no saving me.

Niamh answered before I could even think of my own name, my head was in a spin.

He suggested that we stay for mass and even offered to drive us home afterwards as it was forecast to rain for the rest of the day. He was going as far as Cleggan anyway, so it would be no bother to go to Clifden. What a lovely man his kindness would have me at Mass on Saturday night for sure. It is a shame that there were not more priests like him.

I will have to write to tell Amelia in the morning, I would love to see her face when she hears about all this craic.

The week flew by, and it was Saturday night, arriving in a flash, we were busy getting ready and in record time we flew out the door; we wanted to see if your mano made it up after all. Neither of us could remember his name or if he had even told us his name. Of course, we would have to check out all the pubs first. Off we went, dolled up to the nines. We were disappointed when our search came up empty what else did we expect; the chances are he wouldn't have any memory of giving us a lift in the first place. Later that night we made our way to the disco resigned to the fact he would not be there; we were dumbfounded to see him and three others standing at the bar in the nightclub.

Holy crap, what do we do now - before anyone had a chance to say a word, Aoife marched up to the bar like a

Brazen Hussey and put her hand on his should and said "let me buy my knight in shining armour a drink" We should not have worried as he recognised us immediately and introduced us to his friends. We all got on like a house on fire. By the end of the night, I believe we were all loved up. It was early the next morning that the lads headed home to Westport - no one wanted the night to end. We agreed to meet the following Friday night in the pub at 8.00 O'clock sharp, only this time they would stay for the weekend.

Chapter 11

The following Sunday morning, my life changed for the worst. Never would it be the same again. The doorbell was ringing, and it was half-past five in the morning, I had only gotten in bed a half hour ago, tiredness cried out from all over my body. I could hear my mother giving out as she climbed down the stairs. Shouting at whoever was at the door better have a good reason for getting her out of her bed at this un-Godly hour. I followed her down the stairs as I was surprised that it was not Dad that had gotten up. He must have gone to work earlier than normal this morning.

Standing at the door were two guards and Dr O'Connor. I froze, I could sense that all was not well as I listened to my mother ranting and raving as to why they were at her door. "Had something happened to her mother?"

Everything from that moment on moved in slow motion. "I'm sorry Mrs Wood's, but there has been a terrible accident in the bakery."

"Now, Dr, why would you be bothering me with such a thing, you know well that Eddie looks after anything got to do with the bakery I have enough to be doing here."

"I'm really sorry Evie, but this is about Eddie."

"Eddie is the reason I'm here I'm afraid he was the one in the accident, the tragedy is he has died as a result of his injuries earlier this morning."

Why Me?

"Sorry, Dr, it must be a mistake Eddie is upstairs in bed."

Molly, go get your father so we can put an end to this nonsense and get back to bed before the whole household is running around the place.

"No, Evie, I'm afraid he is not; I pronounced him dead before coming here this morning; he had passed before I got there, there was nothing I could have done. The ambulance has taken him to the regional where they will perform an autopsy, and then we will have a clearer picture of what has happened." With that, the three of them came into the house as bold as brass, "Now ladies please sit down," one of the guards went into the kitchen and started to make tea for us.

He handed us two scalding cups of strong tea with enough sugar to cause diabetes.

I sat there frozen in time, as if I was watching some else's life play out. My mother at this stage was rolling around the floor screaming like the banshee. This can't be true. This can't be true repeatedly until her words blended together, and she was not making sense anymore. She looked like a mad woman. She was screaming at me to call Eddie's mother and brother.

Dr O Connor told us that her mother and sister would be here shortly, as the Garda's have already been dispatched to their house.

Dr O Connor turned to me and told me to run up to the

phone box and call Jack with the news, and that he would stay with my mother as she couldn't be left on her own. Why the hell was he asking me I don't know, what was I going to say to Jack, nevertheless I made the call.

By the time I came back my mother was in bed asleep, Dr O Connor said they had given her a mild sedative to help her get over the shock. He said he would stay with me until my aunt and grandmother arrived.

I asked him if he knew what had happened very slowly. He spoke as if he was talking to a baby. It turned out that my father was working late out in the shed fixing one of the delivery vans for the morning deliveries when the jack snapped and the van came crashing down on top of him, crushing him to death. He would have died instantly; he would have felt no pain.

I must be experiencing an out-of-body kind of thing, as I could hear him speak, but all my mind was saying that, that there has been a terrible mistake.

My father was dead. What kind of fecked up world is this? My life was far from being perfect, but now it is as good as over, my life would never be the same again. The day moved so slowly it was as if there were several hours passed between each minute. My mother was out of it on prescription drugs and alcohol for days on end. She was not coping at all. When she was awake, she just sat there staring into space, talking to herself.

They left me with my siblings, unable to explain what had

happened. I fed them; I dried their tears, held them in my arms. I tried the best I could, but I was not who they wanted or needed. I'm not sure who organised the funeral, as my mother didn't seem to have the where about to do anything. All I knew that there were plenty of raised voices over where he would be waked. His mother didn't want to put him into the cold dead house, she wanted him home. My mother said that this was his home and that with the kids she was unable to have him here. She didn't even want the casket to be open, as she was afraid of the damage that had been done to his body. This set my grandmother into a rage telling her that she had ruined his life and made him miserable and who knows that he might be still alive, if it was not her constantly nagging him, he would have been at home in bed like any normal person instead of working all hours of the day and night trying to make you happy. You had the poor man driven to distraction with all your antics and moaning. Nothing was ever good enough for you. My poor son was under your spell, and there was no one that could break it. We had begged him not to marry you, but he would not listen.

My mother had the last word, and she was not budging. He was to be laid out in the cold dead house. The evening that Dad arrived at the dead house, my mother was nowhere to be found. My grandmother begged the undertaker to bring him home but said he wouldn't go against Evie's wishes. Grandmother had asked a neighbour to come with his trailer to bring him home as she couldn't leave him there all by himself. I just want one more night with my son before he leaves this world. It was heartbreaking hearing hear sobbing, it is not natural for a mother to be burying her son, that is not right. Jack and his brothers had to carry her out of the place and telling her she would be arrested for robbing a corpse and that they only ones that would suffer was his children and by God, they have enough to deal with without making any of this hard on them. She howled that she wanted to give her son a proper send-off, that it was the last thing she could ever do for him and that she was not leaving him here alone and cold. After, sometime she agreed that Dad would not want his children upset any more than they had to be. Reluctantly, she agreed it would be best if he stayed here; she was supported out the door by her boys. It shocked me to hear Gran saying the things she did, I had never heard say a bad word about Mum before. I always thought that they were the best of friends.

Mum's sister and her parents helped her the best they could, but they couldn't reach her. While everyone fussed around her as they were afraid of what she would do next. We were largely forgotten about until Uncle Jack came and took the younger kids to his house to be with him. In fairness he tried his best for me to go with them but, I couldn't leave the house. I wanted to be as close to Dad as much as I could, this way I could walk over to him, even though I was terrified to be in the room with him especially by myself. I was torn on what I should do for the best. After some time I decided that if I sat outside the room, it would work just as well as I would be close enough he could hear and yet I wouldn't be freaked out by his dead body. Why the hell no one ever tells you about these things, I will never know. Nobody else has a problem with dead bodies but me. Sure I had the house more or less to myself as my mother was spending most of her time with her parents, which was a good thing as I would not have been able to deal with her shit.

As Dad was not been waked at home, you would think that the house would be private. But never the less people filled the house for three solid days and nights, drinking and talking about how he was a brilliant man. Nothing like a wake to get people to come out of the woodwork, nobody does a wake quite like the Irish, I had never seen half of them before in my life. In the middle of it all, was my mother sitting there walling like the banshee. It amazed me and I wondered if she believed half of the stuff that was coming out of her mouth.

I was just thankful that the younger ones were not here for any of this so-called ritual. I was on call twenty-four hours a day several people came and often forgot to go home. All I could hear was get this one a drink, make tea, is there any sandwich left, give them a slice of cake would you for goodness sake. As soon as my back was turned I could hear her saying that I was a complete waste of space. He mollycoddled her since the day she came out of the hospital. I told him it was a mistake, but would he listen? No. I told him that no good would come out of it. She is about as useless as an ashtray on a motorbike and now look at her going around the place with a face that God himself would find it hard to look at.

Why Me?

What do you expect your father had her ruined? Ruined, I tell you. I say spare the rod and spoil the child. I felt like screaming at her, they could never accuse her of sparing the rod she had a very heavy hand. I would often hide until dad came home to avoid another senseless beating for nothing. She is the one that would make it her business to collect sally rods from her parent's farm every week. But like a good obedient daughter, I kept my mouth closed and made the tea.

This whole situation was a total nightmare. I prayed it would end, knowing only too well that it was only the beginning and there would be no end. Was I invisible, not for one minute did anyone stopped and think I might be grieving or that I might need something. On the third night, I couldn't take it any longer and I went into my bedroom locked the door covered my head with my pillow and cried like a baby for the night, the saddest part of it all was no one even noticed I was not there.

The day of the funeral was horrendous, hell on earth. The queen bee had taken the front stage again. Not long before the coffin was due to be closed a strange lady entered the room, as soon as people saw her they gasped and whispered, 'would you look at who the cat has dragged in?'

'Where in the name of God did she come from?'

'I wonder what she is doing here after all this time?'

The question was being asked if she came home for her own mother's funeral or not? No one could agree - if she had or not.

I had no idea who she was my mother straightened herself up and plastered a false smile on her face but I knew that smile so well and it meant anything but I'm pleased to see you. The room went eerily silent, as if they were waiting for my mother to say or do something. She approached my mother first and offered her condolences before she walked over to dad's family, they all seemed to know her and they welcomed her with open arms. My grandmother held her tight and shook as she held on to her. It looked like she had tears in her eyes as she placed a red rose with a letter in the coffin with dad before stretching in to plant a kiss on his forehead - afterwards she stepped away and made her way towards the back of the room I wasn't sure but I swear that she wobbled slightly. When she had reached the end of the room, I asked Jack who she was and he said whispering 'she was an old friend of your dad's, her name is Ruth'. I had often heard my mother talk about a Ruth over the years, but right now I could not remember much about what was said. Except for my mother saying that she should have done the same as her, if she had any sense.

Before my mother had a chance to get near the coffin a group of men moved forward placing the lid over my father - the room went eerily quiet except for the noise of the odd roars and the sniffle of noses. I was frozen to the spot as it just hit me out of nowhere that I would never see his face again I wasn't ready to let him go and was glad when my mother stepped forward to place her hands on the edge of the coffin to try and stop them from putting the lid on - it

Why Me?

was no use as they turned the screws there was no more to be done. I should have known that there would never be enough time to say goodbye and the longer they took to cover him only made it harder. Then the men of the family came forward to lift the coffin on to their shoulders and carry him the short distance to the church. I'm not unsure how my legs carried me up to the hill to the church all I know is that my grandmother had to keep nudging me to walk and walk I did, like a zombie. I had no recollection of what happened after that only that it took nearly two hours, as the endless line of people that came to pay their respect went on forever and ever how or when I got home is still a mystery to me.

If I thought last night was bad, I had no idea of what the following day would be like. The mass took forever and once again I sat there as if I was frozen in time, it was more like an outer body experience. I could hear the priest but couldn't understand a word - I moved when I was prodded. Outside the church people came in their droves and shook hands with me offering their words of comfort, it took all of my strength to nod my head as I was afraid if I spoke at all the tears would come pouring down and if that was to happen there would be no stopping them and the last thing I needed was to make a show of myself. If there is a hell this must be it - hell on earth. Once again his brothers, uncle and friends carried his body for the last time to the grave on the hill it was only a short walk from the church but it took forever. As I walked behind his coffin I prayed that my tears would stay silent and for Dad to hold me in his arms one last time as they laid him to rest. With each step I became more like a robot than a human, stopping and starting, I kept my head facing the ground so that no one could see the tears slipping out of the side of my eyes, despite my best effort to keep them from falling. I knew I was surrounded by people but yet I had never felt so alone. I blame myself for his death any sane person would find this nuts; I know myself how it sounds but If I had only known this was going to happen, I would have stayed at the bakery with him on Saturday night instead of going out with my friends. When I called into the bakery to ask him if he needed any help at 9.00pm he just laughed and insisted that I should go out and have fun 'life is for the young' he said to soon you will be an adult and then your gallivanting will be curtailed with the responsibility of adulting'.

I definitely would not have made it through the day of the funeral without the girls, and much to our surprise, the lads came. It was great to see them even though we had not known them for very well they slotted into our group as if they had been there all along. Kevin held me at the right time, allowing me space when I need it. It was strange having him there, as they had never met my family and now they were seeing them at the worst time of our lives. I'm not sure why they came as I could barely speak a word. The silence was now my main method of communication. Somehow I think Dad would have approved that I had someone there just for me to offer the support that I needed to get me through the day.

Why Me?

The short walk to the graveyard was the longest walk of my life, my heart was full of dread as much as I wanted this day to be over, I also didn't want to say goodbye. The hardest bit was standing there as they lower his body into the ground as the priest said the rosary I found no comfort in his words just pain and more pain. I was not prepared for the sound of the dirt hitting the coffin, in some ways it echoes the pain in my heart as it thumped and banged it's way around the coffin filling in space between me and him. The noise of the soil hitting the coffin send knives through my body it took every bit of strength I had not to let the screams escape. Sadly as someone has forgotten to put a cloth over the coffin everyone was taken back by the sounds. As his brother and other members of the community shoveled the dirt onto the coffin at a rapid speed his uncle started to sing I'm a Connemara Man quickly followed by Willie Mc Bride. I had often heard my father sing them as he went about his day I could hear people saying that sure he sang from one end of the day to the other. He had a great voice on him. He loved his music and would often sing in the pubs at the weekends. As another neighbour played the accordion I have to fight to keep my tears to myself as with my eyes closed I could have sworn it was dad himself that was singing. With the familiar words of the rock of bawn nearly killed me altogether. It took all my strength to hold myself together as all I wanted to do was crumble. Nobody ever told me that I would feel this empty, It was like I was hollowed, the lights were on but there was no one home. I was so angry at the world and had cursed all in heaven, and beyond and screamed 'Why

Why Me?

Me,' what I have ever done to deserve this. I was too young to have my dad taken away from me, this is not the way it was meant to be. He was to be here to see me finish graduate, to see me through college and to walk me down the aisle on my wedding day, to hold his grandchildren in his arms. To help me through on my dark days, to make me laugh with his wacky humour. Now, I don't know how I will manage these milestones in my life, each one will be a reminder of what I have lost. There was so much he was going to miss, I'm going to miss. How do I carry on without him? My biggest fear is there is no way back from this and I know I'm not strong enough to do any of this without him.

'Sweet Jesus, Why - Why ME.'

After the final piece of ground had been placed on top of him and the flowers covered the grave, people one by one made their way to the local pub for soup and sandwiches. This was going to be hell on earth altogether. I was trying to work out if I could get away with not going there, but I knew there would be hell to pay later if I didn't. I would make my escape as soon as I can as I need to be on my own where no one would be watching me every minute I moved. I found myself bartering with God that if he could get me through this, I would go to mass at the weekend. Which is a laugh as I didn't believe in him in the first place? Amazing how you cling to any bit of faith to get you through your darkest days. I don't have words to describe accurately how I felt or how I got through the last few days. It was as if it would never end. I prayed for the pain to pass, but with

Why Me?

each new day, the pain got bigger and deeper. The hole was getting bigger and the light was fading. I wonder if this is normal or am I completely Fecked.

The night of the funeral the twins stayed with mum in the pub the younger ones had gone back to Uncle Jack's. I had persuaded my friends that I needed to have some time to myself before the boys and mum came home. I needed to retreat to try and get my head around all of this. I thanked them for being with me today, but I needed some space. I went home and put on a blazing fire and made myself a cup of hot chocolate with extra cream topped off with melted chocolate as if this was going to make me feel better, I think not but hot chocolate has always been my comfort food, Dad would make it for us when we didn't feel well or if we had a bad day. The girls and the lads had stayed on at the pub thankfully. It must have been about 11ish when there was a loud knock on the door my first thought was it was my gang trying to persuade me to go out or that they should be allowed in as they were surprised that I want to be by myself. They said over and over again that, this was the worst idea I ever had.

When I opened the door my aunt nearly knocked me over 'Is Sam here?' she was speaking so fast I struggled to understand what she was saying finally, all I heard is there was a fight in the pub and Sam had gone missing, Kieran had looked everywhere for him and still couldn't find him. Kieran was currently over with Guards to see if they would go looking for him as he was in an awful state. The boys were far too young to drink but that did not stop some amadan from giving both of them plenty of it, of course, my mother had not noticed anything and currently was unaware the Sam was MIA. We agreed that we should split up and look for him.

This was the last thing I needed tonight above all other nights. Was there no God up there at all? I roared up to the heavens to please take it easy as I wasn't able to take much more shite especially today.

We all went off in a different direction, I found myself walking towards the beach as this was the place I find my peace and low and behold there was Sam up to his waist in the water completely of his head. He cried like a newborn baby except it sound more primal as he was in so much pain. He had no idea of what he was doing or how he got there. We held each tight for a long time before we could speak neither of us had any words. Nothing could be said to make any of this better and we both knew it was hopeless to even try. By the time we had it made back to the house Kieran was already there with the Guards. I told the Guards that all was well and they could go. Neither Sam or I ever spoke about that night again. It was best forgotten about as it was not his finest hour.

Chapter 12

Ruth called to the house the following evening to talk to my mother I was told to get out of the house and told not to come back until I was called for. As much as I wanted to know what was going on, I was also so tired of the drama that had nothing to do with me so a little downtime will do me the world of good, off I went over to Aoife's house as I had not seen the girls properly since Dad's funeral. One thing is for sure I would find out eventually as my mother could never keep anything to herself especially after a drink or two. She would only be too happy to tell everyone what was said or not said.

It must have been a week or so after the funeral that I received Amelia's letter. It was upbeat and funny, as expected she found our trip to Westport hilarious. I had totally forgotten that she would have had no idea that dad had died and now I was unsure how to tell her. If I say nothing then I can pretend that he is still here and avoid the reality - instead I just sent her the shortest letter ever telling her what had happened, minus all the heartache that I was feeling. She had lost her dad to so if she was here she might be able to help me understand any of this. I missed her words of wisdom now more than ever she would know what I should do and how to do it. She would have practical advice on how to continue with this alternative life of mine.

Why Me?

Tomorrow I must go back to school and try to get some sort of structure back into my days, being at home was not doing me any favours, I find comfort in school because Dad was a great supporter of the education system. He was forever telling us to stay to the end and get a good education, and the world would then be our oyster. I could hear his voice saying 'there is no price too high for a good education'. He had told us often that the one and only regret he had in his life was that he left school at 13 years old. He said he was one of the lucky ones and many other folk his age, had left a lot earlier as their job was on the family farm or on the fishing boats. With many mouths to feed at home it was more often than not down to the older kids to provide for the entire family. Everyone had their jobs to do from the oldest to the youngest. The only kids that stayed on in school to the age of sixteen or seventeen were the kids that had come from money, their parents were the local doctor, solicitor or something like that. School seemed like a good idea to me, it gave me some distance between myself and my mother, this might do us both the world of good, a bit of normality could do me no harm.

I found myself thinking more and more about Kevin. He was great to have made the journey up to see me a few times during the week. He was a lovely guy, tall, dark and handsome, not to mention kind and caring. I was not convinced this was the right time to fall for someone, never mind for it to be my first love. I'm sure if he knew how dysfunctional my life was, he would run down the hill and I would not blame him. If I could, I would run too.

Why Me?

It was useless being in school. My body was there but my mind was nowhere to be seen. I spend my days sitting in the classroom staring out the window in a total daydream. My saving grace was being surrounded by my friends and the thought of seeing Kevin as soon as possible. They were putting a bit of light into my days where there was no light. I think, in some kind of a strange and weird way it helped that he didn't know about Dad, he saw me as just me and that was easier all round. I didn't feel as he was judging me if I was laughing or messing around. I never once told them how I was feeling or how hard it was at home. I didn't let him or anyone for that matter see how much it hurt on the inside. I was unsure of how to take down the walls that I had put up over the years. It was much easier to put a smile on my face and play a happy person neither he nor the girls could understand what it was like to lose my father; I know they wanted to help but didn't know how. My pain was all hidden, and I learnt very quickly how to wear a mask in front of my friends.

I found some people never mentioned his name, others would say you get over it, or pull yourself together, or time is a great healer. Seriously, how do they come up with this crap? Tell me how will time make it any better are they crazy or what. Time will only be a reminder of what I'm missing. If I mention my dad to my family I was told to be quiet that talking about it does not help it would not bring him back, every trace of him was removed from the house.

I was surrounded by people yet I was alone and desperately unhappy. Grief is a very lonely place. Alone at night, I would speak to him and at times ending up roaring at God why did you take him. He was all I had in this world and I was unsure how to navigate this life without him. No one ever asked me if I was ok.

I had a lot of screwed up emotions, and in truth, I was lost. I knew I needed help but didn't know where to find it. I was alone in this mad crazy world once again I would ask Why me, What did I do to deserve this.

It scared me, I was falling for Kevin and when he saw the chaos of my life, it would be over and I was not ready for that. I was afraid to tell him that I didn't come alone as I needed to look out for the younger ones, I would come as part of a package either he liked it or not.

My mother drank more and more, there were days she was never sober some days I never saw her and in many ways, these were the good days. I had not got a clue where she would go after the pubs closed. She completely abandoned her responsibilities as a parent. She was no longer functioning as a living, breathing human being, within six months she no longer resembled the woman she once was and had given up trying to pretend she was not drinking. She had fallen apart in her own grief, also afraid to admit she needed help or that she missed him terrible. The whole town knew of her for all the wrong reasons. She was either passed out in a ditch or been thrown out of the pub for fighting. Nobody knew if she was drinking to forget her own actions or Eddie. She was drowning in her own sorrows. More and more I was beginning to feel sorry for her. She too was lost and her entire life had been changed beyond belief. To be fair to her, she never asked for any of this and when she said her vow's everyone would have thought the death, do us part bit would be way down the line. It was not unusual to get a knock on the door asking if I could go downtown and try to calm her or to bring her home. As you could imagine when I would turn up it only made matter worse and of course, in her mad mind, I had killed my father if it was not for me he would still be alive. What kind of messed up logic is that, talking like this was not the words of a sane person? She would nearly always threaten to kill herself when she didn't get her own way or if someone said anything to upset her. God forgive me please but under my breath, I would whisper I wished you would in fact, be doing us all a favour. But I knew in my heart that she would never do it behind her big voice, she was a coward.

It was just another guilt tactic, to push the knife further into me. It was at times like this I would prefer the beatings. The words would swim around in my head long after the bruise would have healed. These words would haunt me for the rest of life. If I had a broken leg or arm or if my head was hanging off me, it would be obvious that I was not coping very well, but no one can see the scars that run this deep inside. They can't see the turmoil that goes on in my head or that my heart is screaming in pain. This pain is invisible. I just wished that someone would have told me about the void that Dad had left behind. I can honestly say that I'm no longer a whole person.

Why Me?

There was no way of getting through to mum at the beginning many people tried but they all backed away one by one. Her verbal abuse only got worse every day there was always something else my fault. Yet, no one would intervene as they were afraid of her, she was so unpredictable. When you see her coming, you never knew which person she would be. These days her bad temperament was clearly to be seen by all. Even Marion no longer calls to see her. I have seen her on more than one occasion crossing the street to avoid her. Whenever she sees mum coming out of the pub or walking down the street, she takes off in a different direction.

Then one day after school my life came crashing down around me. There was not a bit of food in the cupboards and to make matters worse there was a line of irate people at the door looking for the money they were treating that they would take us to court and call social services. I didn't know what they were talking about most of the time and I hadn't seen some of them before, but I understood they wanted their money, and they were not willing to wait any longer for it. They didn't seem to realise or care I was not my mother, I did not owe the anything.

I was screaming on the inside as I thinking they have all forget that I was only a child and not an adult, surely there is someone else they could talk too. The principal from the kid's school had also called to say that the younger ones were missing too many days and they would have to report them to the department unless their attendance improved, not to mention their behaviour.

Why Me?

I found all of this overwhelming, it is too much for me to deal with what am I supposed to do? I decided that I needed to talk to someone, so I eventually picked up the courage to talk to my grandparents but as it turned out they had not seen Mum much since the funeral as the last time she called to see them they had a blazing row. She turned their house upside down, knocking dishes of the press, she had gone as far as punching her father when he told her to calm down or get out. I told them about the recent callers and they were horrified as they had already given her money to pay for the funeral, they hadn't got the faintest idea of what she had done with all of Dads money as he had left her fairly well off. She got a very good price for the Bakery when she sold it, there was no way she could have gone through everything so quickly. They had heard she was drinking but not as much as she was or that she was never home. My gran said that her tongue was twisted with all the praying she has been doing for her. They promised they would try talking to her again. But their words fell on deaf ears.

If anything, she was worse than ever; I had to decide should I stay at school or not, it wasn't long before that decision was made for me, I would have to give it up and get a full-time job at least this way I could make sure that the younger ones would get to school in the morning and to see to it they would have proper food to eat, at the moment there's not much point going there as I'm not able to concentrate on anything that the teacher's are saying. My grandparents paid all the people she owed money too and they told them they should not give her any more drink or anything else for that matter unless she was paying in cash as they would not give them any more money. They warned them that under no circumstances were they to ever approach me or any of us ever again about any problems they had with my mother. Now looking back I can see this only aid her escape from her motherly role and reality. As you would expect she hates me even more for talking to her parents, she is taunting me more and more, there is never a stopping point. It was not uncommon for the shouting match to go on long into the night and she would turn physical at times when she would whack me with Dad's belt or anything she could get her hands on. Furniture would go flying around the room often through the window. Even when I went to my room and locked the door she would not stop, she would kick and bang on the door for hours calling me a chicken because I was afraid to come out and talk to her. I was more afraid of me than I was of her as I knew it was only a matter of time before I exploded and I was afraid of what might happen if I did. I knew there would be no way back if I did, so it was best to stay out of her way for everyone sakes.

Then one night I snapped and when she hit me, something inside broke and I hit her back with such a force that she fell to the ground and as I was walking away, she caught my leg and I tripped and hit my head of the tv stand. There was blood flowed from my head covering my clothes in blood. When I saw the blood on the floor that is when I lost all control of myself and jumped on top of her and had my hands wrapped around her neck with every intention to keep squeezing until she shut up I think I would have choked her only for the twins came and pulled me off her. It felt good to hit her back and not to be the punching bag for once in my life. Over the years I let things slide, but from now on I did not think I can do that anymore. I bandaged my head and cleaned the blood off the floor when she went to bed, I was still raging inside I knew I had a temper but this was totally out of control, and it scared the life out of me, this is not who I was or wanted to be, my mother needed help not this, it was my biggest regret that I had behaved so out of control, it was unacceptable and could never be repeated. I left the house that night with a heavy heart walking towards the beach knowing I couldn't continue like this no matter how much I needed to be there for my siblings, going to the beach is my calm place it is here that I feel at one with myself and the world. I would be of no use to them if I ended up in jail or the nut house I was ashamed of myself I had to control my temper, sure now I was no better than she was, I was worse as I knew better, I had no excuses I was not full of whiskey I was not angry at the world, the last thing I wanted was to turn into another version of her. The world couldn't handle one of her never mind two.

When I told the girls and Kevin that I lost control they were so supportive, it surprised the girls that it didn't happen a long time ago, they said they never understood why she disliked me so much. I was surprised that they had noticed as we had never spoken a word about any of this before, I was shocked when they said they had known for years she was unkind to me and they didn't want to upset me by saying anything, they were waiting for me to say something. They tried to reassure me that this was a normal reaction to everything that was going on but I knew this was anything but normal and if this was to be considered normal I did not want to be part of it. Kevin suggested that he would get a job in Clifden so we could see each other more and maybe help me out a bit this was really sweet of him and I was really touched by the offer but I didn't want him anywhere near this toxic place also I knew that he would become a new target for my mother.

I was still only seventeen going on ninety, I could see my life playing out in front of me and it was not a pretty sight it scared me more than anything else ever had. I tried to put that night to the back of my head and I would never mention it again and in fairness neither did she I was never sure if it was because she was embarrassed or she couldn't remember, we all knew she had a very selective memory at least she was trying to behave better for now, long may it last. I thank God for every quiet day for every moment without the arguing these days we didn't speak, and that was a blessing I was in no hurry for her to start speaking to me again I was just as stubborn as she was on that front, we are well matched in truth, life was easier this way on both of us.

It must have been two months later or so when she kicked off again this time because someone in the pub told her to go home and look after her kids, it ended up with her been taken to the Guards Barracks and spending the night in the cell to help her cool off, you would think she might have been a bit humble given that the other person had decided

Why Me?

not to press charges but oh no that would be too much to ask for sadly that was never going to be the case. The next day she headed for the town as bold as brass to find the pig who had insulted her even though she was unsure of who it was it didn't stop her, she had no clue just how much havoc she caused, that day or another day for that matter. I could no longer take any more I passed my breaking point. Life came to a standstill the night she turned the house upside down in a mad rage. Once again I waited till she went to bed and I set about the place tidying the place and removing any trace of the damage, I had enough and without thinking too much about anything else I took a load of pills that were in the kitchen, I could no longer take the pressure of my life of the hatred my mother forced upon me, it was if somehow I brought out the worst in her. It was the same thing day in day out no matter what I did or would do it was never going to make any difference if this was how my life was going to be I no longer wanted to be part of it, I was sorry I had to do this to my siblings but they would be better off without me. I couldn't think about them or anyone else too much for that matter I was only thinking about myself. I know you might say this was very selfish of me but that was the way I felt maybe if I was not here Mum would calm down a bit and take more responsibilities and grow up. I swallowed the box of tablets and took a large glass of water to make sure they went down as they tasted disgusting. I climbed into bed as happy as Larry I couldn't remember the last time I felt this contented, I could feel all the pressure lifting off me as I drifted off into another world knowing that I would soon

Why Me?

be with dad again. I prayed to God for forgiveness as I knew what I was doing was a sin.

Much to my disappointment, I woke up the next morning. No surprises I was not feeling the best my head was spinning I was in so much pain, the room was going round and round I was going to be sick all over the place if I didn't move and quickly. It took me a while to sit up and all of my strength to get to the bathroom before I was violently sick, I was grateful that there was no-one else in the house. After an hour or so, I could just about move only if I held my head in my hands and as for my stomach it was in bits, it was like someone had taken a knife and cut it into two, the whole room was spinning around and around. I spend most of the morning in the bathroom vomiting up all sorts of crap I'm sure that part of my stomach had come away. But could I say anything? No, chance. I was due to meet the girls later that evening, and I had to scrape myself off the floor and make my way down the town to meet them for an hour or so, I just needed to tell them there was no way I would be able to make it to the Disco tonight.

The girls were flabbergasted at the state of me.

'Molly, what is the matter? You look like you have been pulled through a hedge backwards.' Whispered, Aoife

'Not Funny, I'm fine I didn't put on any makeup,'

'By the state, you are in it has nothing to do with makeup,'

'Sorry Girls, I only came down to say that I wouldn't be

going out tonight as I'm not feeling too hot at the minute. I think I will have an early night,'

'No Shit, Sherlock, what's the matter? Now spill the beans!

'I'm fine I just was feeling a little under the weather,'

I could tell they were not buying it, so they suggested that they walk me home. Not long after we left the town I lost my footing or fainted not sure which but I fell to the ground banging my head on the road. The next thing I knew I was in the back of an ambulance with the sirens blaring, it was like a drill going off in my head. I tried to tell them I was fine, and that I wanted to go home, that I didn't want any fuss it was just a fall it was no big deal, that they were overacting for no reason.

'They said it was more than their jobs worth not to take me to the hospital, as I had been of out it for nearly 20 minutes so there was no way that the doctors in A&E would allow me home as it was more than likely I was suffering from a concussion,'

I couldn't focus on what they were saying I was seeing them in the double with all sorts of funny looking heads on them. I guessed this must be what it is like to be off your head on speed or one of those drugs they always talking about in school. The lads were right as I was admitted to the hospital almost as soon as I arrived. I spent the next week in the hospital and it is honestly a relief not to be at home. It gave me time to pull myself together. Kevin visited every second day even though I had asked him not to come. The doctors

Why Me?

asked lots of question I think they might have suspected something was amiss, but not once did I let my guard down, I couldn't tell them that I had tried and failed to end my own life. What kind of Sado would I be? I couldn't speak those words out loud to anyone once again I was so ashamed of my actions I swore I would never tell a living soul. I was not sure how I would have reacted if they asked me straight out; I was very thankful they didn't. They said that I had a concussion, and that I was underweight for my height and age. I told them I have always been this way and that I eat like a horse. It helped that Kevin would bring me a Supermac when he was in I knew they were watching me when I was eating but I did not care as long as they were looking at me eating they were not asking tricky questions. I was not ready for the funny farm just yet.

Not once during my stay in the hospital did my mother come to see me, not that I wanted to see her. In many ways, it was a blessing in disguise. I knew that when I went home, I needed to change my life as there was no point in expecting my mother to change there was no one that could do this for me, it would have to be down to me. I wished that I knew what those changes would be or how I would go about them. I prayed that I would find the answers and the strength that I needed when the time came.

Chapter 14

I left the hospital feeling like a new woman it was as if the weight of the world had been lifted off my shoulders the rest had done me the world of good it gave me time and space to be me for a change it gave me a new perspective on life. On the bus on the way home I promised myself that I would have a life better than this one, a life that I deserved. Dad would not be happy to see me like this, I knew he would want me to be happy. When I arrived home the best my mother could manage to say was 'Ah you're back then' Thank God, at least she was sober I was relieved. I was home four days when without knowing where I was going to go or what I was going to do I packed my bags and walked out the door with no destination in mind. I told no one where I was going, partly because I didn't know and partly because I didn't want anyone to follow me or to try and stop me. My mother cursed the living days out of me and cried in equal measures that I should stay as I walked out the door. She promised that she would change and in fairness, she had not had a drink in over a week and a half. Then she tried to guilt trip me using my siblings as bait, there was no way I couldn't back down now as I knew it was now or never. I didn't even give Kevin a second thought, I was afraid he would try to change my mind or come with me. I will send him a letter and try to explain the best I can and I hope he will understand that I need to do this on my own for myself. My friends were not impressed and they tried their hardest to get me to change my mind. They were afraid, 'this is madness, no one in their right mind would do this' I smiled to myself as everything they said was true and I had to agree with them that I was not in my right mind. Even so, I knew I was doing the right thing for me. It didn't need to make sense to anyone else but me, and in a weird way, it makes perfect sense to me.

They begged and pleaded, as they were convinced that I had lost my mind.

They blamed the bang on the head. In their words it had to knock any sense I had out of me. It was hard for them to understand that I was leaving not because I wanted to but because I needed to and they couldn't get their head around it. I promised that I would come back, I just couldn't say when that would be. I couldn't answer any of their questions, I totally understand why they were concerned I would be too if it was one of them leaving.

I knew that if I had any chance of the life I deserved I needed time away from here.

The guilt I felt about leaving everyone was heartbreaking the little ones cried and cried begging me to stay they were too young to understand what I was doing or why I need to do this but I hoped one day, they would understand and forgive me. I would try to make it up to them when the time was right.

If I had been thinking logical or took the time to plan this properly, I could have gone to Canada to visit Amelia there I would be looked after and allowed the time I needed to come to terms with everything that had happened over the years, when I get to where ever I'm going I must write her a letter she will think that I have gone completely mad deep down I know she would be delighted for me.

Sitting on the bus on the road to Galway, I could feel my excitement growing I was a little apprehensive as the big wide world was now at my feet. I planned to spend the night in Galway and in the morning have a look around and see what takes my fancy I had enough money for a month or so if I looked after it.

The following morning I walked into the FAS office in Galway City and spoke to an amazing lady who after an hour or so had laid out several options, the one that took my fancy was a hotel in Cobh County Cork, they were offering training and accommodation to work in the bar & restaurant. The pay was not great, but it was the best option available for now, beggars couldn't afford to be fussy.

Without a second thought off I headed to Cobh, I had never left Galway before so I could have been setting off for Australia it is the same excitement it would have been. Several hours later I arrived at the hotel tired and hungry my nerves had kicked in as soon as I saw the hotel it looked very posh and expensive, normally I would never dream of entering anywhere like this but it too late to walk away, now that I'm here I have no other choice but to go in. I should not have worried as soon as I stepped inside I fell in love with the place on the spot. The feeling of peace and serenity washed over me and I knew that I was in the right place, it was at the end of the harbour with spectacular views of the sea in so many ways, it reminded me of Clifden so I knew straight away that I was in the right place. The place was owned and run by Mr & Mrs Kelly, a charming couple in the forties. They told me that they had bought the dilapidated building a few years ago after they had returned home from the states, they lovingly restored it to the beautiful building it is today. After dropping my bag off to my room I was brought into the kitchen to meet the other staff, we had a quick bite to eat and then it was off to get my uniform, I guess there was no rest for the wicked as I was due to work in the restaurant tonight. Mrs Kelly told me that they were delighted to have me as they were short staffed and that I would have to learn the ropes very quickly as they were fully booked in the restaurant and there was a large function in later as well, so it was all hands on deck 'A baptism of fire' she called it, if you survive tonight you will be ready for anything, and I mean anything as this place is all sorts of crazy, we have a saying here "that you don't have to be crazy to work here but sure does help." We referred to it as if we are swan's gliding across the pond looking elegant and efficient when in fact we are paddling like crazy underneath. As long as the guest is none the wiser we have done a marvellous job. She gave me a crash course on how to set up the tables, what cutlery went where and on how to serve the guests, she would take the food orders for this evening so all I would have to do is serve the food and clean the tables. Depending on how the night went I might need to go to the bar afterwards, we will show you what to do in the bar later. She told me it was going to be a long night, and by God she was right the place was crazy busy, I didn't get a chance to bless myself all night it was nearly 3.30 in the morning by the time the last guest left the bar my feet were hanging off me you would swear I was walking on broken glass all night.

Mrs Kelly said 'soak them in cold water and they would be as right as rain in the morning.' Little did I know it but this place would be the best thing I ever did. It would be home away from home the work was hard and fast paced, you never knew what was going to happen next. I loved the unpredictability of it. Life in the hotel was complete madness most of the time there was never a dull moment the busier it was the more I liked it. It meant that I had no time to be homesick, or to sit dwelling on the past. This place became like my drug if I was not at work I missed the place so much, more often than not I would end up working on my days off. I now knew that I didn't like the silence or being by myself, I need to be where there were lots of people. By the end of my first month, I wrote to the girls, my family and Amelia. I couldn't wait for them to reply as I was desperate for news from home.

A letter from the twins was the first to arrive, and I was over the moon to hear that Mum was no longer drinking as much and she was spending more time at home, she was back cooking wholesome dinners and occasionally she would bake a cake or two. They said that everyone was doing well in school and that they were delighted that I was happy, they were very much looking forward to seeing me when I could get some time off.

Why Me?

The girls wrote to say that Kevin was livid that I had left without talking to him first, he was hopping mad that I never gave him the opportunity to have his say. He is up every weekend wanting to know if we have heard from you or if we knew where you were. They gave me the lowdown on what was happening in school and at the disco. Needless to say, they were missing me as the place no longer felt the same. They suggested that I write to Kevin to let him know that I was all right. They said they would not be surprised if he followed me to Cobh they agreed that they wouldn't tell him where I was until I was ready.

Funny, but this was the first time I had thought of Kevin, and it amazed me that I hadn't missed him more. I will have to write and let him know that all is good and that it would be best if we were to call it a day. Somehow being away from him I now know that if Dad was still alive, we would have fizzled out long before now, if we had ever started seeing each other in the first place. I understand that I would have found life more difficult if he had not been there to help and support me leaving as I did was not very fair to him. I pray he will realize that this is for the best for both of us.

Little did I know but he turns up a few days later with an engagement ring, declaring his undying love for me. He would not listen to reason no matter how many time I said we were too young to get engaged, he would stamp his feet and say he was ready and he couldn't fathom what my problem was. He would be more than happy to move to Cobh so we could be together, I was blue in the face telling him that it wouldn't work as I was not ready to make such a big commitment, I did not want to be somebody wife anytime soon.

He said, 'that we could wait for a bit before we got married as it would take us some time to get the money together.' I tried to explain that for the first time in my life I only had to worry or think about myself and that was the way I wanted it for now.

He roared that 'I was a selfish bitch and that I must be seeing someone here. Why else would I be here? Anger and rage took him over. There was nothing I could say or do to help him. I couldn't tell him, Yes, and that is all he wanted to hear.

'I asked him to calm down as he was scaring me.

'Calm down you say, Are you mad? that may be easy for you to say, but I'm the one standing here breaking in two, my dream crashed and shattered. You walked away leaving me thinking all sorts, not knowing where you were. What kind of person does that? Answer me that, will you? You know, that I loved you from the first time I laid my eyes on you. You are all I ever wanted, you are all that I need. I promise I will make you happy and I will be the best husband you could ever ask for me. I love you Molly-Rose with all of my heart. There will never be anyone else in this world for me. I beg you please marry me, say Yes, and make me the happiest man in this place. I love you more than I can say I'm nothing without you, my life means nothing to me if you are not here to share it with me.'

Why Me?

'Molly, please say you will at least think about it? We are perfect for each other, can't you see that. I can wait for you, we don't have to run down the aisle this minute. I promise I will do everything in my power to make you happy, I know you love me too.'

After seeing this side of Kevin, I knew without any doubt at all that I had made the right decision. There would be no going back now I could see what my life would be like flashing before me if I was to marry him and it was not something I could live with. I could see him wanting to be in control all of the time and there was no way that was ever going to work for me. I have already lived like that for long enough, there was not a hope in hell I would choose it ever again, I knew he was more in love with the idea of love than he was with me. In the end, Mr Kelly came to my rescue and asked him to leave or he would have to call the Guards, very reluctant by he walks out of the hotel with his body shaking with a mixture of tears and anger, shouting 'that he would be back that I was not going to get rid of him that easily. I can't just let you walk away from me Molly we need to talk after you finished work I will be waiting in the pub next door for you'

Mr Kelly told me I had a very lucky escape from him as he didn't like the cut of him, there is something wrong with him that he couldn't quite put his finger on.

I felt sorry for Kevin, I never for one minute believed that he would be like this, I was shocked that he was so in love with me, I never thought that getting married was on the cards, I could say that I now know that I didn't feel the same way about him and, for that reason only I will meet him after my shift ends and I hope he will have calmed down enough to listen to reason, I owe him that much at least.

Why Me?

Chapter 15

I continue to thrive in the hotel every day I became stronger and stronger, I guess you could say I was slowly healing, my wounds were closing bit by bit. The icing on the cake was that I loved Cobh I had become part of the community, they accepted me for me, there was nobody here to feel sorry for me or talking about what my mother was up to behind my back. There are no tales being told, no idle gossip, no one bats an eyelid if I'm wearing a new dress, there's no one whispering who does she think she is. Life is wonderful, and although I do miss home, I'm happy to be here. I regularly send gifts and money home in the hope it was of some help.

I knew Amelia would be back in Clifden soon, and I was itching to see her. I couldn't wait to catch up as so much had happened I need to share with her. Nevertheless, I was fully aware that I was not ready to go back yet, I still had a lot of work to do on myself I was still coming to terms with my life and trying to balance the old and the new.

Tonight was going to be exceptionally busy in the hotel and we had a building firm from Dublin hosting an event, apparently, he has property all over the place and that he is some big shot up there in the big smoke Mr & Mrs Kelly were beside themselves all week getting the place ready for him. You would swear he was royalty at the way they talked about him. They warned us over and over that they wanted nothing but the best, will do, that whatever he asked for he was to get, as he could put the place on the map with his connections so we all have to be in top form and looking our very best. The evening was running like clockwork everything was working out better than had been expected. All the planning had paid off, as everyone was happy and singing our praises. The bar tab was colossal not to mention what it would be like at the end of the night as it was still early, the food bill was still to be added on, I was grateful that I was not the one paying the bill at the end of the evening. It amazed me how the other half lived. They spend and spend without giving it a second thought a girl can dream that one day I would be able to do the same. My heart skips a beat at the mere thought of walking into a shop and picking up whatever took my fancy without looking at the price tag. A girl can dream, can't she.

Some of the guests had arrived much later than everyone else and the group welcomed them with a massive roar. I was so busy that I had not noticed who they were until a lady approached the bar and asked 'if it was me that was in it'

Before I even looked up 'I said it is indeed, it is myself in the flesh,'

She was laughing so hard that I had to turn around as she looked kinda familiar but I was not sure from where or who it was only when she called another lady and as she approaches the bar that the penny finally dropped you could have knocked me over with a feather, I nearly fainted, I almost dropped the drinks I was holding, I couldn't

Why Me?

believe my eyes, she looked just like Amelia, surely it couldn't be it was a moment or two before I realise it was her twin sister Sara. I had forgotten just how alike they were, I let out a squeal at the same time as she did. She threw her arms over the bar and gave me a massive bear hug I was astounded that they had remembered me as I had only met them once before at Amelia wedding and that was a long time ago, we spoke for a few minutes before I had to serve someone else. They said they would be here for the night and when I finished my shift for me to join them afterwards for a drink.

'I said that I didn't want to intrude before I could say another word they echoed each other with Nonsense, we would love you to come over we have lots to catch up on.' It was the first time anyone I knew anyone from home that had come into the hotel I was taken back by how lovely it was to see someone, anyone I knew. It was a bonus that it was Amelia's family.

The Kellys were impressed that I knew them and told me I could finish early if I wanted to go and join them you can call it a guest relationship if you want. 'I can't believe you know these people and you never said a word, you're a dark horse Molly'.

'Off you go, you can thank me later said, Mrs Kelly.'

With that, I took off my little apron and sprayed a little perfume and made my way over to where the group was sitting. I felt awkward, and unsure if I should join them or just go back to work but as I walked across the floor. I need not have worried because as soon as Sara caught sight of me she was out of her chair beckoning me over ordering the guy beside her to pull over another chair, she quickly introduced me to the group as a dear old friend that they had not seen for ages. After we had finished hugging each other - Stuart had the place in stitches with his comments 'of all the joints in the town and in the world and we happen to walk into yours' Funny said Elizabeth, Stuart go to the bar to get the poor girl a drink she must be parched the poor love has been run off her feet all night.' 'Here, here the others cheered we can all vouch for that'

Stuart said, 'drinks all round, I take it.'

The group were in top form, they were jolly and full of wit they were all very friendly and welcomed me into the group. We spoke non stop for hours, the banter was great it was a lovely treat to sit here and be sociable I had not realised how good it was until now. Not once did I feel like I was an uninvited visitor at their table. Late into the evening when most of the crowd had gone to bed. Sara and Elizabeth told me that Amelia had told them about Dad's passing they were so sincere in the words it brought tears to my eyes even though it was a few years since he passed I had not heard Dad's name in so long and it had taken me by surprise the emotions that came with it. I was not prepared for it they held me in their arms while the tears slowly flowed and then they took over completely, it was a long time since I had cried and the first time I had cried in front of anyone I was so embarrassed, I just wished the ground would open up and swallow me now.

Why Me?

'I apologised and said that it would be best if I left'

'Nonsense, you will do no such thing, you're with friends now and what kind of people would we be if let you go now. Besides, Amelia would kill us if we did. Take your time, there is no hurry.'

'Do you know that Amelia and Dermot are coming home at the end of November for good?'

'Yes, she told me in her last letter, she said that they will come down to see me before she starts back to work. I'm really looking forward to seeing her, it was great getting her letters, but I have to admit I have missed her.'

'We all have it will great for us all to be together again. We went over to visit them a few times but it is not the same we will have to have a party to welcome them back.'

Sara, spoke about her upcoming wedding and that, of course, I would have to come no excuses as I'm almost family.

Oh Lord more tears, 'I'm sorry, but you guys just seem to have this effect on me you're all just too kind.'

Elizabeth, turned to me and said ' tears are good, and letting them out is the best thing you can do, too many people fight to keep them in and that causes more harm than good never apologised for your tears as they make you into the person you are we all have scars we carry, there is no shame in that.'

Why Me?

In the back of mind, I was wondering where did these ladies come from as I'm sure they are a rare breed they are beyond kind and sincere. Normally people who have their kind of money have a certain amount of self-importance, these three are made from a different mould altogether.

I told them that I had not been back to Clifden since as I had left in a hurry, and I wasn't sure if I would be welcomed as I didn't leave on the best of terms, this was the first time I had spoken those words out loud?

'That's not a problem you are always welcome to stay with us that is if Amelia doesn't keep you all for herself. As for problems with your family, say no more about it as I know all about what that is like, so don't you worry about it.'

'When is your big day?'

'That the best bit of all, it's a Christmas Wedding it on 26th December, and we are getting married out at the house in Ballyconnelly'

'I'm hoping for a white Christmas, can you imagine how good that it would look up at the lake. The photos would be amazing. I can hardly control myself with the thoughts of it, It would be like a fairy tale.'

'I have to agree it would, that is, if you don't get hypothermia,'.

'Funny, Funny I can promise you that will not happen as all of the marques will be heated, not to mention we will have a big fire pit outside for those that might need some fresh air and to prevent anyone people from freezing in the progress.'

'It sounds amazing, you will have a fab day, but I'm not sure about snow, Clifden is not known as a snowy destination in fact, I have no memories of it ever snowing there.'

'Laughter roared around the room, That's a good one Molly'

' That's true, said Elizabeth'

'That just means it's about time for it to change, so get down on your knees and pray for snow everyone,'

Stuart and George joined the conversation by saying that if the Good Lord had any sense he would provide the snow as he would not like to see Sara disappointed on her big day if not, we can always get the crew to provide us with fake snow just like the movies, Sara said.

So no, Snow is not an option, that's enough about the wedding. What about you Molly is there someone special in your life?

'No, no one at all, I have no time between work and college, there is not much time for romance plus I think I prefer to be single as I can't ever see myself settling down and getting married anytime soon.

'Nonsense said Elizabeth, you're young and have not had a

chance to meet that someone special, believe me when you meet them you will know. Then settling down will be exactly what you will want to do.

'Ok, I will take your word for it, when it happens you will be the first to know.

'That's a deal, I will hold you to it.

 We stayed up talking till nearly six in the morning, we were all feeling a little puckish, we joked saying that there was no point in going to bed now as we may as well wait for breakfast. I had to agree, I got up and went to the kitchen to make some coffee and brought out some croissants just to keep us going. In the kitchen, I send out a silent thank you that I wasn't due to start work till dinner service, as I was wrecked it would be next to impossible to serve breakfast or even lunch, I needed to get some sleep. By half-past seven I was leading the group into the dining room for breakfast.

 When Mr Kelly, said "you look like you've not gone to bed, my dear,'

We couldn't stop laughing, to which 'I replied you're right but I will be there shortly.'

'Well, for now, stay and have breakfast with your friends and then you can have the evening off and try to get to bed at some stage or you will be like a bag of cats tomorrow, Lord of Mercy on us. We all know you and no sleep don't mix well.'

Why Me?

'Are you sure?'

'Yes, enjoy the rest of your day and we will see you tomorrow.'

'Thank you, Mr Kelly'

As we sat down for breakfast, I found it strange to be at this side of the table as it was an alien concept to have someone else waiting on me, especially here. Sara, 'remarked that the Kelly's seemed like a nice couple to work for?'

'I told them that I was very lucky as they are the best bosses I could ask for, they had been very good to me since I started. I had learnt so much. The Kellys were the ones that pushed me into going to college to do Hotel Management. They had offered to pay the fees and I could continue working here so I could have the best of both worlds. At first, I was very reluctant, but they were relentless and now I'm at the final stage, I have the last exams soon and then I'm finished. I was terrified to go back to college as I was so afraid that I wouldn't be able for the coursework but with their ongoing words of encouragement and not taking no for an answer, I found myself loving the course and now I'm the assistant manager here. The two years have flown by so quick it is hard to believe it is nearly finished. They had always known that my mother gave me a hard time more so that any of the rest of them, they guessed it was because I was the oldest

'Do you miss Clifden at all?'

Why Me?

'At times, I miss my brother and sisters the most, the twins came for a visit at Easter and it was lovely to see them, they wanted me to go home, but I feel more at home here, than I ever did there. Which I know is kind of strange.'

'Not at all, it is possible to feel at home in more places than one, and if you're lucky enough to have two places, you can call home it is the best of both worlds. I have to admit I was a little sad to say goodbye to them after breakfast, I was so tired that I headed back to the flat and finally crashed into bed and quickly drifted off to dreamland.

Chapter 16

Life returned to normal after the surprise visit from the Reid's, the months passed quickly and in September I finally got my result to say that I had not only passed my exams but got a distinction, I was over the moon. It was safe to say I was floating on cloud nine. The Kellys opened the champagne, and we partied the night away. It was the end of the month I had an invitation to Sara and George's Wedding the paper was a beautiful linen finished card it was so soft it felt like a version of canvas, I couldn't help but run my hand across it. The text had a clean, classic look that had been beautifully engraved in silver ink.

Why Me?

TOGETHER
WITH OUR FAMILIES
WE INVITE YOU
TO THE WEDDING OF

SARA
& GEORGE

ON 26ᵗʰ DECEMBER
AT OUR HOME IN
BALLYCONNEELY

Why Me?

I read it with tears in my eyes, it was lovely of them to invite me, there's part of me that would love to go, but I was not sure I should go home. There was a lot of words that have been spoken and it may be best if they are never had to be said in the first place, but once said there's no way to taken them back. I had written to mother many times and I sent cards and gifts every Christmas and Birthday and Mother's Day, but not once did she ever answered. I had not had a Birthday Card or Christmas Card from her, nothing, not a single word or a grunt. The kids often sent letters keeping me up to date on all the gossips, I can't help but wonder if they are telling me everything. Even after all this time I still worry about them, silly I know but I can't help it. The old saying out of mind out of sight doesn't work. I have to believe that my leaving was for the best thing for them as well as me. It would be lovely to see them, I guess I could stay with the girls even though I'm not sure if that would make matters worse with Mum. If I go, I would have to stay at home for better or worse, if thing went downhill I could move out on the flip side it might force her to talk to me if, maybe as we have both changed we could have a normal conversation with each other although I can't see us being the best of friends we might be at least be civil to each other now we both had some space. Surely, it couldn't get any worse than it is now. I could feel the excitement of seeing the girls and Amelia, getting their letters was great but nothing compares to sitting beside them chatting and laughing like mad things it is what I miss the most from home. It is great having my friends from here but it is different as we don't share the history of our childhood in common. The weeks flew by and before I knew it; it was the beginning of November and only for I got a letter from Amelia saying she was over the moon to hear that I was going to the wedding and she couldn't wait till to see me as we had so much to catch up on she gave me her telephone number to call and let her know when I would be getting into Galway and she would pick me up I was stunned as I didn't remember ever saying that I was going to the wedding, in fact, I sent a card last month to say that I couldn't make it. I had my mind made up that it would have been best if I gave it a miss as I was sure it would be best to let sleeping dogs lie for everyone. I wished I could give her a call when I finish work to let her know I wasn't going instead of sending a letter I wonder if Sara even got my letter. The hotel was so busy these days and to add to my workload the Kelly's had gone on a two-week holiday and leaving me in charge; it was their first holiday in years and they had every confidence that I could manage better than anyone else. When they first said that they were going away leaving me in charge I nearly had heart failure, they even joked that maybe they could take earlier retirement if all went well. The thought of this freaks me right out as I'm counting down the days till they come back praying that there will be no disasters. The good news is that everything was running as planned and everything was on schedule. There were a few minor issues when some of the staff went out sick but after running, around like a headless chicken, everything worked out in the end. I was covering the reception on a dreary Monday morning when I answered the phone to a familiar voice; it was Amelia; I let out a squeal in shock as she was the last person on earth I expected to hear from, thankfully there was no-one in the lobby. The first words out of her mouth," there is no way you're not coming to the wedding even if I have to go to Cobh and drag you here so now that is sorted, are you free to talk for a bit or I will call you back? "

"No, I'm good for a few minutes."

"I can't believe you're going to be home soon, How was Canada?"

"Canada was wonderful, but I miss Clifden much more than I ever thought I would. I'm so glad to be coming back. I'm disappointed that I have to wait to see you; I'm really looking forward to catching up properly."

"Me too. I want to know all about Canada; I'm sorry that I never made it out to you, I would have loved to have gone but with the way thing where here it just never happened."

"Never mind that now, when are you getting back to Galway?"

"I'm not sure as I have not said anything to the Kelly's about taking time off, I'm not sure if they will let me at this late stage as the place is so busy. Can you believe that the hotel is fully booked from the 24th of December to after the New Year? I'm always surprised that so many people choose a hotel to spend Christmas in. Who would have known?"

Why Me?

"Stop that, Moll, I'm sure that they will give you the time off and if not I will get Stuart to have a word with Guy and get him to call them to cancel all future booking if they say no."

"Funny, Funny that is taking it a bit too far. How about I ask before you go blackmailing them?" I knew that the Kellys would only be too happy to give me the time off, as I have not taken any proper time off since I got here and they are always on my case to take a break. Now, I will not be able to use not getting time off as an excuse not to go Amelia has called my bluff.

"Sounds good to me, we really want you to be part of the wedding so not coming is not an option ok."

"Ok, Okay, leave it with me but sadly I must go for now as there are guests waiting to check in, I will talk to you soon."

"Great, take care."

I went about my day, I was on a high it was the most excited I've been in years, I so wanted to go to the wedding despite my reservations about going home, may be going home for Christmas might be the best time after all, my mother would normally be in good form as she loved Christmas, peace to all men and all of that. I suppose I have to go back and at some stage it may as well be this year I can't keep putting it off forever. I guess I will have to face the music and dance as dad would say. It will take all of my courage to go back but please Dad stand beside me and help me and please let Mum be in a good form. The twins have said repeatedly that she is a different woman from the woman she was when I left. As much as I miss the place and want to go back it would be so much easier to stay away.

Just as I thought, the Kelly's were delighted to give me the time off, on the condition that I would come back to them, they thought it was a marvellous idea and wouldn't it be lovely to be at home for Christmas. If only they knew that, I would have been really happy to never go back. The hotel was so busy it was easy to forget about the trip home, which suited me just fine. I loved Christmas in the hotel, the place was a hive of epic excitement with all the office parties it would put the strongest bah humbug in the mood, everyone was so happy it was easy to join in the joy of the season. It is my favourite time of the year in the hotel, most people hate it but there is something about the way the hotel looks like it has been taken from fairytale book. I love the smell of the real trees and the flicking of the lights and the sound of the logs burning on the fire, it like heaven on earth. On the 23rd of December, I started my journey west with mix emotions I no longer knew how I was feeling, all I know is I cried all the way to Galway. Thank God the weather was so cold that I could hide my face with my hood and scarf, I kept my head down so that nobody could see my tears just in case anyone was to ask me if I was ok I was afraid I would have a full on breakdown. The last thing I needed was someone asking any questions that I couldn't answer. What kind of gombeen would I be, having to tell them I had no idea why I was crying, it would kill their cheerful buzz. The noise on the train was deafening as

Why Me?

everyone was in high spirits there was laughter and bags everywhere, I wasn't meeting Amelia till this evening so I had plenty of time to pick up presents for everyone, as I didn't want to be carrying too many bags on the train and now I know that was the best plan as there was barely anywhere to sit never mind to store the luggage. Arriving in Galway felt strange yet so familiar and yet different I dry my tears and went to the café to get lunch and to make a list of what I needed to get. It was great that Amelia was collecting me which means that I don't need to rush for the bus; I was so looking forward to seeing her we had so much to catching up to do; it is going to be a long night. I walk out to Terryland and bought presents for Mum and the gang. Then to Eyre Square to get the girls some makeup and smellies. I already had gifts for Amelia, Sara and Elizabeth. I bought the Wedding Gift a while ago from a sales fella that was in the hotel, apparently it is the newest coffee maker on the market; it makes all the coffees that you would buy in the posh coffee shop. He had delivered it himself as the thing was huge and I didn't fancy carrying the thing around with me, at this moment I was very grateful to him as I was now loaded down with bags it was becoming impossible to get around without banging into people and knocking things over in the shop. I made my way into the Imperial to have a G&T while I waited for Amelia; I was exhausted. I had hoped for a quiet corner but I must have been out of my head as the place was packed I was lucky to get a seat at all never mind a quiet corner. As I sat down to rest my aching feet I prayed that I wouldn't meet anyone from Clifden as I was not yet ready for the questions, also Mum would know I was on my way before I got there and the element of surprise would be gone. I thought it would be best to just walk in, maybe that way she will not tell to me to get the hell out as I was not wanted there. She could be very stubborn at the best of times and now I'm hoping she didn't mean what she said as I was leaving. Her tone often haunts me late at night 'if you leave now you are no longer part of this family, don't come back with your tail between your legs'. I could still hear her angry tones ringing in my ear as if it was yesterday. I'm optimistic that she will be better now that she is off the drink, I would like to say that I'm hopeful we can put the past behind us and build some kind of truce. Let's pray that time has been great healer.

I almost fainted when Amelia walked in she was as beautiful as ever, she was radiant, tall and elegant it looks as if she glided across the bar, people just moved out of her way without her even asking she was totally unaware of her beauty and the effect it had on everyone. Men and women alike were enthralled by her she stood beside me and gave me the biggest hug I ever had in my life, we stood there for ages holding each other half afraid that the other one would disappear, she broke the silence first right ' let's get out here and go somewhere where we can get some food in peace, Let me help you with your bags'. Before I knew it she had bags in hand and was making her way through the crowd. Outside the cold breeze bit hard against our skin, it was certainly cold, a lot colder than it was earlier 'You would never know Sara may well get her to wish for snow after all it is definitely cold enough', I said as we wrapped our scarf around our necks.

Why Me?

'Now that would make her very happy.' We battled our way against the crowds of people that were rushing to get the last of their shopping, it took us nearly fifteen minutes to get to the across Eyre Square. We were both relieved to be loading the bags into the car. Amelia suggested that we made our way out of the city before everyone had the same idea. We stopped in the Westwood Hotel on the Clifden road it was a lot quieter than the city and we found a cosy corner, ordered our food and chatted for hours, it was nearly ten o'clock by the time we looked at our watches part of me wished that I could stay here. I told Amelia that I was half afraid of how my mother was going to react when she saw me.

'Nonsense, she said, you will be ok. She has changed a lot. Do you know she is working in the supermarket and was promoted to duty manager a few months back? She has done an amazing job with all the kids. She looks amazing since she started working, with her new haircut and the make-up she looks years younger she seems a lot happier. Losing your dad hit her much harder than she would ever let on. Half the men in the town have been trying to go out with her, all of them have failed she hasn't touched a drop of drink in years. '

I almost fell off my chair, 'No, What, When.'

Amelia laughed and said, 'There had been a lot of changes since you were at home and I think you will be nicely surprised.'

'I hope so, now let's get a move on or we will need to take

B&B here for the night.'

She must have seen the colour drain from my face, 'You will be ok, I'm here and if she doesn't want you to stay, that is a bonus in my eyes as you will stay with me, and I would love that.'

'Thank you, Amelia,'

Off we headed on the bendy roads of the N59. Sadly it was too dark for me to appreciate the beauty of the journey I was so lost in thought that we had arrived at my mother's house before I knew it. I almost didn't recognise the place, even in the dark I could see someone had painted the outside, there were new curtains on the windows, the place seemed like it was loved once more. There was a warmth coming from the place, I stood at the door not knowing if I should knock or let myself in, when a dog started barking I jumped back, it was James that came to the door to see what the dog was making a fuss over. He opened the door and let out a roar; he engulfed me in his arms as the twins and the girls came from their rooms from the corner of the eye, I could see my mother standing in the background, I could swear I could see a lightness in her eyes that I had never seen before. She looked amazing; I had never seen her look so good; she had an air of happiness about her it was lovely to see before I could get a word out of my mouth.

'She told the gang to allow me in and for Sarah to put the kettle on.' Amelia dropped in the remaining bags and quickly said her goodbyes. We had already planned to meet

Why Me?

tomorrow for lunch.

Mum eventually 'said hello and that she knew I would be back for the wedding. Standing face to face with this lady who I believed hated me all of my life now looked at me with a softness I had never seen before, it was as if I was looking at her for the first time. Maybe the old saying that time is a great healer was true. If I wasn't my imagination, I could swear there was a thaw in the coldness between us. Standing here now it certainly feels like we found a truce, maybe now we can rebuild a more normal relationship. I had hope in my heart of hearts that new level of respect for each other and that as she has turned her nightmare around. It was heartwarming to be around these guys again, I had missed them so much and we had a lot of catching up to do.

We stayed up late into the night chatting, playing board games and acting like fools. The following morning I planned on popping down to the girls for a quick coffee as are meet up later in the evening at my house for a pre-Christmas drink, then I was meeting up with Amelia for lunch then for the rest of the afternoon we were going to help with the preparation for the Christmas Dinner, mum has already made the mince pies and the Christmas Cake, my job was to make the trifle it had always been my job every Christmas for as long as I could remember, each of us had our jobs to do and we were happy to do them we filled the kitchen with laughter and the smell of the wonderful food made our mouth water. We finished all the prep just in time to go to Midnight Mass, which for some reason was now at 9.00pm rather than midnight. It was a lovely feeling walking to Mass as a family, the church was full and I must have spoken to half the town by the time we walked down the hill. Only for the girls rescued me I would still be there, it was good to be home.

It was agreed that we would all go to the pub, I was nervous as I was unsure how Mum would feel and I didn't want her to go home by herself, I was shocked when I found out it was her that suggested it. She must have read my mind as she laughed so hard 'It is ok, the first drink is on me.' I was dumbfounded, it was like I was in a parallel world as we walked to the pub my Mum put her arm into mine and said that she was happy to be going to the pub these days without having a drink I have not had a drink since the day you left, you leaving was a wake-up call for me one that was long overdue. So thank you for leaving and for coming back. I was unsure at how to take this, was she been genuine or giving me the daggers, it was hard to work her out at the best of times. Christmas Day was like old times, we had eaten way too much so our trousers needed to be loosened, we laughed till the tears flowed. we play board games until it got too heated as we fought over who was cheating as if we were five all over again, finally we had to give in so, we sat and watched movies late into the night. The biggest surprise of all was when Mum raised a toast to Dad with a croaky voice she called him her true love and that he would be thrilled to see all of us here today as he loved Christmas and most of all his family.

Chapter 17

We were woken the following morning at 8.30 with a loud knocking on the front door. As I was the nearest to the door I crawled out of the room to answer the door who in there right minds could have been at the door this early the interruption suddenly brought back the memories of the morning when they came to tell us about dad. The frosty air took my breath away as soon as I opened the door Amelia was standing there jumping from one foot to the other telling me to hurry up as we need to be put in Ballyconnelly as soon as possible. I was so relieved to see her I was in such a fog as I had almost forgotten about the wedding.

'What is the rush the Wedding is not till four.'

'It is but we are having breakfast before the craziness starts, the hair and makeup ladies will be arriving at twelve. They put the marques up two days ago, the lads are up to ninety with the finishing touches, so all we have to do is to get out there to get ourselves pampered. So get your bum into gear.' Thankfully, I had got my glad rags ready yesterday, just as I was walking out of the room Amelia asked if I had my PJ's as it would make more sense to stay over for the night.

'Grand give me a minute with that, I was out the door Amelia's excitement was infectious, it was hard to not get carried along. Seeing Amelia been so out of sorts was a new experience, I don't recall her being this nervous at her own wedding it just amazed me the way these three ladies interacted with each other, currently, they were all a bag of nerves it was hard to tell which one was worse, the normally cool calm women of yesterday have been replaced with three raving lunatics. They were so close to hysteria, which had everyone baffled as no one had ever seen this side of them before. Apparently, for the two previous weddings, they were as cool as cucumbers, both of those weddings went like clockwork and there was no reason to think today would be any different. Amelia said it was because this was the last family wedding and that she and mum had enjoyed their day so much that they want that and more for Sara. After we had breakfast Stuart opened a bottle of champagne to help calm their nerves. I was not sure it was having the desired effect I could watch them any longer without taking charge before the day spiralled out of control. I was so used to dealing with frantic brides and their families it is second nature to me, it was a place where I felt most comfortable and confident. I sent the boys up to the marquee to check all was in order and to make sure the heaters were all on as it was getting pretty cold out there, the frost from this morning was yet to clear, so they had to make sure the paths were safe, they were going to add more salt to help. I directed the caterers to their station, and they were so organised that you would forget that they were here in the first place. Next to arrive was the florist, the flowers were simply breathtaking, followed by hair make-up ladies who were friends of Sara from the theatre, they were wired to the moon, they brought with them a certain buzz of crazy they were full of fun it was no doubt about it, tonight was going to be a lively night that possibly will last till the early hours of the morning. They were going to party hard that's for sure, it was hard to get them to start, with hair and make-up I was beginning to think that Sara wouldn't be ready in time when I said this to the girls they roared with laughter.

'Well, we would never let that happen as she would be sure to kill us afterwards.'

In fairness to them once they started, I had never seen anyone work so fast these guys were certainly very skilled and in a very short space of times the Bride, Amelia and Elizabeth were ready. They all looked so radiant, they were three of the most beautiful women I had ever seen. When the Reid ladies were getting changed Janice turned to me and said 'Come on Molly it is your turn'

When she was finished she handed me a mirror. I nearly fell I was gob smacked I was the best version of myself I had ever seen. I couldn't believe my eyes for the first time in my life I felt beautiful. Since I started working in the hotel I had lost so much weight and now had a figure most girls would die for, but I had never seen myself as anything other than a plain Jane, the image that is looking back at me now is a beautiful one even if I say it myself. Janice must have seen the tears build and let a roar out that I better not start crying as I would ruin the make-up and there was no time to fix it as she was on her way up to the marquee, she was off before I could mutter a word. Just then Stuart came bouncing in to tell us it was nearly time to make our way up to the lake. I didn't want to see Sara until she was walking down the aisle so Stuart nipped into the other room to see his girls and afterwards he would escort me to my seat. I went into my room and quickly changed into my dress; I wrapped my shawl around my shoulders as I was afraid everyone would get pneumonia this was not the weather for an outdoor wedding.

Finally, it was time for myself and Stuart to make our way to the lake and I was struck by the Baltic air as soon as the door opened and that was before I had a chance to even step outside.

Stuart laughed and said: 'Once we get up there you'll be fine, it is lovely and warm, Just you wait and see.'

' I certainly hope so, as Sara might just regret this outdoor winter wedding,'

Once we turn the corner my mouth literally hit the ground as they had turf fires burning on both sides of the path. I knew it was an old west of Ireland tradition that had long since died out; I guess many old folks would say it was the cost of modern Ireland, the only person I ever heard talking about its magical effects was my grandmother and by God; she was not wrong this had an astounding effect, the smell of the turf the sparking and crackling of the wood overloaded the senses. In days gone by the fires would be kept burning till the bride and groom returned home. I bet there wouldn't be a person here that wouldn't be in awe of its effects. It set the scene for what was to come I was on total overload when I walked into the marquee it was a sight for sore eyes, once you step inside you could immediately

Why Me?

forget where you were, there were straw bales covered in sheepskin blankets, and hand-knitted wraps for the guests in case they got cold. It was so cosy in here it was easy to forget about how cold it was outside. The lads had outdone themselves this time as there was no venue as beautiful as this. There were several Christmas trees dotted around the place, candles and fairy lights surround every available space. It was better than any of the wedding venues I had ever seen, there was nothing even close to it in the hundreds of magazines the filled the back office in the hotel. They are full cover to cover with all sorts of ideas on how to decorate your venue but there was nothing that came close to matching this in any of them. It had to be one of the most romantic settings ever. The musician played softly in the corner; the sound coming from the harp was enchanting. There must be at least one hundred people here, a lot more than I had expected. I was still taking in the details of my surrounding when the music changed to let us know that the bridal party was on their way.

The soothing sounds of An old Marriage Song; (author unknown):

Marry when the year is new, always loving, kind and true.

When February birds do mate, you may wed, nor dread your fate.

Why Me?

If you wed in March winds blows, joy & Sorrow both you'll know

Marry in April when joy for maiden & for men.

Marry in the month of May you surely rue the day

Marry when June roses blow over and sea you'll go.

They who in July do wed must labour always for their bread.

Whoever wed in August be many a change you sure see.

Marry in September's shine, your living will be rich and fine.

If in October you do marry love will come but riches tarry.

If you wed in bleak November, only joy will come

Remember

When December's rain falls fast marry & true love will last.

Amelia was the first to walk down the red carpet she was radiant, she took her place beside Dermot who was looking at his wife as if it was the first time he had ever seen her.

The room gasped a few minutes later as Sara walked in arm in arm with her mum. She looked as if she had just stepped out of heaven she was almost angelic like. George had tears in his eyes as he watched his bride approach, the closer she got the more he looked as if he was going to faint. She stopped halfway to remove an elegant modern-day version of the Galway Shawl a unique full-length handmade mohair and silk, crochet stitched with honeycomb pattern, which is believed to symbolise good fortune, a Celtic knot symbolising loyalty, faith, friendship & love, only one thread is used in this stitch to reflect life eternity, no beginning no end. To reveal the most stunning sweetheart illusion lace and tulle neckline gown with a mermaid fishtail, with the most exquisite buttons running down the back of the dress, as she walked the lights shone showing off on the metallic thread. She wore a simple headdress made of out the same flowers that were in her bouquet. Her veil was a simple lace with embroidered sparkling beads around the edges gentle trailed down the back of the dress. Elizabeth has outdone herself, I have no idea how she can create such amazing gowns. It is no wonder she is so successful.

The official was the same guy that had married Elizabeth and Amelia. He welcomes everyone and gave a brief rundown on how the ceremony was going to proceed. Then he began.

Friends and Family so fond and dear, it is our pleasure to have you here to celebrate the union of George and Sara to be a witness to the love they share not just for today but for many years to come, and years from now when grey hair takes over and our bodies frail may everyone remember this day with the fondest of memories. George and Sara when your love may be shaken by the difficulties of life may you both remember the love you shared today, the dreams and hopes that you have for the future will carry you through. Today we will have a drink of Irish mead in your honour and ask the universe to good and true to bless you with its gifts that will see you through your hour of need.

He tied their hands together in ribbons of gold and afterwards; he hands them a cup of mead.

Let raise our glass and say, on your special day our wish for you both be the goodness of the old and the best of the new be always at your door, the full blessing from this world and the next always surround you. Now drink this mead and that your needs will always be filled before you need them.

An Irish Blessing; (Author Unknown):

May your marriage bring you joy and your evening bring you peace.

May your troubles grow few as your blessing increase.

May the saddest day of the future be no worse than the happiest day of your past.

May your hands be forever clasped in friendship and your hearts joined forever in love.

Your lives are very special God has touched you in many ways, may his blessings rest upon you and fill all your coming days.

Why Me?

After the final blessing, he introduced the new Mr and Mrs Spencer, loud roars echoed the room for several minutes as they walked down the aisle. After the beautiful ceremony, we moved to the back of the marquee where the champagne flowed and canapes gave us a sample of the feast that was to come. Needless to say, the evening was full of great food, music and laughter. Every person here was in high spirits, they partied hard and well into the night, not even the freezing cold could put a damper on the occasion. I danced so much that I thought my feet were going to fall off, there was no end of eligible young men to keep me on my toes, but I had only eyes for one young man named Ronan Farrell, we chatted for most of the evening, much to my disappointment I knew I would not see him after tonight as he was working in London for one of the big city banks. Maybe it was knowing this allowed me to relax and throw caution to the wind. A high flyer like him would never be in my league, but it was nice to be flirted with as I hadn't given anyone a second glance since Kevin. Sara was granted her wish when the first snowflake fell to the ground, and with two hours the place was covered in snow, it was the perfect touch. All her praying had worked against all the odds. I might have to start praying if this was anything to go by. I had never before seen so much snow in my life, a few of the men wrapped their coats around them and went out to build snowmen, it was a sight to be seen with the mix of alcohol and excitement lead to some very strange looking snowmen most of them had a bottle of beer in the hands. The birds were singing as we walked back to the house, as happy as could be, we all fell into bed in the hope of getting forty winks before breakfast. Sara thanked me for all of my help for making her day run so smoothly, to which she would brush off any attempts I made to say I did nothing.

'Stop that Moll, you kept me calm and I will not forget how quickly you stepped in to get the day back on track, you were amazing at organising everyone. You're very talented. So thank you. The Kelly's are very lucky to have you I hope they know that,'

'Honestly, it was no bother at all. I was only too happy to make myself useful It stopped me from feeling like a spare part. I was very grateful to be part of your special day, so thank you for having me.'

'What are you like, you are very dear to us? It was our pleasure to have you as always. Just don't be a stranger, when you head off back to Cork.,'

This was the most perfect day ever I can honestly say it was the happiest day of my life so far, I pray that this is the start of something new and wonderful, it is about time I had some fun in my life up until now it has been all work and no play. I fell into bed with a mixture of tiredness and excitement, I felt alive rather than my normal half zombie-like state. Today has shown me that I once again need to make changes and start living life rather than being an observer, I need to take control and get out of the hotel more and see what life has to offer. It wasn't too long before I could hear the kettle boiling and the smell of toast, so I decided to get up and make my way to the kitchen, to my surprise all the Reid ladies were not only up but looking fabulous, the words were out of my mouth before I could stop them.

They just turned around and laughed. We were sitting around the table reliving what a magnificent day yesterday was, we were all astounded to see it was still snowing it was picture perfect. Amelia slipped into the conversation that she was pregnant so subtle that no one picked up on it at first until five minutes later Elizabeth said: 'Did I hear you right did you just say you are pregnant?'

Before Amelia had a chance to answer, Sara said 'You are, aren't you? That's brilliant, the best news ever. The men walked into a room, full with a mixture of tears and laughter, it was not long before they too joined in the celebrations. It was not long afterwards that there was a knock on the front door, it was Isabella saying that she had a sixth sense that she was missing something important and that would never do, she too was overjoyed when she heard the news.

She turned and winked at Elizabeth, 'Well it definitely looks like you will be spending more time here once this little munchkin is born, Now maybe it's the right time to start seriously thinking about opening a shop over here. We talked enough about it over the years.'

'Never mind, the shop people would pay a small fortune for a venue like this, it is unique, there is nowhere else in the country like it even the weather didn't put a damper on the day, in fact, it added to the magic, and if you were to introduce more of the old traditions that haven't been used for years I think you would get a lot of Irish from overseas coming here to get married especially the Americans they would go mad for it. '

'Molly, you are a genius girl, I think that is a brilliant idea. There is so much you could do and you have everything that you need here and when Poppy adds her marketing skills to the mix, you are on to a sure-fire winner.'

'Would you two stop talking ráiméis, I think the drink from last night has gone to your head there is no way I'm opening this place to the public this is my home.'

'Molly, how are you getting on with your mum since you have been home?'

'It's has been ok so far, I wouldn't say we are the best of friends, or anywhere close to it but we are polite to each other and I guess that is a good place to start. To be honest I'm relieved that we are not at each other throats, she is much calmer without the drink and it is the first time I have ever seen this side of her and I have to say it suits her. I think there has been too much hurt for us to ever be bestie I'm trying to let the past stay in the past and hopefully, we will eventually be able to sit down and have a conversation without tearing strips off each other. For now, I'm just happy taking each day as it comes. The fact she is working is really agreeing with her, she is not as angry as she was. I would love it if she found someone to share her life with as she is still such a young woman. For now, I'm loving being home, I hadn't realised just how much I had missed everyone. It is true to say that you never really appreciate what you have until you to lose it.'

'Tell us what you think of the gorgeous Ronan Farrell, you two seemed to be getting on very well last night, you looked very much like a couple.'

'Stop, Amelia, it was not like that at all. We had a few dances, he was a nice guy alright, but that is all. How could it be anything more than that, we both live in different countries and are not going to see each other again.'

'I'm not too sure on that Molly, as he was asking an awful lot of questions about you last night, replied George. He seemed very keen to me not to mention, I have invited him to have dinner with us tonight and I have already told him you would be going, so there is no way you can back out now.'

'For Feck's sake please tell me you are joking?'

'Sorry, I wish I could, but no. We are all going to the hotel in town for dinner tonight at 8 pm sharp.'

Stuart nudged Dermot and said, 'Hey lads, we might have to have one more wedding here yet.'

I didn't know whether I should laugh or cry as the thoughts of seeing him again had me in a tizzy.

'I'm glad you guys are finding this funny. But I think you need to stall the ball there, you are both off your heads talk about putting the ass before the cart.'

Chapter 18

Before I knew it, my holiday had come to an end and it was time to go back to work. I was looking forward to getting back to the hotel, I had missed the hustle and bustle. The bus journey to Galway had me mesmerized by the beauty of this place it saddened me to be leaving this time for different reasons. I had gone on a few dates with Ronan which surprised me more than anyone else he went back to London two days ago promising to write as soon as he got back part of me was convinced that I would never hear from him again, but I was very thankful to have met him as now I knew I was ready to start dating again.

Once I got back to the hotel it was all systems go, as usual it was frantic, I barely had time to unpack I was glad that I had washed and ironed my uniform before I left. One of the girls was out sick, another was away at a funeral and the new fella never showed up it was a brilliant start to the day three members of staff down. We had a Wedding in the function room the dining room was full house for dinner and to top it off a large stag party arrived into the bar all wanting bar food, thankfully they were so busy singing their heads off that they didn't notice that the food was taking ages to come out, by the end of the night we were all shattered and to make matters worse the night porter was running late again, we pulled straws to see who would stay until he came in it was just my luck that I would have pulled the short one. Welcome back to the madhouse Molly, I guess there is no rest for the wicked. Life returned to

Why Me?

normal and as I suspected I had not heard a word from Ronan, I have to admit I was just a little disappointed even though I knew it would be impossible for anything else to happen it was best that it ended before it began, it saved the heartache in the long run. I had planned to go back home for two weeks at the end of June by then Amelia should have had the baby I couldn't wait to see everyone especially the baby but for now, it was work as usual.

I was like a child on Christmas morning every time I thought of my trip back to Clifden, Amelia had the baby a few days ago, in the end she was ten days overdue, to say she was climbing the walls waiting for the arrival of her little bundle was an understatement as there was only so much nesting anyone could do. She started her maternity leave at the beginning of May, earlier than she had originally planned as the hospital had predicted that she would have the baby early, as the baby had dropped quite a lot, and with the high number of Braxton Hicks, it was a shock when she went over her due date. Everyone thought she was going to have twins despite the ultrasound showing one baby, she was carrying such a huge bump you would think if it was not twins that the baby would be a bruiser, but no, she had a 7lbs little girl. By the end of the pregnancy, she was just wobbling around the place like a penguin. I was going home a day early, so I got the bus from Galway to Clifden which is my favourite part of the journey. To be honest, I prefer to get the bus rather than go by car, from the bus I have the advantage point to take in the ever-changing scenery, no matter how many times I have travelled these roads I'm always astounded by the beauty of the place it never looks the same, each time it is as if I'm seeing it for the first time.

When I arrived at the house, there was no one home, I dropped my bags into my room and headed to town to see if Mum was working. When I walked into the shop I was surprised to find Mum was over the moon to see me. We ended up going for a coffee, where she gave me the update on all the local gossip, all the girls were still working so I walked over the sky road to Amelia and baby Chloe. I barely recognised the house, Dermot had done so much with the place. Before I had a chance to ring the doorbell Amelia was opening the door.

'Wow, the place looks amazing, I love your kitchen. It is the perfect space for entertaining, Dermot has worked wonders with the place.'

'Yes, he has an amazing vision when it comes to anything got to do with buildings.'

'I can't wait any longer, where is the star of the show?'

'She is finally asleep, come with me.'

My eyes filled with tears as Amelia placed baby Chloe into my arms.

'She is just perfect, easily the most beautiful baby ever.'

'Well, I glad you think so because Dermot and I would love you to be her Godmother with Sara?'

'What? Are you sure?'

Why Me?

Amelia just laughed and said, 'Of course, you will be a wonderful role model for her, and don't forget the job comes with a catch!'

'Okay, what is the catch.'

'Plenty of Babysitting.'

'I would love to spend loads of time with this wonderful bundle, but I'm not sure, how much use I will be on that front it might take me a while to get here. I replied.'

'You have an excellent point there, we would still love you to be part of her life.'

'Well, don't keep me waiting? Will you just say yes?'

'Yes, yes, I would love to, how could I say no to these big blue eyes. But I have to warn you, I'm way out of practice.'

'Believe me, it will all come back to you in no time at all it is just like riding a bike you never forget.'

I stayed with Amelia for hours, I just had to feed Chloe, I was not as brave when it came to changing her smelly nappy, I was more than happy to hand her over to mum.'

I was completely taken in with baby Chloe. I was going to be putty in her hands I could see it now I was honored that I was going to be such a big part of her life

Just as I was leaving Amelia said that Elizabeth and Sara would be home on Saturday and that Elizabeth had said she wanted to meet up with me. Amelia had no clue what it was about, only that she definitely wanted to meet up before I went back to Cork. I was intrigued why Elizabeth wanted to meet up. It sounded like she was up to something, I guess I will just have to wait and see. If you are free on Sunday we would love to have you here for dinner.

'Sure, I would love too then I can get to see this little cutie.

It was around 9.00pm when I walked into the pub to catch up with the girls and it was going to be a fun night as so much had happened since we had last seen each other Aoife had gotten engaged to John last weekend. Sadhbh recently started a new job in Dublin, and Niamh is doing a steady line with Tony. There was no doubt about it, it was going to be a long night. Once we started chatting there was no stopping us I was looking forward to making a wish on Aoife engagement ring. According to folklore it's guaranteed to come true. I just need to work out what to wish for may be to meet my one true love. We were three sheets to the wind when we left the pub at six o'clock in the morning, we decided to walk to the beach to see if we could sober up before we went home, lucky for us it was a lovely morning, we headed down towards the beach road it was just like we were teenagers again. I had forgotten that the pubs of Clifden were famous for its lock-in. A fifteen-minute walk took us close to an hour with all the laughter and messing about. We sat at the edge of the beach, our feet dipped in the cold water trying to sober up, eventually the hunger took over us, so we headed back to town for breakfast. Before finally going home to get some shut-eye.

Why Me?

Saturday lunchtime I sat in the local café waiting for Elizabeth, my mind was in overdrive trying to work out what she wanted, I guess I will just have to wait a little longer, otherwise, I will drive myself around the twist. Thankfully, I didn't have to wait that long as Elizabeth arrived a few minutes later, after we ordered our food, she wasted no time in getting down to the reason she wanted to see me. I was gob smacked, in my wildest dreams I would never have come up with anything close to her latest plans I thought she was partially mad. She wanted to open a Bridal shop out in Ballyconnelly. I found it hard to get my head around what she was saying I couldn't imagine that anyone from the city would travel so far out of town, so after we finished our lunch she took me for a drive out to Ballyconnelly so I could see it for myself. Elizabeth stopped outside the old rope factory and went to the boot to take out a pile of drawings. She explained as we walked around the crumbling walls, that she planned to renovate the old building keeping as much of the old walls for the Coffee shop, would add a two storey extension for the main bridal shop, with plenty of space for the seamstress to create one-off design, and for any alternation that maybe needed to the dresses from off the rail. Giving the bride total control over how she wanted her dress to look. There would also be a section for bridesmaids and flower girls. I was hoping to open a section for the mother of the bridal party, giving them the options to have bespoke outfits made. We will stock all kinds of shoes to suit all types of budgets and of course, we can cover them in any colour to match the colour scheme of the wedding. On the bottom floor, we will have a range of suits for the groom and his party.

There would be space for catering, wedding photographers, wedding bands, DJs, cake makers, florists, videographers, pre-dinner music, Ceremony music, wedding planners, hair stylist and makeup artists, wedding invitations and stationery, gifts and favours, wedding cars and buses, Registered Solemnisers, photo booth & selfie mirrors, décor and event styling. You name it, we will have it anything a bride will need for her special day you will find it here. We will also link in with the local hotels to provide our guest with accommodation.

'I think it is a fabulous idea, but do you really think people will travel all the way out here?'

'Well, Molly, the idea came from you at Sara wedding, and what I have not told you the best bit yet! So follow me.'

Before I had a chance to say a word, Elizabeth marched off towards the lake. I had to virtually run to keep up with her. I was thankful when she finally came to stop, I was covered in muck up to my knees. Elizabeth was so animated and unaware that she was covered in muck too, it was a strange sight, this glamorous lady in these unfamiliar places she was talking so fast it was hard to understand what she was saying. When she finally took a breath, I got a chance to ask her what was she talking about.

'Sorry, Molly, but I have not been so excited about anything in a long time, in fact, the last time I felt like this was when

Why Me?

I first opened the doors to my shop in London that's how I know in my heart and soul that I have to do this.'

'Ok, tell me again what the plan is for here?'

'Well, remember when you said that I should do weddings for the public back at the house and I said I couldn't have anyone there as the place was too close to my heart.'

'Yes.

'Stuart finally, got me to try a game of golf a few months back and as we were passing here I thought that this would be the perfect place to put your idea into action. If we build a barn here so we can use it as a wedding venue I plan to put a permanent marquee up over here and gazebo overlooking the lake for when the weather is nice. Just think about it, it will be amazing.'

'Molly, I want you to manage the coffee shop, the suppliers, the shop space, and the Wedding venue. Poppy will do all the marketing and promotion with her skills, the place will be a tremendous success in no time, Dermot and his team will look after planning and have the building work done. Isabella has been trying to get me to open a shop over here for years and up until now, I had not wanted to be here but, now Amelia has had Chole and with Sara talking about, if she should move here as well it seems like the logical thing to do as I want to spend more time with Chole and further grandchildren, the thought of me being in London and not part of the grandchildren's life doesn't appeal to me.'

Why Me?

'Why me, I don't think I would be able to take on such a project, it is a huge undertaking.'

'Stop talking rubbish, I have seen the way you organise everyone at Sara's wedding and I watched you working at the hotel, you are more than capable. You just need to believe in yourself. Furthermore, I will not take no for an answer. I can promise you I will support you in any way I can whatever you need you will get. Isabella and Poppy will also be on hand to get everything up and running, you would be in safe hands with us. Not to mention I would be willing to double your current salary and a percentage of the profits. With great company perks, we will provide you with any training you need. I believe that you are the best person for the job and there is no way can I have someone else managing the place you will have plenty of time to get your head around the job and everything that goes with it, as I have yet to get the final set of plans drawn up and planning can take ages. So, can I count you in? just to let you know that anything other than yes is the wrong answer'

'I guess in that case, I have no option but to say yes.'

'That is great news altogether. Welcome on board.'

With that, we walked around the place and I was seeing the plans come alive in front of me. We spoke about different options and tweaked the plans a little before heading back to the car. When we arrived back to Clifden we went straight over to Amelia to tell her the good news it goes without saying she was over the moon for us both.

Why Me?

'I guess that means I have another babysitter for this little one. I also, have been thinking about some changes I would like to make to the surgery and now that I have increased my babysitters I will have the time to start the ball rolling.'

We both looked at her, with a confused look on our faces. She just laughed and said she would say no more until Sara was here tomorrow. Well, well, this was without doubt turning out to a week of new beginnings. Elizabeth and I tried to guess, but Amelia just laughed and said she wouldn't say another word until everyone was here. Curiosity was going to get the better of me. Amelia opened a bottle of champagne to celebrate today's good news.

'Welcome to Wear with Confidence, Moll. I wish you both every success in your new adventure may you love working with us so much so you will never look for another job again. one thing is for sure you will never get bored or lack excitement with Mum and Isabella around. The best part of all you will be coming home and I know everyone including your family will be delighted with that you have been away for too long, Clifden has missed you.'

'Stall the ball there Amelia, it is going to be some time before I come back to live.'

'Yes, that's true as we need to get the plans approved before we can do anything and that could take months at the earliest. I'm hoping that there will be no objections, as it will create new jobs for the area I plan to employ as many locals as I can. There are loads of very skilled and talented people here, so I see no need to look anywhere else. If people are willing to work hard and take a chance, then I'm willing to give them a chance and invest in their future, any training they might need we will be happy to provide it.'

'It will certainly put Clifden and Ballyconnelly on the map. I think most people will be amazed to find such an amazing facility here. Most people would think you have finally lost it, you would expect to see the like in the big cities, not in a small rural village.' We're all very excited about what the future would bring for Wear with Confidence one thing for sure it will never be boring.

Chapter 19

Sunday lunch was crazy. With the news of the plans for the old ropes factory, Sara announced that she was pregnant and to top it off she was also moving to Clifden to be near Amelia and baby Chloe. George has been offered a manager's job with the bank and was looking forward to getting away from the cut-throat world in the city. Sara has an offer in, for an old building just outside of the town with plans to convert it into a studio for acting and dance, with space for kids to perform. She had meetings with all the local schools planned for the next few weeks, to see if they would be interested in putting a programme together. "I plan to get transition students involved in training the younger kids and getting them to organise the shows, from stage production to lighting and directing, props, advertising and costumes and make-up. Hopefully, they will get on aboard in writing the scripts. The idea is to get everyone involved, even the kids that are not interested in acting or music. There are so many other roles that people don't even think about, so there are no excuses for anyone to be left out. It will help the young adults to build their self-esteem and confidence and hopefully get them to interact with each other in a more positive way. It will give them somewhere to go in the evening and keep them off the streets. If we are going to bring our children up in this beautiful place there needs to be something to do outside school especially for those children that are not interested in Gaelic football and soccer.

Why Me?

'It will be nice to have a choice of something, I think this will be an amazing experience for any young person, it will tie in nicely with Clifden Arts Week. There are fantastic music and Irish dancers around the place that will be delighted to get the chance to get involved. I would love to say I would help but I can't sing and I have two left feet and can't act if it was to save my life.'

'Well, Molly, you can't be good at everything. Don't you worry I will find a way to drag you on board.'

'Good luck with that Sara, you have not got a hope to get me on stage.'

'Dermot, it looks like you are going to be very busy over the next year or two. These two will keep you on your toes.'

'Dermot gave a very hearty laugh It's not Sara and Elizabeth that has me worried. Tell them, Amelia, what you're up too? The fact she is on maternity leave is wasted on her as she is busier now than before. So, my darling, enlighten them.'

'I have been planning to open up a new medical centre, I have not yet found a building, but it needs to be in the town so it is easy for everyone to have access to it.'

'Amelia, you are being very modest as it is nothing like anything we have in the county, never mind dear old Clifden.'

Amelia took a deep breath in, her face came alive as she

explained that she wanted to model the clinic similar to ones she had seen in Canada. It is a genuine challenge for lots of people to get into Galway for appointments, plus the fact the Galway Hospital is so overcrowded and with the extensive waiting lists, people are going without the intervention they need. Many of our patients avoid going in as they either have no transport or have children and they have no one to mind them, if they are not back before school end. It is madness in this day and age that we don't have the facilities available here. The plan is to get all the GP's in the town to come together in one building and to work closely with each other to help each other out when necessary, hopefully, they will agree to have a 24-hour call out service. The clinic will have an X-ray machine, a Scanner for expectant mothers, counsellors, psychologist, play therapists, occupational therapist, and speech and language therapist. A room for an acupuncture, a physiotherapist and a massage therapy, a chiropodist. Meeting rooms for AA groups and for parental support groups, mindfulness workshops, etc. We would be able to do information evenings on different health issues with a large room for yoga and meditation. It would mean that we can take a more holistic approach to treat the person and with all the services working together it would improve the communication between everyone, hopefully, then no-one would get lost in the system. I would love it if there was a spare room or two so we have the option to expand as time goes on. The possibilities are endless. It would be great if we could have a mother and babies group and first aid course running as well. The more I think of it, the more and more I'm convinced that the town would benefit as a whole. Clifden had such a wide catchment area if you take in all the surrounding areas. I'm in the process for applying for grants from the HSE and the National Lottery and in talks with other professional to come on board and so far the response has been overwhelming. I have been contacted by a dentist, orthodontist and a chiropractor would all love a room. Now, all I need is a building big enough and with scope for growth. Fingers crossed we will find something soon.

Dermot laughed and said, 'That he for one was very happy that you have not found anywhere yet, as it gives me a chance to crack on with Ballyconnelly. We should hear back from the planning any day now, we are hoping we have supplied them with all the information that they had requested and much more. I'm fairly keen to get started as I have a lot of work coming up next year. It would be great to get ahead start.'

'Clifden is going to be the place where everyone wants to live by the time you three are finished.' Replied Moll'

'It will be for sure, hopefully, other small towns around the country will try to follow.'

'That is so true, Dermot.'

Molly said, 'she was sure that Clifden was not ready for these three mad ladies, they will have no idea how to keep up with ye.'

'Everyone roared with laughter, I think we should raise our glass to these wonderful ladies and may God give us the strength and energy to keep up with them, replied George.'

Stuart and George were being very quiet, they were both looking at Dermot with an anxious expression.

Stuart said, 'If you are not very careful Dermot, these three will be the death of you with all that work! How are you going to get it all done on time?'

'Thankfully, I have a great gang of lads that are not afraid of hard work. There is no doubt about it the schedule will be tight, but rumour has it that these clients are very easy to work with.'

'Don't be fooled my dear man, these women are all slave drivers at heart, so watch out. We will be on hand to supply the beers.'

'Thanks, lads, I knew ye wouldn't let me down.

'No Worries, Dermot, we will never let you down.'

I was absolutely in awe of these people, the love alone that filled the room had me praying that one day I would find someone that would love me the way they all loved each other. I was not convinced that I would ever be able to keep up with their pace never mind the standards that they have. It must have been well after midnight when I left Amelia's. My head was dizzy and I was not sure if it was from the alcohol or if it was the mammoth tasks that were

Why Me?

ahead of me.

Four days later I was on the road again on my way back to Cobh and to be honest I was full of mixed feelings, part of me was looking forward to getting back to normality and the other had half was heartbroken to be leaving Clifden. It was easy to get carried away with the Ladies and their plans, their minds must always be on full steam ahead. I guess the best thing about going back to work would be it would give me a chance to really get my head around Elizabeths wonderful offer. I was still in shock with Elizabeth's job offer, the reality of the situation, never in my wildest dreams did I imagine my time in Clifden would have gone the way it did. My head was in a tailspin, with all of the what if's, part of me had always hoped that I would go back to live there in the future but I didn't think it would be so soon. I'm not sure if I'm excited or terrified. I loved catching up with everyone but it would be a different kettle of fish living there. It was definitely food for thought, I will have to have a serious talk with Mum about me going back as I'm not sure how she would feel about it, I know we are getting along a lot better these days but living so close may be pushing it a bit too far. I hope we will be able to work out our differences for once and all as there was going to be lots of changes that is for sure, for me and for the town. It would be my idea of a nightmare, if going back meant that we would return to our old ways and be at each other throats the whole time, it wouldn't be good for either of us. I know for sure that I never want to return to the old me, the angry me, the one that always felt I was not good enough, that I need to prove myself over and over again while being partly invisible. I've spent too many dark nights looking into my soul trying to find out just who I was, and truthfully I'm still not sure that I have fully answered that question, but I do know that I'm not that person anymore and I never want to be again. Have you ever asked yourself who you really are? Where you're going, what are you supposed to be doing with your life? What makes you happy? These are tough questions and are difficult to answer, all that soul searching takes it out of you and I don't want to end up back there again, at times I was convinced that I was losing my marbles on more than one occasion was ready to sign myself into a home for lost causes. Enough of that maudlin for now it's onwards and upwards the only way to go. Focus on the now as there is no use in looking back.

On the other hand, I'm not convinced that the town will know what is happening to them. Once the Reids ladies get to work. If the Bridal shop will be half as successful as expected, it will be guaranteed to bring a lot more visitors to the town and would be good for all the local business even if they would kick up a stink that the charm of the place is being ruined. It will be wonderful to see that there will be more jobs in the place, it might just stop all the younger generation from leaving, as most kids leave as soon as they finish school. I know for a fact that many of them would have preferred to stay, as it is a wonderful place to raise a family, it will be a win-win situation for everyone.

Why Me?

I'm lucky to be part of the adventure.

The new medical centre will mean so much to so many people, I really hope that Amelia finds a suitable building soon.

Once I was back in the hotel, life returned to normal very quickly, there were days when I didn't even think about the shop or going back to Clifden. I would just fall into bed exhausted and had to dragged myself out in the morning. The hotel was getting busier and busier every day, even after we had hired more staff it didn't seem to take the edge of it. I guess we were blessed that the business was doing so well as there were many hotels across the country that were struggling to keep their doors open. So I guess I should be thankful for small mercies, although right now I could do with some quiet time my feet are ready to fall off and I could easily scratch my eyes out with tiredness. It was hard not telling the Kelly's but for now, I wasn't ready to tell them just in case I ended up jinxing everything. Only for the texts and emails from Elizabeth to keep me up to date with the plans, I could have easily forgotten about the whole thing. Last week she was a nervous wreck as they should have had the final decision from Galway County Council regarding the planning permission but as of today there is still no update, we all believe it will be a yes as they can't possibly look for anything else with all the extra information they have been looking for, the more that has been supplied to them the more they are looking for. Even the locals that had initially objected to the plans have come on board and we now have their blessings as everyone in the community will benefit from the shop in the long run. The Chamber of Commerce, local business and residents have all issued a letter to support the application, so now everyone was sitting at the edge of their seats. I felt guilty at times that it was at the back of my mind, unlike Elizabeth and Dermot. Dermot swears that the fine head of black hair is going to be a thing of the past soon as the grey hairs are showing themselves every time he sees another request for more information. Once planning comes through, it would be full steam ahead for Dermot and his team so he had all of his ducks in a row ready to go. Dermot and Amelia have planned a trip back to Canada for a break before the madness begins. Once building starts it would be impossible to take five minutes never mind a few days off it will be their last chance for at least a year if not more. Right now I was very envious of them, as I would love to be flying off to anywhere, preferably somewhere peaceful and quiet. A girl can dream, will have to add that to my to do list. Elizabeth and Stuart came to stay at the hotel a week or so after Dermot and Amelia left for Canada with the good news, the planning had been granted it was champagne all round.

Elizabeth said, 'Now we have the planning, we should be able to start the building work in a month or two at the most. Have you said anything to the Kelly's about you leaving there Molly?'

'No, not yet. I was waiting until I had a better idea of when I would be starting it will be a long time before you will be ready for me, Surely?'

'That's true, Molly. I reckon it will be at least twelve months before all the building work is finished, but we will need you to start six months before we are due to open the doors. There will be loads for you to do, you can help with the recruitment of the staff, your input will be invaluable as you would have a lot of local knowledge.'

'There will be so much to do we will all be running around like headless chickens no doubt.'

Why Me?

Chapter 20

The months passed slowly to begin with, there were times I didn't think Elizabeth would be able to get the council on board, what clinched the deal was she had agreed to share the cost for the roads to be upgraded. Then it all moved in a flash and before I knew it, I was heading west for the last time, I was going home. It was a weird sensation to know that I was going back to work and live there the closer I got to Galway the more excited, I was getting I had not seen the building since Dermot had got his hands on it and I was unsure of what to expect. I was planning to stay with mum for the first month while I looked for a place to rent, hopefully, at some stage in the future, I will be able to buy something small, fingers crossed, that would take a year or maybe two. I was lucky as I was able to save a lot of my wages and tips up until now, that's one of the advantages of living on site. Both myself and mum are worried about living together again we will both have to be on our best behaviour.

The first thing the following morning Dermot was collecting me to bring me out to Ballyconnelly, Elizabeth would meet us there. Dermot drove at a rapid speed and he spoke nearly as quickly my head was spinning not to mention I was none the wiser as to whether the schedule was on track or not and what he has done so far. I was not up to speed on builders speak. The one thing I now know for sure was, that putting my driving license on the back burner was a big mistake. Now I will have to make it my top priority as I think cycling in and out of town is going to old very quickly, especially if it is raining. My mouth hit the floor as he drove the car around the corner, the old stone building that was once faded and jaded, with its missing roof and most of the back walls on the floors, and the wall that was still standing that were crumbling down, was now standing tall and proud, it was lovingly restored and looked every bit as good now if not better as it did on the first day it was built over a hundred years ago. Elizabeth greeted us as we got out of the car, I just followed the pair of them inside.

'WOW, WOW, was all the words I could get out. Inside was even more beautiful than the outside, they had kept the stone wall exposed, it was impossible to know what was new and what was old. It was remarkable.'

Dermot just laughed and said 'That the place was far from finished as there was still loads to be done, all the different sections need to be sectioned off, the first fix electrics and plumbing were yet to be done, all the top floor needed to be finished and that was before we even think about the wedding venue by the lake or any landscaping. The list of things that needs to be done is endless, we are still a long way off opening our doors.'

'The only place that is finished was the workshop out the back, come and see. By next week we will receive the delivery of the sewing machines and all the materials we need so we can start training the staff here, we are blessed that some of the guys are willing to come over from the UK to help get the new staff up to speed, as we speak we have five new members of staff currently being trained in the London workshop to try and make the transition as smooth as possible.'

'This is so exciting and with the list of jobs to do is overwhelming, I'm not sure what I can do to help?'

'Nonsense Molly, come and have a look at where the coffee shop will be. I would like you to work on the plans with Dermot as to which would be the best way to lay out the kitchen and the restaurant, you will need to order all of the equipment from cookers to tables and chairs as no-one else know anything about catering, it would be up to you to organise suppliers, staff and anything else you might need. Oh, I almost forgot, do you know how to go about getting a liquor licence?'

'Yes, I can get that sorted, but I know nothing about setting up the kitchen from scratch or what would be the best equipment or dining room furniture, so I'm not sure I will be much help, I would be more of a hindrance than of any help. "rubbish Molly, you know more than we do and anything else you will learn as you go. Dermot will be able to guide you, so I have no doubt you will excel yourself. When I opened the doors to Wear with Confidence, I didn't know what I was doing either you just make it up as you go along, If something doesn't work, you simply just try something different. At the end of the day, we are all learning together on this one as this will be so different from anything I have ever done before. So we will all have just roll up your sleeves and see what happens.'

'Elizabeth, I think you are crazy.'

'I have heard it all before, you are not the only one to say it. But, what I do know is to always follow my gut and my gut is driving this project. So, my darling, you will get used to me after a while. If you have any ideas, feel free to let me know.'

'If you say so, Elizabeth. I'm willing to try anything once.'

'That's the perfect attitude to have, we are going to work very well together as I can see you are a girl after my own heart. We will be just fine, you just wait and see. Have faith, even if that is all you have.'

With that, we walked down to the lake where the builders had placed markings on the ground for the Marquee and the arch for the wedding ceremony with the awe-inspiring backdrop.

'Elizabeth, I was wondering if it was possible to build a permanent structure made from the same stone as the main building, if the walls at back had big glass doors that could be opened up so you could have the full view of the mountains and the lake, and on a fine day it would to bring the outside in, it would be a magical venue. Also, if there was a small cottage for the bride and groom to stay in on their wedding night. Who knows, some couples may even want to stay here the night before, it could make their lives a lot easier then they could have the hair and makeup done in the main shop and come down here to get dressed and if there were any problems with the dress, there would always be someone available to help fix it. It would give the couple that little bit extra peace of mind.'

'Molly, you are a genius have I told you that before if I have I really mean it, It's a fabulous idea it would be the icing on the cake so to speak, I will talk to Dermot and see if he can get planning, I don't think it will be too much of a hassle as there is the old building at the back we could just convert it.'

On arrival, the wedding guest will be welcomed with pre-drinks and canapes for the guest before being escorted into the Marquee or the stables.

From the day I arrived back in Clifden, it was full steam ahead where sleep had become a luxury, and I love my sleep and normally don't function too well without it, somehow I was more energised than I had ever been. My days started at 6.30am and rarely finished before 2.00am five days a week. My days were full to the brim between the builders, suppliers, recruitment and training of staff. I was proud of myself these days as I no longer feel like a pleb talking to the builders, the days off having no idea of what they were talking about were gone, I was almost fluent in builder speak, I had even developed the art of swearing like a pro. My nights I spent researching different products and going over the schedules. My saving Grace was the wonderful Poppy, she was a Gods send on the other end of the phone

Why Me?

day or night, she had so much patience and was kind and full of advice, she was always calm and reassuring, I was learning so much from her, up until now I had not given marketing much thought. When I took on the role, I knew I would have to be a quick learner but I had well and truly underestimated the sheer volume I need to get to grips with was overwhelming. I was looking forward to meeting Poppy in person, most days she was the one that keeps me sane.

It was another late night on site when I said jokingly to 'Dermot, "that I may as well live in the building as I was spending so much time there and that was even before we opened for the weddings. There are days when I was only home for forty winks, quick shower a bite of food if I was lucky and I would be off again. Once we open I might need to take up lodging in the farmer's cowshed over the road. Most days I was still cycling in and out unless I was lucky enough to grab a lift from someone, the best thing about being so busy and the cycling everywhere was that I was the skinniest I had ever been and I had even seen the inside of a gym. I was so busy with work that all plans for a driving lesson were on the back burner again.'

'Molly, that is an outstanding idea, I will have a talk with Micky tomorrow to see if he would be interested in selling, as they have not used it in over forty years or more. I could kick myself that I didn't think of it first.'

'What, you've got to be kidding me! you have completely, without doubt lost your marbles? I was only joking. There is no way I would live there."

Why Me?

'No joking, it would be perfect, it would make a beautiful cottage for you. You might be lucky enough to catch up on your beauty sleep think about it, it would be the perfect answer and you did say that you were looking for somewhere to live. Planning will not be a problem as we could use the footprint that is already there and put an extension on the back.'

'Stop, will you, I'm not going to living in a cowshed, that will do my street credit no end of good I will never find a man when I tell him that I live in a cowshed. There is no way I would be able to afford the place never mind the cost of the renovations.'

'Micky, will not be asking for much I bet he would be happy to see the back of the place as it is an eyesore, as for the renovations I will only charge for the cost of materials, on the grounds I can sign you up for more babysitting.'

'Fat chance of that at the moment, I would only love to spend more time with Chloe, as I have not seen her or Amelia for longer than a few minutes in weeks.'

'Don't worry that will all change when everything is up and running'

'Can I hold you to that?'

'You can for sure. It is me you should be feeling sorry for as soon as we finish this place, I have to make a start on the Medical Center and Sara's Dance studio, between the three women, I don't have time to bless myself.'

Why Me?

We both roared with laughter as it was true it was a hard job to keep up with them. They were unstoppable once they got an idea into their heads.

A week later Dermot came into the office jumping from foot to foot like a child shouting 'Guess What, you'll never guess, Micky will only be delighted to sell the shed to you the best part of all is that he had a great time for your dad, apparently your dad helped him build the house he is in now and as a thank you to him he will sell you the shed and the land around it for only fifteen thousand, which is for nothing, even though the land alone would be worth a hell of a lot more.'

'That's very kind of him, Is he aware that he could sell it for quite a lot more?'

'Yes, I had offered him the going price but when I told him it was for you he wouldn't hear of taking another penny, he said it would be his way of saying thank you to your Dad for everything he had done for him over the years.'

'I have just over fourteen thousand in savings so I will need to speak to George about getting a mortgage for the difference and for the cost of material and for furniture. How soon will you be able to give a rough idea on the cost?'

'I have some rough drawings in the car to give you some ideas of what we could do with the place, so you just need to tell me what you think and I can get started on the planning application. I have also taken the liberty to call

Why Me?

George and he will meet you here at five to go over the mortgage application.'

'Well, Dermot you don't let the grass grow under your feet, do you I think the girls are rubbing off on you?'

'Very funny, besides I had to move fast, so you didn't get a chance to change your mind.'

I had no doubt what so ever that he would turn it into a marvellous house. When Dermot showed me the plans my mouth literally hit the floor, I could feel a tear escaping from the corner of my eyes, I had never seen the likes of it before it was beautiful. His words that it was only a small job and would be completed in no time was wasted on me I did know that this was a huge undertaking and was bamboozled to see how this could be a finished house in less than fourteen weeks, I thought he had lost his marbles, there was no way he could get all that work done in such a short time frame. Never the less a few days later I had signed the paperwork for the cowshed or should I say my new home. Eight weeks later the planning was granted and Dermot wasted no time in getting started, I would go over every day for a few hours and do my best to give them a hand for what I lacked in skill I made up for in enthusiasm there was nothing that I wasn't will to try. Each time I walked through the building it amazed me at how much work that was done the day before. To say that I loved going shopping for furniture was an understatement, I was like a woman possessed.

Right on schedule, Dermot handed me the keys to my new

Why Me?

home, and it was outstanding, I was so overwhelmed it was mind-blowing to know this was my home, there was no evidence of the former cowshed, just a magnificent home that would rival any posh house in the country. I spent my first night here in total bliss, it was still like I was dreaming. I could never see myself living anywhere else, the life of Molly was good now really good. As I walked around the house trying to take in everything I had the tremendous feeling that I was home that I was exactly where I was supposed to be, the sense of contentment flowed through my body. On the kitchen table there was a bottle of champagne and flowers from Amelia and a little box, when I opened it I roared with laughter it was a sign with "Welcome to Cowshed" as the house was anything but now, I loved the sign so much that I will have to hang it outside. I had arranged a small housewarming for tomorrow night, I was a little nervous as mum and the gang were coming over as well, they had not been near the place since I bought it and mum wasn't shy in telling me I was making a big mistake taking the place, she had outright refused to come and see the place as far as she was concerned the Reids were a bad influence on me, I had not got a clue of how she came up with that one, still I was hoping that she would fall in love with the place as much as I had. I have no idea why I was still looking for her approval it was complete madness as I knew that she would never give it, that was not part of her psyche I guess I can live in hope. I pray that she will be at least polite to everyone, I would be mortified if she was rude especially to the Reid's if she says she didn't like to place in front of

Why Me?

them I would be so humiliated, as they have only ever been kind and supportive towards me. I would not have a wonderful job to go to everyday, and I certainly would not have a house like this. I'm often left wondering as to why mum is so negative towards them and in fact, she is the same with nearly everyone she meets, she a Devil for talking behind people's back something that I hate with a passion. Fingers crossed for tomorrow, but there is nothing she could say that would take away the way I feel about my fabulous house. I wished that Dad was here to share it with me as I know he would love the place and would be so proud of everything I have achieved so far, I found it of some comfort that in someway he is responsible for helping me as I could never have afforded it if Micky hadn't given it to me at the price he did. Thank you, Dad.

The housewarming was a wonderful success Micky came down with a bottle of poteen and a bag full of vegetables from his garden, he just loved the place and wasn't shy in telling everyone at how marvellous the place was. At one stage it looked as if mum was going to clock him one if he said it great job one more time. Elizabeth, Stuart, Sara, and George were seeing the place for the first time needless to say they loved the place. I knew I was going to be very happy living here, I was going to enjoy coming home in the evenings. I even had a surprise visit from Ronan which made my night complete I had not seen him since the wedding even though we spoke to each other every week. My God, he was handsome he was even better than I had remembered. Sadhbh was poking me in the back pulling me into the kitchen 'You need to come with me now, we have a minor emergency, she will be back in a minute.'

In the kitchen, it was like standing in front of a firing squad, with Aoife starting the inquisition, Who is he? Why haven't you told us about him? Where have you been hiding him? We can't believe that you are holding back on us, you sly horse. 'Girls, there is nothing to tell, I met him at Sara's wedding and we got on well so we have kept in touch we speak to each other every now and again since and that is it, nothing to tell as it happens he works in London and you may have noticed that I'm here, so there is no chance of anything happening. That's not saying that I wouldn't have wanted to keep on seeing him as he is rather cute so that is the complete story.

'If that is the case, Why is he here now.'

'I don't know, I was not expecting him in fact he was the last person on earth than I had expected to walk thought the door, believe me there is no-one more shocked to see him than me. Now, ladies, I think it's time for me to go back out there otherwise people will think I have done a runner and I need to keep an eye on mum to make sure she doesn't say anything to offend anyone.'

'Alright, you're off the hook, for now, we will have to come over tomorrow night after work for the real gossip unless he is still here.'

'Stop it, and let's get back to the party, I will call you in the morning if there is anything to report otherwise I'll see you for dinner tomorrow.'

Why Me?

The party was a roaring success. I was exhausted by the time everyone had left Ronan said he would stay behind to help me tidy up, we sat up till the early hours of the morning chatting gosh it was good to see him again I was taken by surprise when he said that George had offered him a job and if it was ok with me, he would love to take it as it would mean we could spend more time getting to know each other better.

'Are you asking me out?'

'I Guess I am, I have wanted to since the first night we met but I figured it would never work with us being so far apart, now that is no longer an issue there is nothing that would make me happier than getting to spend time with you. So what do you say?'

'Well, I suppose I would be ok with that'

'Just ok?

'Alright, I admit that I would love to spend more time with you too. So when do you start?'

'the end of next month on a part-time for six months to start with as I need to finish a few projects I will have to split my time between here and London until then afterwards I'm a free man.'

Life was mental there was so much to be done as the opening day got closer and closer it felt like the more tasks that were completed the more there was to do, the list was getting longer not shorter everyone was in overdrive from time to time tempers flare and even erupted. The official opening was on the 2nd January all of the suppliers will be on site by the 15th December which allows time to put the finishing touches on everything. At the last minute, Elizabeth thought it would be a good idea to have a completion party so everyone could meet each other and it would be the best way of saying thank you to everyone for all of the hard work they had put in over the last year. With the holidays around the corner, it was a great way to complete the year everybody would be in great form and looking forward to the break before the madness begins in the New Year. A lot of the staff from the UK will also be coming over according to Elizabeth it will be a marvellous way to build the relationship between the two parts of the company. On one hand, I was in agreement that it was a brilliant idea and on the other hand I was freaking out as it was more work, more pressure. I had invited the Kelly's, and they were delighted to come they eventually agreed to stay with me and I was over the moon it would be one way to say a big thank you for everything they had done for me in the past and still continued to do today, they still are always there to help when I need help with suppliers or the best place to go for the best deals. I couldn't have done it without their support. They were disappointed that they couldn't make it down on the 2nd for the opening but this was the next best thing it will be great to see them again. I was really looking forward to having some time off as it would the first time since coming home to have more than a few hours off.

Chapter 21

Now that all of the work was completed inside and out the place looked impressive, the main build gave little away it was only once you stepped inside you were transported to a fairytale. As for the wedding venue itself it was remarkable, it was no ordinary venue the views were out of this world, the mountain stood majestically as if they were standing watching, on a day like today the lake looked as if it was made of glass, it reflected all around it. There is no doubt about it it will be excellent for the photos. No matter where you looked you couldn't be disappointed there was also the bonus that the beach was a short distance away.

On the evening of the party, I was overcome with emotion the place look so good I was so damn proud of myself just knowing that I was part of the journey was just WOW.

Elizabeth made a wonderful speech to welcome everyone and with a very long thank you list. However there is one person who has made all of this possible and before I begin, I'm sorry if this causes her any embarrassment, but that is not going to stop me as this lady normally likes to hide in the background as she goes about her business, Without further ado can I ask for everyone to give a huge round of applause for Molly.

I have prepared a few words for you Molly, you can kill me later but for now, I want to say a heartfelt thank you for all of your work. For anyone that's doesn't know Molly let me tell you a little about her.

Why Me?

Well, where do I start she is efficient and eager to please there is nothing that was too much trouble for her, no problem that couldn't be solved. No matter what is going on around her, she remained calm and in control. It was sometime later I would discover that she was frazzled 90% of the times trying to find the right solution. Things have run smoothly under her watchful eyes and I have no doubt that will always be the case. There is no way we could have got this project off the ground without her. She moved with gentleness. You would think people would walk over her but underneath she was tough as old boots. Sorry Mol but it is true.

She is well able to negotiate with the builders and suppliers, with an incredible easy, so much that they would agree to prices that I'm sure no one else has got.

She easily calms the most irate customer, they would come in all guns blazing and they would leave as calm as could be.

She is a force to be reckoned with. She knows her craft better than anyone I have ever met. There would be many of the top hotels biting at the bit to get her on board and all I have to say about that is sorry she is ours. There were many times that I would be worried that the project would be too big for her, but if she ever felt the same I don't know, Molly looked so in control and would brush away any such talk as nonsense. It was only earlier this evening that she referred to herself as a swan, calm and graceful on top but paddling like mad underneath. Frequently I can see

Why Me?

a younger version of myself. A determined and capable youthful woman, there was no job too big or too much trouble. She had an endless amount of energy so that the builders and staff alike referred to her like the energizer bunny. Day or night she was bright and breezy. When the builders started to fall behind schedule, we could see her driving the digger or with a sledgehammer knocking a wall, watching her occasionally I didn't know who to feel sorrier for the wall or the sledgehammer which is nearly as big as her. According to the builders, she is the woman if you need anything demolished, although they say she needs a bit more practice for the repair jobs. She painted the place as good as any professional painter. At first, the builders thought she was a crazy woman, but it didn't take long for her to earn their respect. Dermot and his site manager have said that if she ever needs a job that they would hire her in the morning. The day I saw her swinging the sledgehammer over her head, she scared me half to death. She looked like a crazy lady. She would laugh it off and said that it was a marvelous way to remove stress and keep fit at the same time.

Her genuine personality is what warm's everyone to her. She may be just short of 5 foot, she may be still mistaken for a thirteen years old, playing at dress up but don't be fooled, she is a wise intelligent young woman. I could never get tired of watching her deal with an upset customer as they demand to see the boss, the look on their faces when she tells them she is the boss, is priceless. She would ignore all the hostile comments about how she should be at home in bed or in school, after they had left she would laugh and would pray that when she was in her fifties that they will be saying she only looked like she was in her twenties. There is so much more I could say but by now I scared I have said so much I'm afraid at she will do a runner on me and I'm sure you would much prefer to get back to your drink, and the food is almost ready. So can I ask everybody to raise their glass to Molly, Thank you seem such a small word for all that you have done and I'm in no doubt at all you will continue to achieve amazing things?

Elizabeth brought me to tears with her speech, I was taken off guard as I knew for sure the speech she had made, I knew her words came straight from the heart, I didn't like all of the attention and now I was very self-conscious as all the eyes in the room were staring at me, so much for the wonderful make-up I had on, I can only imagine what it looks like now a big red nose like Rudolf himself and panda eyes. I was so outside my comfort zone it was not funny, never before has anyone ever said such kind words about me or to me. The Kelly's look as if they were about to burst with pride, telling everyone in earshot how wonderful I was and when I worked for them I was a real trooper, the best member of staff they ever had they had been devastated when I left. Elizabeth's words weren't familiar to me as they were a far cry from what I was used to hearing growing up, words like this were not used in our house anything but, I can honestly say. Sadly, before I had a chance to enjoy the moment I could always rely on my mother to bring me back down to earth as she tapped me on the shoulder and whispered 'now don't you be letting your head get any

Why Me?

bigger or you'll never fit through the door." Even the loud clapping and the roars here, here couldn't silence her words, the sharp words were booming in my ears. By now, I didn't know if the tears were from what Elizabeth had said or from what my mother had said, I guess I was lucky that no one else had heard her, thankfully for small mercies she didn't make a scene. Even now after all, that has gone on between us she still can't pass up the opportunity to spit out the venom. I was so sure that our relationship had moved on from the past that we were somehow working on healing the past, but here I am being humiliated all over again. Stupid, gullible me. Once again I was asking myself why I even bother trying to have a relationship with her as it was clear that she wouldn't miss an opportunity to knock me down. Why couldn't she be like all the other mothers and be glad that I was doing well for myself, but no, life was never that simple in our house! Why the hell was she so bitter I would love to know but before I had a chance to dwell on the matter too much, Ronan thankfully, was on hand to help and at the first opportunity he had, he whisked me into the safety of the office, where I had a chance to re-apply my make-up to make myself look more presentable. For now, I need to put aside my frustrations otherwise I might explode and now is not the time or the place, maybe I'm just overreacting or been too sensitive I plonked a smile so I could enjoy the rest of the night as I wasn't going to let her see that her words still cut like a knife. I often wondered if she knew what she was doing, was she doing it deliberately or was she clueless to the effects her words have! The best way forward was not to let her know just how hurtful her words were or how much they upset me, I wouldn't give her the satisfaction of knowing that she had the upper hand. Just once it would be nice to hear her say something nice to me, for her to say well done, would it kill her to say it for once in her life. She was like a Jekyll and Hyde character when she is with someone else she is so nice you would think that butter wouldn't melt there is no way they would ever believe me if I told them half the stuff she has said and done over the years. So once again I will brush myself off and smile my way through it. Hopefully, I will be able to stay out of her way for the rest of the night. The evening was a huge success everyone was buzzing with the excitement. What a way to start the holidays. One thing for sure everyone was exhausted and need the break as we were running on fumes. Christmas was wonderfully quiet and relaxing, in front of the fire.

In no time at all, we were opening our doors to the public, there were so many people here including the Mayor of Galway, who was on hand to officially cut the ribbon and declare the shop open and the press to record the moment. Sara had roped in a few of her actor friends from the theatre to model some of the dresses. It was a wonderful sight to see locals and the celebrities mingling together as if it was an everyday event. Both worlds blending better than anyone could have ever expected. We had predicted that it would be fairly quiet when we opened, oh boy! did we get that wrong, from the minute the doors opened we were run of our feet it was all hands on deck even the ladies from the sewing floor had to come out and help, a few of the local's came in to complain, that they couldn't get over the road, that we would have to do something about the cars parked in their way that it was ridiculous in a small village that they couldn't go over the road. Elizabeth offered them a drink while Stuart, George and Dermot headed out to try come up with a solution, needless to say, it didn't take long for them to forget about going over the road. All of this was before the wedding venue is even opened, God above help us. It was just after 9pm when the last of the guests left, the fact we should have been closed at 6pm was irrelevant, we all crawled out of the place. I was dog-tired, and this was only after one day, the break over Christmas was already a distant memory. Knowing that Ronan was coming over to cook dinner took the pressure of me as I was starving, I hope that dinner will be still ok he was expecting me at 6.30pm. The wedding venue should be finished just before Paddy's weekend with the first wedding booked for May Bank holiday. Roll on Easter and I'm off for two weeks, myself and Ronan are going to Lake Garda it will be my first time on a plane, first time going abroad, I get goosebumps thinking about it; I was so excited it was hard to wait, on more than one occasion I had to pinch myself, to remind myself that this is real I will burst with anticipation every time I think about it, I get a flurry of excitement flowing through my body. Fingers crossed that the time will fly.

Chapter 22

I often wondered what my life would be like if I had never met Amelia, she has been my saving grace in so many ways, without her words of encouragement and support I would have been lost. It is a mystery, the way life works out. Neither of us could have foreseen our friendship all those years ago when she was making a routine house call. What has surprised me more, was just how the rest of her family have included me in their lives, I will be forever grateful! Late at night, I wonder if Dad had anything to do with bringing them into my life, it helped me to believe that he did. No-one ever told me that I would miss him more and more, as the years passed the pain has changed but it's always there and when I least expect it that rawness comes from nowhere and leaves me on my knees. There have been so many times when I begged to every God known to man, to allow me to see him and talk to him for one more day, I know deep down that I would always want the one more day. In my heart of heart, I know there could never be enough time to spend with him. I would give my right arm for him to hold me in his arms, to hear his voice. I have so many questions for him. When I was a small child, he had often spoken about what it would be like to be dead and he promised me that if there was a life afterwards that he would find a way to come back and tell me about life in heaven. Sadly, this is the one promise that he had not fulfilled it is the only promise that he has ever broken. I know that he would be very proud of everything I have achieved but I ache to hear him tell me, knowing it is not the same. Some nights are harder than others and it is on a night like tonight I call his name to remind him of his promise. I pray that I could feel his arms hugging me so tight that I can almost smell the tobacco from his pipe. The only thing I know for sure is that my life would be very different if he hadn't died that night. What hurts the most is that I never got to say goodbye or told him just how much I loved him and that he was an exceptional father to all of us. I hope that one day I would be lucky to find a man that would have the same qualities as Dad.

I had adjusted much better to my life back in Clifden, a lot better than I had ever imagined. I loved my job which helped, I had my dream house, I knew I was very lucky as the girls were always complaining about their jobs and they were afraid that they will never have their own place as trying to get the deposit saved is near impossible. I thank my lucky stars daily for that chance meeting with Amelia as without her I'd never be where I'm now. I would even go as far as saying that myself and mum are getting on better these days although she would still have the occasional dig at me, to which I no longer react. She still tries to play her old game of putting a wedge between me and my siblings thankfully it has only brought us closer together. None of us knows why she has such a dare on me, but they can all see it and have told her it wasn't good enough. On her bad days, she would phone me to scream that I should be ashamed of myself, to abandon my family when they needed me the most, that I was the worst daughter in the world. Her last line would always be that my father would be turning in his grave in disgust at the way I had carried on. Thankfully, for me, I had grown up a lot and ignored all of her rants and when I would refuse to get drawn into an agreement after the fifth call, the best thing I ever did was to put the phone on the side until she ran out of steam, then I would simply pick it up and say goodbye she was never any wiser that I wasn't listening. I figured that there was no point in hearing, the same old story over and over again, once was more than enough I had no intention of reliving it every time she was on her "poor me days." On more than one occasion I had thought she was back on the drink but she swore she hadn't touched a drop it would have been easier to accept this abuse if she was drunk at least it would offer some reason for it. Even when we were on the best of terms she would never say sorry or admit that she had hurt me in any way. There wasn't a cat in hells chance that she would ever admit that she had done any wrong in this lifetime. She was convinced that she was the mother of the year material. Once upon a time I craved her affection and needed to hear her say I'm sorry more than anything else in the world, nowadays I know she is not capable of ever doing so as I have gotten older I no longer need to hear it, I have forgiven her and as a result I'm a much happier person these days. Her memories on the past are very different from mine and that is ok as we don't need to be on the same page or best friends. There have been times when she has wanted me to say that it was all my fault or that she was the best mother in the world, but no matter how hard I tried I couldn't get the words out. Deep down I knew that she was very fragile and broken and there was no way she was strong enough to hear the truth, normally I would make my excuses and leave as quickly as I could. I also knew that she never had these conversations with my siblings, sometimes I wonder if it is her way of trying to say sorry, but at the last minute would bale. Believe me, I have tried to say she was an amazing mother on many occasion, in many ways it would have been easier if I could, maybe then we could move past whatever it was that was between us. I have read all the self-help books out there and they all say that the best thing to do is to forgive the person and by forgiving them you are really releasing yourself from the situation and it is only then that you start to heal and move forward. I have no ill will towards her, quite the opposite I want her to be happy and to forgive herself, for her to find peace within herself. It would be the icing on the cake if she would lose that chip on her shoulder. It has to be exhausting being that angry all of the time.

My bags are packed I'm ready to go Sadhbh is outside beeping the horn like a woman possessed we are off to Kilkenny for Aoife's hen weekend it is hard to believe she will be married in a months' time. She will be the first of our group to get married as for the rest of us there is little chance of us following her down the aisle anytime soon. It will be the first time we have been away with each other since the nutty weekend in Westport all those years ago. I was just about to lock the front door when the phone rang, I was tempted to ignore it but I thought it might have been Ronan so I ran back inside to answer it. I was startled to hear it was Sam's voice on the other end, it was hard to understand what he was saying as he was speaking so fast he was not making any sense, thankfully Marta took the

Why Me?

phone of him to tell me that mum has been rushed into the hospital earlier as she collapsed at work, they were both with her now and she wasn't looking so good the doctors were with her now doing all sorts of tests at the moment, they weren't giving anything away but they are asking all sorts of questions.

'Molly she is not making any sense, she seems really confused she is talking a lot of seafoid. 'They think that it is down to the bang on the head when she fell. I know you're going off with the girls this weekend, but is there any chance you could call into the hospital before you go?'

'Sure, no problem, it's on our way, I should be there in just over an hour and 15 minutes depending on traffic.'

'Thanks, Mol I know you will be able to make sense of this.'

I was flabbergasted, I'm not sure if I was more concerned or annoyed. Sadhbh went nuts when I told her, as she was sure she had done it on purpose, as she never liked you hanging around with us she was afraid we were a terrible influence on you.

'Well, I think she might have a point there,'

'Shut up, and let's collect the bride to be and Niamh, hopefully, they will be ready by the time we get there,'.

By the time we had got to the hospital mum had taken a turn for the worse and the doctors were recommending for all member of the families to come in as it was touch and go for now, they had her heavily sedated to see if the swelling on the brain would go down, they were still running tests as they were unsure if it was as a result of the fall or something more serious, the next twenty-four would be crucial. I told the girls to go to Kilkenny, as planned and if mum improved that I would follow them, they didn't want to go as we knew that the chances I was going to make it was slim to none. Aoife wanted to cancel the weekend altogether, but there was no way I could agree to that. 'Please Aoife, you have to go the other girls will be there already it won't be fair on them to cancel at this late stage besides there is nothing you can do here.,'

The next few days just dragged on and on with no answers, just more and more tests, myself and the twins took turns going into the hospital. I was at home on Friday morning when Kieran called to say that the doctors are asking all the family to come in to discuss the results we agreed that it would be best to wait till we hear what they had to say before calling James or the girls as there was nothing they could do at this stage. Sam was already in the hospital, Kieran was going to collect me so we could travel together as we weren't expecting to hear anything good. Within two hours we were walking the long walk through the corridors to the ward, it felt like it went on for miles, neither one of us spoke a word, Sam was pacing the floor outside the ward where mum was, he took one look at us and shook his head 'Jesus, lads this is not going to be good, I tried to get to them tell me something but they wanted to wait until we were all together.'

Why Me?

The nurse took us straight to the relative's room to wait for the consultant, Sam looked like as if he was about to faint, his whole body was shaking, thankfully, we didn't have to wait for long before the consultant came crashing into the room with his arms full of files. He must have been at least 6'6 with the dark brown eyes, he was a vision to be sure that I had almost forgotten why we were here, I was brought back to reality as soon as his deep voice spoke, "I'm sorry but as you may have guessed the news is not good, there is no easy way to say this but your mother has stage three ovarian cancer which we believe has spread to her liver and lungs. There are a few things we can do, first we are recommending surgery to remove the tumor on her lungs we will have to remove part of her liver and a full hysterectomy, then we will follow with chemotherapy to kill off any cells that may be left." He spent ages detailing the advantages and disadvantages of everything. He was very clear that the cancer was so advanced that all of the options would only buy her time that there was no way her life would be saved long term it should also give her a better as the quality of life for her remaining time. After the operation, she will be in the hospital for three to four weeks depending on how she recovers. Once she is home she will need full-time care for six weeks possibly more. We spoke to your mother this morning and she is happy to go ahead with the operation tomorrow, she is fully aware that there is no cure at this stage and there is no guarantees on how long she will live, at the best we can hope for is around 18 months maybe two years but it could also be shorter as there is no real way of telling. After the vision had left the

Why Me?

room the nurse from earlier came in with a pot of tea and a plate of biscuits. We needed to pull ourselves together before we went back into the room to see mum. I've had to admit that I was shocked to the core, as I didn't think that it would have affected me at all, but now I'm an emotional wreck. The boys were equally upset. We agreed that I would call Kitty & Sarah and they would call James, it is going to be so much harder for them being overseas even if they wanted to be here for the operation there is no way they would get here in time,as they are the three youngest they had a very different relationship with mum and were much closer to her than we had ever been. Sarah was so young when dad died that she didn't remember him at all and Kitty would often say that she had difficulty in remembering him, they were known as the unofficial twins of the family they were always together. James was just so happy go lucky, he was the peacemaker in the family, he looked the most like dad and had many of his mannerisms, he was a younger version of dad no doubt about it. Once the others heard about mum, they booked the first flight they could get on.

Mum's operation was scheduled for ten the following morning, and by all accounts, everything was going according to plan. She was over the moon when she woke up and saw that Sarah & Kitty had come all the way from Australia and she nearly collapsed altogether when James walked into the room with his dark brown, tan courtesy of the Dubai weather he looked more like a dad than ever before. A few hours later she developed a fever which turned out to be the MRSA bug needless to say she was moved to isolation within the intensive care unit for the next few weeks we were all living on the edge of our nerves, every day the news was full of ups and downs with more downs than up. The only good thing is that we were all together for the first time in years, luckily we all get on like a house on fire. We talked a lot about what was happening with mum and what would happen if she made it through this bug. The girls would have to go back to Australia by the end of the month, James had his business in Dubai so he couldn't stay indefinitely. So the care of mum was going to fall, at the doors of myself and the boys between us, we said we would work out a plan later but for now, we wanted to forget about what is coming down the road and enjoy being in each other's company. They loved my house, the girls said that they were very jealous but happy for me as I deserved it. It was wonderful spending time together, it is something we need to do more of we will have to make more of an effort, being at the end of the phone doesn't compare to being together. It was hard to believe the guys had been home for a month already, Mum was home for two weeks now and in fairness to the girls and James, they pampered her as if she was a newborn baby, they were going to be a hard act to follow. She lapped it all up as if she was the queen of the castle I was petrified at the thoughts of how I was going to cope when it came to my turn to take care of her as I know for sure that I was not cut out to be a nurse to anyone especially to a woman who has made my life a misery, not to mention the fact that my mother has made it perfectly clear that she did not need my help and was adamant that she didn't want me around. The day we had all been dreading finally arrived it was time for the guys to go back home, dropping them all off at Shannon Airport was one of the hardest things I had to do so far, it didn't take me long to work out that I hated goodbyes as we stood teary-eyed at the departure gates, I found myself agreeing to visit the girls in Australia and not forgetting James in Dubai I was going to be a global trotter after all, who would have ever thought it. We must have looked a sight for sore eyes, the crowds moved around us as we hugged each so tight none of us wanting to let each other go, we could barely breathe this was a rare show of emotions for our family as our number one rule was showing emotions was a sign of weakness. We were relieved that mum was not here to see us as she would have never let us live it down.

Chapter 23

The hospital had been very clear on what we were to expect as the time progressed and it was not a pretty picture they were painting; it was going to be a tough road for sure. but nothing they had told me prepared me for just how hard it was going to be.

Looking after mum was a nightmare, the boys were brilliant and helped enormously but she was much harder than anything I could have ever imagined, every day was unique sometimes I was left wondering if she was suffering from a split personality disorder. She would be so good for the boys she would be upbeat and grateful for the smallest of thing they did once I come through the door she would transform into a beast from hell, lucky old me.

I had so many emotions flowing through me from shock to anger to why this was happening and what did I do to deserve any of this, to sadness and sorrow of how I was going to be able to look after her as she was never the mother that I need. Most of the time I was exhausted and extremely frightened I didn't think I could make it through another day I was so tired that I often thought about giving up and walking away, I know that if the shoe was on the other foot, she would run to hills without looking back. I question myself daily as to why I felt the need to look after this nasty woman who gets a glorious sense of achievement from making my life hell and all this is before she needs 24-hour care. For now, at least I could get away with calling to see every day making sure that she had food in the fridge, and a clean house, the boys were doing all of the trips in and out of the hospital for now, she was on her final round of chemo in the hope that it would buy her more time. She has already told them that there is no way she will take any more treatment unless they were going to cure her, deep down she was still hoping that they had made a mistake or that they had found a miracle cure.

Some days I would swear she was back on the drink, the other's thought I was losing my marbles that was until the day I got a call at work asking me to come into town quickly as my mother had fallen in the pub and was refusing to leave, before she fell she had thrown a glass at the bar staff when they refused to serve her any more drink. They didn't want to call the guards on her with her being so sick. How in the name of all that is Holy did she get down the town, most of the time she can't get out of the bed with help. My eyes nearly fell out of my head at the sight that laid in front of me as I walked through the doors, I was mortified at what was coming out of her mouth as I tried to help her up she belted me as if I was a punching bag not to mention what was coming out of her mouth it was vile. The staff tried to help but she wouldn't let them near her. In the end, I had no choice but to call the twins to help, as soon as she saw them, she was all sweetness. The bar staff were astounded at how quick she changed. I would like to say this was the last time I had to deal with this nonsense but no she started to drink in secret at home, I would find empty bottles all over the place, once she even managed to set the bed on fire with her cigarette. We had asked

Why Me?

everyone not to bring her any drink but there was a traitor in the mix and if I find out who it is I will wring their necks. She would make me so mad that I thought I was going crazy or I would do something stupid I questioned daily if I was going to be able to carry this burden to the end. It was going to be a test of character and strength, Ronan or the girls couldn't understand why I put myself through its my new mantra was one day a time. I was lucky so far with work as I could arrange everything around when I needed to be with mum. Each day just gets harder and harder, we will have to get some help from the home care team soon. As she was getting weaker and weaker in some ways it was a blessing, which is not a very kind thing to say but she could no longer go down the town to buy any drink and at these times she was too weak to be nasty. There was no easy way of dealing with the task changing her after she had been sick or when she was not able to make it to the bathroom in time, it made my stomach sick and I would spend a lot of time vomiting in the bathroom, she was spending more and more time in bed and had started getting bed sores it was obvious I would have to move in with her and take some time off work which was going to be very hard, work was my everything and the thoughts of not going home to my own bed was hardest of it all there would be no escape . I was lucky as the boys were always on hand to help but in fairness, to them, my mother didn't want them washing her or changing her nappies so all that fell on my doorstep, and they had their own families to look after which was not easy with the kids being so small.

Amelia helped us organise the house to make sure that it

was accessible for mum to get around for as long as she could, she made sure we had every piece of equipment that would make our lives a little easier, our beautiful home had changed so much, some of the furniture had been moved to sheds to make room for the wheelchair her bedroom looked more like a hospital room with the instalment of the hospital bed, hoist and the commode in the corner of the room. The doctors had suggested that she went into a hospice for her final part of her journey, she told them if that was why they were here they could leave as they were no way she was going into one of those places as it was full of sick people. For the last few months of her life, we had to get the help of specialist palliative care, as we needed someone to give her injections and change her dressings and to keep her as comfortable and pain-free as possible. Without them, we would have been lost. The months that followed were incredibly hard and each day there were new challenges. The Palliative care team went about their business with such care and compassion it left us speechless, they not only looked after mum, but they made sure we were eating properly and gave me a much needed break. They told us about what signs to look for as she would approach the end, apparently knowing what to expect helps relieve the anxiety or worries we might have, and it would allow us to plan for it better. It was impossible for them to predict how long she would have, as a lot depended on the person themselves and how much they would fight it, at the moment she was getting weaker by the day and spent a lot of time sleeping she no longer wanted to get up and sit in her chair watching the world going by from

Why Me?

the porch, the smallest of tasks left her exhausted, she had lost so much weight she was almost skin and bone, and for a woman that loved her food she was eating very little. Her voice had turned to a whisper. You could hear the pain in her voice and she required more and more drugs to make her comfortable. She still loves to hear the gossip from the town. It was painful to watch her in so much pain, you see her breathing getting slower and slower, when she was sleeping each breath gave off a rattling sound that you would think it would wake her up but it never did, her once radiant skin which was the envy of everyone was soon replaced with a strange shade of grey and hands and feet were so cold that it was a full-time job keeping the hot water bottle warm, the electric blanket was on all of the time. She would often speak about dad, she would get annoyed at us for interrupting her when she was talking to him and couldn't understand why we weren't speaking to him, she told us that he was coming to collect her soon for their date night that we needed to stop delaying her as she needed to look her best. Every time she spoke about him, she had a massive smile across her face, every now and again she would turn to us to tell us that she loved him and that she would marry him as soon as she could and that there wouldn't be a woman in the world that would take him from her not even that Ruth one. At that moment I soften towards her as I never believed that she really loved him but watching her now it was clear she did love him very much and must have been devastated when he died. She was a young woman when he passed and although we knew she had been seeing other men after his death she never

Why Me?

once entertained the idea of remarrying.

I found it hard most of the time knowing that I should be able to provide her with the words of comfort, I knew what I should be saying and I had always known and maybe if I had not been so stubborn I could have said them years ago then maybe we would have had a better relationship, even if I had half of what the younger girls had I would be happy, and I was afraid that once she was gone, I would regret not saying them but no matter how hard I try to say that I loved her or that I forgave her I just couldn't get the words out, the words would get stuck in my throat. All I could do was attend to her physical needs the best I could, so I changed her sheets daily, I would gently move her in the bed to try to make her more comfortable I would offer sips of liquid through a straw or from a spoon, in an attempt to keep her lips moist. I wasn't able to apply lip balm as this seemed to be an actual act of love.

The others had no problem offering words to comfort her, I would love to be able to say– 'It's ok everything is all right or we are here with you and we love you so much, we are all together to support you and each other. We took a turn sitting there with her talking, gently touching, or holding her hand. The two girls had returned home and loved combing her hair and applying her make up as she would hate anyone to see her without lippy. They would often fall asleep squished up beside her on the bed. Such acts were all normal, but I found this expression of love for the mother who has spent a lifetime of hating me and who I never really knew, strange. I more often than not would sit in silence. Thank God the rest of the family could do this for her even if it made me feel like a total failure, some daughter I was, perhaps there was some truth in her words after all. I knew I was lucky that the other didn't judge me and understood that was the way it was. Amelia, would pop in every other day to say hello and her arms would be full of delicious home-cooked food just to make sure we were keeping our strength up, I had never seen such an array of foods as the neighbours also brought us food every day, not one of us had cooked or made a sandwich in the lasts few months there was always more than we could eat, so the twins brought food home to their families. If we were not careful, we wouldn't be able to leave the house after all the home cooked goodies were beginning to make our clothes feel tighter.

The only thing that makes the days easier was the fact we were all together, James and the girls stay in the house with mum which meant that I could escape the odd night to go home without feeling guilty. Thank God for Ronan he was an angel. When they needed a break, they would stay in my house or with the twins, it was good that we could get a break away from the house. The palliative care team would often send us all away telling us to go downtown and have dinner together that it was important that we spend time together.

One of the evenings when I was alone with mum she was having an exceptionally bad time and everything I was doing just upset her more I was at my wit's end, I asked why she was like this with me, well her response was

Why Me?

ruthless she didn't hold back in any way. She blamed me for ruining her life, having me was the worst thing she ever did, before I came along, she had a wonderful life full of promise. She ranted that it was a crying shame that the church forced women into giving birth and if she were a way right in the head she would have gone to England and had me an aborted. All her other children were perfect, not a bit like me. She was in no way repentant or remorseful. All I could say was that I was sorry that she felt the way she did, as all I ever wanted was to be loved and accepted by her. Deep down her words ripped through my whole body cutting me to the core. Once again, she had pulled me apart piece by piece and for what? After all her ranting, she pretended to fall asleep, it was her way off saying that she no longer wanted to look at me. How could she hate me the way she did? Or why for that matter I was still none the wiser of what I had done to make her feel this way. What is it about me that brings out the worst possible side to her? It never made any sense and now it made no sense at all, if only I knew. Little did I know that the girls were outside the door listening to every word she said. They were truly horrified and completely in shock as they had never heard her speak like this before to me or anyone else. I left the room with my head spinning before I had the chance to burst out crying. There was no way I was going to let the selfish and bitter old cow see my tears not now, not ever. I nearly knocked the girls to the ground in my rush to get away, I did not see them standing there. They grabbed me and hugged me so tightly that I could hardly breathe, which I'm so grateful for, otherwise I would just crumble into a heap on the floor.

They said 'That they were so sorry that I didn't deserve any of that, there was no truth in any of it. They asked me if she was always like this or was it in part down to the drugs and the pain she was in?'

'I replied, No, that this is the way it had always been for as long as I could remember always quick with snide remarks. No matter what I do I can never please her.'

'We have always been aware that she was on your case more than the rest of us, we thought it was because you were the oldest and nothing more than that. We never understood it as you have always been Miss goodie two good shoes, the rest of us have always broken the rules and pushed the boundaries.'

'We are going to talk to the boys later and afterwards they would speak to her together as what she was doing just was not right.'

'Do you mind, if I'm not there as I cannot take anymore more crap for now.'

They were at a loss of why she was like this, there was no excusing it. Shortly, afterward Kitty went in to check on mum to see if she needed anything and told her that once everyone was here that they wanted to have a serious talk to her.

True to their word, at 8pm the troops gather in my

mother's room to ask her why she was so unpleasant to me earlier, that they heard everything, so no use in saying it was nothing. Molly was really upset'.

To which she replied as bold as brass 'That she had her reasons, and she was not about to discuss the matter with you lot, if Molly thinks sending ye in here is going to do her any good she is more delusional than I thought. You would be better off minding your own business rather than sticking your noses where they were not wanted. Of course, it is not my fault for her being so unruly as a child.'

We all knew that she was hiding something, but we were not likely to ever find out.

The following evening, it was my turn to go into Mum but, after yesterday I was not ready to face her, after work I had arranged for Ronan to come over for dinner and a nice bottle of wine. A cosy night in watching some chick flick will work wonders no doubt.

James decided he would talk to mum by himself about the way she has always treated me, to see if they could get to the bottom of what was going on. He was the golden child, and he was sure she would tell him or at least give him some clue. It did not go the way he had hoped as she went berserk.

If I had known what he was up to I would have told him not to bother as there was no way she would tell them anything, that it would be best to ignore the nasty comments as it was not worth it at this stage, as she was

Why Me?

unlikely to change a lifetime of wrongs.

She was in so much pain for the last few days we could tell that her time was coming to an end that she was probably scared and was trying not to show it, better to go out kicking and screaming than admit she was afraid, or God forbid to say sorry. The priest came to visit her this morning and she ran him out of the place, we have not got a clue what she said to him but, it was not anything good judging by the look of him. The poor man was as white as a sheet going out the door. It was four days later when she finally passed we were all by her bedside even though we knew that she was fading and that there was not much time left we still were taken by surprise at just how quick it was, we were in awe at how peaceful she was at the end, she simply closed her eyes as she was sleeping, it took us a few minutes to realise that she had left as she looked as if she was asleep, The lines in her face seemed to had faded away, in an odd way she look younger. We sat there motionless not knowing what to do next, the silence in the room was eerie. Kitty was the first to break the silence with the sound of her crying, the others soon followed, their tears rolling down their faces. I, on the other hand, was numb, frozen in time, unsure of how I was feeling, on the one hand, there was this great sense of relief and on the other hand a sense of nothingness. The only way I could come close to describing it was I was surrounded by a mist. It was nothing like how I felt many years ago when Dad had died that is for sure. As I watched the other's tears falling, I could feel a sense of anger rising inside me. It was like a volcano waiting to erupt, as I knew the only tears I had inside of me were

Why Me?

ones of regret and the pain of never knowing the gift of a mother's love. Never knowing the power and strength of having that bond. If any tears were to come, they would be ones to finally acknowledge I had lost my mother many, many years ago. In many ways it was a relief or acceptance that it was something I never had or would have.

The palliative care team arrived not long after she passed thankfully they knew exactly what to do and swept into action and took care of everything, in no time at all the doctor was there to declare her death officially, the undertaker came and took her body to get her ready, we all agreed to wake her in the house rather than the dead house, we couldn't go back there, a little bit of me was vexed that she got to come home when she wouldn't allow dad to be here. I need to let it go, so I said nothing. The undertaker said he would have her back to us tomorrow evening as there would be no delays, he left taking her clothes that she wanted to be laid out in with him, she had already given him a strict list of what she wanted. The priest phoned to make the arrangements for the funeral mass. We all agreed for him to call to the house at ten the following morning, just to give us some time to get our heads together. We agreed she would not go to the church as she had made it perfectly clear she was not to be taken inside the door of the place or she would haunt us from the grave, she had said as much to the priest himself before she ran him out of the place a few days earlier. She was to come home for two nights and then go straight to on to graveyard to be buried beside Dad, Fr. Murphy said there was no point in waiting, as everyone was home, it was best to get it over with as quickly as possible as the last few months had been hard enough on all of us. No surprise that the house was full of people, long before she arrived back from Galway and remained full until she was taken on her final journey. In all fairness, the priest had done a lovely job with the services, once again we found ourselves standing by our father's grave watching them as they lower mum down to finally be with Dad. It is hard to say how I feel it would take me some time to get my head and heart around this. There are so many emotions running thought my head as I'm now officially an orphan, even though I have felt like that ever since my father died many years ago.

Chapter 24

Before the girls and James went back home, we agreed that we should keep the house and then they could use it whenever they came home, maybe in time rent it out. It was a few months later I was in the house packing up mum's clothes and giving the place a good clean, someone had already come to collect all of the medical equipment, so now was the time to bring back the furniture that was in the shed. Whilst I was packing away mums clothes at the bottom of the wardrobe I found an old suitcase, it was full with bits of paper, old photos many of which I had not seen before, at the very bottom were some old diaries which I was surprised to see as I never saw her writing, I held them in my hands for a good while trying to work out if I should read them or not, after some time curiosity got the better of me. So, I turned on the heating poured a glass of wine and looked to see if they were in any sort of order most of the entries were very ordinary day-to-day stuff. That was until I opened the following pages.

September 1st, 1966

Well, today is here at last it's the D-day, it has finally arrived in a few hours, I will be the next Mrs Woods, and I will spend the first night away from my family in my new home where I will have all the new mod cons, thankfully there be no more getting water from the well or having to boil the kettle and wait till everyone had gone to bed to get some privacy to have a wash, no more outdoor toilets for me or trying to

Why Me?

read under that flaming gaslight . I will be free from my parents and all their prying eyes, and the disapproving looks of my sister. I will be able to come and go as I please. I know that they are delighted to hand me over to Eddie as I will become his problem forevermore. They didn't want to be the talk of the town when the news that I was unmarried and pregnant got out. I was terrified when I had to tell them I was pregnant, I was afraid of how they would react and it made matters worse when they were suspicious that Eddie might not be the father, I was sure that dad was going to skin me alive I had never seen him so mad in all my life he refused to speak to me for weeks. They thought Eddie was a saint for asking me to marry him and knew I hadn't told him that he might not be the father, they were disgusted at my decision but more afraid of the alternative, so they kept quiet. Eddie is a real gem, one in a million, in time I will learn to love him with all of my heart. I know there is plenty of talk going around but that is only jealousy, as he is the most eligible bachelor in the town, when they were making Eddie they broke the mold, handsome, kind and a true gent. I can't wait till he sees me in my dress it will take his breath away. I'm truly blessed. The one thing I know for sure is that he will be my rock. We're heading off to Clare for a few days as a mini honeymoon we had planned to go to London for a week as Eddie was keen to show me the sights and revisit old friends. I had never gone further than Galway I was so looking forward to getting on a plane. I was fuming when mum said she couldn't find my birth certificate there was some nonsense about the priest had forgotten to give it back although he was adamant he had. I was afraid to push him too much in case he would refuse to marry me, so like a good girl I kept my mouth shut until after the wedding even if it could be found now it was too late to apply for the passport so we agreed that we would go after the baby was born in a way that suits me as I get to have two holidays instead of one.

Why Me?

We were getting married in the local church at 1.00pm and afterwards to the village hall for the wedding breakfast, I still have no idea why they call it the wedding breakfast as it will be nearly three o clock when we will be sitting down to eat?

Eddie's mum and sisters are doing the food which will be delicious as they are fabulous cooks.

My mother had taken care of the flower arrangements dad is looking after the drink and my uncles have taken over the music so there is no doubt that the craic will be mighty, it will be a long night if not an early morning, there will be plenty of sore heads in the morning. Sadly, I will not be drinking much as my mother still thinks I'm a pioneer, the fools think I have never broken my confirmation pledge.

My best friend Marion is my maid of honour and Eddie's brother is his best man. My sisters went berserk when they weren't asked, to be part of the bridal party why they thought they were going to be in the first place amazes me. They have spent every day for the last 26 years slowly tormenting me, there was no way I was going to have any of them standing there trying to take over my day, the thoughts of it gives me shivers down my spine. One word for the lot of them B.... s. They have always looked down their noses at me and treated me like an outcast, just because I was the baby. So, sod them and their feelings. Today is all about me.

December 10th, 1966

I woke up this morning I didn't have a clue of where I was all knew was, my head was throbbing as if I had the worse hangover ever and where is all the noise coming from? Before I had opened my eyes there was someone tapping on the shoulders asking me what I wanted for

Why Me?

breakfast. Oh fuck, now it is all coming back to me I had the baby last night, today I was an official mom, and I was clueless of how I should be feeling, I can't even remember if it was a girl or a boy where was the baby now? In a panic I called for help, nurse, nurse, where is my baby, I was relieved to when she told me that she was being looked after in the Scuba unit and that I could go down after I had eaten something to see my little girl my heart was racing at the thought of meeting my baby girl.

There is nothing that could have prepared me for the feeling I had when I saw her she was so tiny my hand looked so big I couldn't wait to hold her in my arms for the first time, I was aching to have her in my arms, any doubts that I had vanished at that moment and were replaced with fear that I would never be able to protect her, as I stared into her big blue eyes that seem to dominate her whole head she was beautiful and she was mine all mine. It was the only time in my life that I had felt so contented so at peace with myself. I promised this little angel that I would love her all the days of her life. I prayed to God that I would always be able to fulfil that promise. For a short while I had myself believing I could be an amazing mother, the reality of it had torn me in two and I was unsure why deep down I felt it had something to do with the argument I had with my mother a few days ago, she was acting very weird over this birth cert that still hadn't turned up, I had a very uneasy feeling I couldn't put my hand on it. When the nurse came to register the baby later that day, Eddie asked what we would have to do to get a copy of my birth cert, she was very helpful and directed us to the office to pay a fee and in a few days, they would have someone bring it up to me if I was still here, otherwise they would pop it in the post. When I received my birth cert I was so excited which was very short lived, I was traumatized to see that where my mother's name should have been was the name of Tina Dillon and

Why Me?

father was unknown, this was not my birth cert they have given me the wrong one idiots, after I had pulled myself together I made my way down to the records department to sort this out once and for all, to make a mistake of this magnitude was unacceptable and they were going to hear a piece of my mind and that was for sure, by the time I knocked on the door I had worked myself into a rage, I tore strips of the lady behind the desk as she went off to get me my real birth cert. However, when she returned fifteen minutes later with her manager, I was sure it was so she could apologise for their unforgiveable blunder. The stern woman quickly told me that there was no mistake; this was the only birth registered in the area for that day under my name. 'How could that be?

'She said that sometimes with home births that the information can be incorrectly recorded and if I had any questions that I should speak to my mother as she would be the only person able to answer what had happened.' I was hysterical, which one, Tina Dillion a woman I had never heard of or Polly O'Toole who up until now I believed to be my mother?' In the end, they called for the nurse to try to get me to calm down which didn't work, the next thing I knew I was injected with a needle, the orderly caught me as I fell to the ground, I woke up sometime later that evening completely confused. Where do I go from here, my whole life was in shatters. Who the hell was I? What will I say to Eddie when he asks if I got my copy, I feel so ashamed and dirty? Why would my parents lie to me and who else knows, do my siblings know and is that why they have looked down on me for all these years am I the only one that doesn't know about this sick secret or is it one colossal mistake? My head is spinning with what ifs. The only thing I know for now is that while I'm stuck in here, I will have to act like normal whatever that is. I guess on one hand I'm lucky to be in here as it gives me time to work out what I'm going to do, if I

ask my parents all guns blazing there is no way they will entertain me. I can safely say that this changes everything.

Every time I look at Molly-Rose I can feel that temper burning inside me. She reminds me of my own mistakes; I thought I could carry on as normal now, I'm not sure. Every time I see the big blue eyes it feels as if she is judging me, laughing at me, taunting me. I know this is ridiculous, but knowing this does nothing to help.

When the doctors tell me she is a fighter, part of me is praying that she doesn't that way I can't let her down there would be no way I could fail her then I would feel guilty. I'm not proud to write that in many ways it would be easier if she didn't make it. I'm so mixed up I no longer know what I want. I wish I never went looking for my birth cert, I should have left good enough alone.

January 1967

I arrived home today with mixed feelings, maybe with some distance between me and Molly, I will be able to sort myself out. But, first I will have to talk to my mother and ask her if she has found my birth cert as maybe this is still one big mix up.

My conversation with mum today was rather peculiar; she said no that the birth cert wasn't found, that she would send away to Galway for a copy. I couldn't believe that she was still lying to me. When I told her not to worry for now as we wouldn't be going anywhere for a while, she just nodded and said she would send away for it just to have it when I needed it. When I asked her if she knew a Tina Dillion she never battered an eyelash and responded that she was a local girl that she

Why Me?

had not seen or heard of for years, she showed no signs of anything out of the ordinary which only raised more questions. They must have got it wrong in Galway. She said that mistake like this happened all the time. I still have not said anything to Eddie, and he is so besotted with Molly-Rose it has totally slipped his mind.

February 23rd, 1967

Molly- Rose comes home today hip, hip hurray, I think. No idea how I will be able to look after a baby for the last few weeks I had just me to worry about and Eddie has pampered me no end, I hope that will not end as soon as the baby is here. Eddie will be an amazing Dad, even if the baby might not be his. When he found out that I was seeing Stephen while we were together he was so hurt I was sure that he would want to end our relationship on the spot, but he was kind and quick to forgive he made a promise that I would stop seeing Stephen if I wanted to be in a relationship with him, as he was not about to play second fiddle to no-one not, even for me. He would prefer to remain a bachelor for the rest of his life. I cried when I saw the hurt in his eyes, and I made him a promise that I planned to keep that there would be no one else but him. When I found out six weeks later that I was pregnant neither one of us spoke about who the dad was, he dropped down on his knees and proposed I didn't need time to think I was over the moon to say yes. I guess he must know that there was a chance the baby might not be his but he never mentioned it directly, he simply said that he would love the baby more than anything else in the world. He was a proud as punch when people said the baby was the image of him, he would stand that little bit taller, even though I knew the baby looked more like Stephen than Eddie.

Why Me?

March '67

I finally picked up the courage to bring the baby over to Stephen so he could see her, I felt that I owed him that at least, I waited till I knew his mother went over to the post office to collect her pension she hated my guts and I was not brave enough to face the dragon lady. When Stephen sees us his eyes filled with tears. All he could say was he was so sorry at the way things had worked out but there was no way he could go against his mother. When I placed Molly-Rose into his arms his whole body shook and for a big burly man he wept like a baby, I love you, Evie, I always have and always will do.

'Is she mine?'

'Yes, I believe she is, when she is sleeping she pulls the same faces as you do. There is no question about it, the dates match to when we were last together.'

'Looking at her she is the spit out of my grandmother.'

Right on cue, she gave him the biggest smile I had ever seen. We were lost in our own worlds and totally lost all track of the time we didn't hear the back door opening; it was too late for me to move I was trapped his mother was standing over me with the poker in her hand with so much rage in her voice that she would put the fear in the devil himself.

'Get out of this house, you dirty little slut and take that petty bastard with you. I told you before you are not welcome here and that has not changed By Jesus you have some neck, or else you are stupid, I have no idea where they found you, your parents should be ashamed of themselves having you whoring around the place.'

Why Me?

'Stop, Ma please stop, I love Evie I told you this before, she is beautiful and kind and this little angel is your first granddaughter.'

'What, she is not my granddaughter, and never will she be I give you this you have some neck showing your face here or are you that stupid to think Stephen will have anything to do with the likes of you. 'I suppose you're here looking for money. Well, lady muck you will not get a penny from us, not a penny I say.'

'Please stop Ma, I love Evie and this is my daughter if you would just take a look you will see she is the image of nana.'

'GET OUT, before I wrap this poker over your head and if you have any brain in the stupid head of yours at all you will never show your face around here again. I don't want you sniffing around my boy again, do you hear me you trollop. I pity poor Eddie having gotten himself laden with you when he could have done so much better than a tramp like you.'

'Now, you have gone too far, who do you think you are just a dried-up old hag, there is no reason why you should speak to me like that, do you know what your problem is, That you're a judgmental old cow, your head is so far stuck up your backside that your head is so full of shite. I have never done anything to you or anyone else for that matter; I have no idea why you are so hateful, you stuck-up bitch."

Stephen just stood there like a buffoon the tears streaming down his face not once did his eyes leave the ground he never stood up for me or himself why a grown man was afraid of his mother, I will never know or understand, maybe I had a lucky escape there as I would be done for murder if I had to put up with her. I was totally lost as to why she hated me so much it didn't make any sense yet when she would meet

Why Me?

my parents at mass or in the shop she was all sweetness and smiles. This was another thing that didn't make sense in my life. What a mess. I had never felt so humiliated as I did at that moment I wrapped my baby in her blanket and walked out of the house with my head held high and a smile on my face as I refused to let her see just how hurt I was. I can't remember what I said as I passed her in the doorway, I do remember the look on her face as if she was fit to kill. To steady my nerves I had to head to the nearest pub and ordered a double brandy as knocked it back in one gulp, as it slid down my throat I could feel my body return to normal the shakes were beginning to fade and the tears no longer were burning the back of my eyes now, if I had any sense I would have stopped with one and made my way home but no, what was I thinking one was never enough, as usual, I had the one that tipped me over the edge. I stumbled home and went straight to bed that way I could pretend that I was tired then Eddie will never know where I have been and by the time I wake up I will have put the whole experience behind never to be spoken about again. The story of my life shut up and put up. God forbid I ever speak my mind.

Three months after Molly-Rose was born, my heart stopped when I realised that I was pregnant again. I was not coping with one, never mind another one, thanks be to God two months later I lost the baby. Even though I did want another one I was not ready yet I was totally ashamed of myself when I had miscarried and nothing could have prepared me for the emotions that followed for sure I knew that I was never cut out to be a mother that was all there was to it.

Why Me?

September 1967

By now I had worked out a routine that works for both of us and I had the morning to myself as Eddie had taken the morning off it was safe to say I was beginning to enjoy being a mum after all.

Mum and Dad are due to come home tomorrow after their annual holiday to Donegal, the weather is unseasonably cold for this time of year so I decided that I would call over to their house with a few bits of shopping and to put the fires on to heat the place up. God forbid that dad wouldn't have his cuppa and rasher sandwich when he gets in. This also gives me a chance to have some quiet time without someone knocking on the door every five minutes that is one of the disadvantages of living in the middle of town. Gosh, it's cold in here I'm glad I came over as the house is Baltic. The first job is to get the fires going and put the kettle on, while I was waiting I ran the duster over the place. I loved being in my childhood home especially by myself it is a rare as hen's teeth for no-one to be here, normally the house is always full and the kitchen table is filled with mum's home baking. I have so many happy memories of growing up here, it was a home that was always full of warmth and love. I took my time dusting all the photos on the walls there were so many of them but I loved the ones of my grandparents the most there were pictures of family members that I had never met as they had passed away long before I was born but somehow I felt as if I knew them all perhaps it was because of all the stories and pictures I was surrounded by, as young child I would climb onto my grandfather's knee and he would tell me many different stories about all of them that it was as if they were right here with us. We would spend hours and hours chatting as I was the only one in the house that was in any way interested in the family history, the others were always busy with going here or there. Molly-Rose was still asleep

Why Me?

so I walked in to my parents bedroom to find the old photo albums I spend so many hours studying as a child, I hadn't had a chance to do it for years. Thankfully my mother still keeps all the boxes together in an old wardrobe that was well past its sell-by date, by the amount of dust on it no-one has been in here for years. I was in my element sitting on the floor surrounded by all these photo albums I was lost in time until Molly-Rose started to cry I guess it was time to fed her which made me realize that I was starving as well so it was a good time to take a break. After Molly-Rose was feed and changed I went back to the wardrobe to tidy them back into place, when I saw a small old battered box tucked away in the corner I don't remember ever seeing it before so I was intrigued, I took the box into the kitchen and made myself a cup of tea and a sandwich I throw some more turf on the fire before curling up on grandmothers rocking chair with the box on my lap. My heart was filled with pride and love as I looked over at Molly-Rose sleeping in her crib. She is the image of perfection, I was surprised at just how much I loved her, any fears I had about motherhood had long since disappeared. I was truly happy for the first time in a long time. It was so peaceful I could easily fall asleep only for curiosity always got the better of me, there was no way I could wait to find out what was in the box. The inside was filled with photos of a beautiful elegant young girl, she was someone I had never seen before she was stunning, I wondered who she was? She was holding a baby in many of the photos, she looked so happy. The last photo she was proudly holding a baby in a christening gown, if I wasn't mistaken it looked a lot like me as a baby but, I never saw her before not even in any of my baby photos, I turned over the photo and scribbled on the back was Evelyn and her godmother Tina. I was stunned as I was sure my godmother was my aunt. It took me a while to join the dots where had I heard of a Tina before, Panic began to rise inside of me, if I'm correct

Why Me?

I'm sure that's sounds like the name they said was on my birth cert, no, it can't be I asked mum if she knew of a Tina Dillion and she said no never. This must be a mistake they made when they were recording my birth if that was the case why did mum say she never heard of her. I looked at the photos again with a lot more interest and unless I'm losing my marbles I swear that I could see similarities between us maybe it is my mind playing a trick on me. After I calmed myself down I promised that I would have to keep my cool and ask mum again, second thought maybe I should ask dad as he can't lie to save his life. I must have fallen asleep as I was woken up once again to the sounds of Molly crying and the fire had gone out. I picked Molly up and fed her and I must be going mad as I could see more of the lady called Tina in her than before, I must be getting home as it was getting late and Eddie will be wondering where we are. As I was placing everything back into the box I saw a two-envelope stuck under the flap, when I picked them up one of then had my name on it and the other one addressed to Mum and Dad. How had I missed it the first time I don't know. I opened the sealed envelope with my name first a sheer fear took over me, do I really want to know what was inside, and can I live not knowing what it says, can I live not knowing who am I, who am I kidding there is not a chance in hell that I could live not knowing what's inside.

Why Me?

My Dearest Evelyn

By the time you read this I have no doubt that you will have grown into a beautiful young lady, I'm sorry that I will not be around to watch you grow up and to be part of your life it is my biggest regret in all of this. Having you was the best thing I have ever done, know whatever you do with your life I will be super proud of you. I need you to understand that leaving you has been the hardest decision I have ever made, but right from the beginning, I knew that this is something I had to do for your sake as well as mine. I know that the O'Toole's will make far better parents than I could ever be. If there was any other way, I could have kept you for myself, I would have. I want you to know you were never a mistake, and I was at my happiest when you were in my arms. No matter what you might hear, I do love you and always will. Please forgive me for my failings, none of this is your fault, I promise that I will watch over you from heaven. I love you with all of my heart, my beautiful sweet little angel.

Love forever mum XX

Why Me?

Mr & Mrs O Toole.

Dear Polly and Phil,

There are no words that can express my thanks for all of your kindness you have shown to me and Evelyn. I know that you are going to be great parents to Evelyn and that she will never want for anything. I love Evie to bits but I can't be the mother she needs me to be. I can do this knowing that she is in safe hands. I feel it is only fair to tell you the full story. You have been such good friends to me. I'm grateful that you have never once pushed me to tell you or to question me as to how any of this happened. Only for Phil found me that night both I and Evie would have never made it through the night. I believe that he was guided in some way to me that horridness night to save us. Anyone else would have called the guards or the doctor for sure then I would be locked up in some madhouse and there not knowing what would have happened to Evie. The way you both took care of me that night was out of this world, not even the doctors could do a better job. There are not many people that would have done what you guys have done for me. I can't thank you enough for taking Evie as your own and not telling a soul that I was her mother, Thank you for making it possible for me to be such a big part of her life I know that I could be here as often as I want and it means so much to be called her Godmother but there is no way I can continue as we are, the pain just gets worse with each new day. I could move away but that would only drive me completely of the rails I need you to know that I never planned any of this, and in all honesty I was not aware of what was happening at the beginning it started one evening when I was walking home from work I was on the late shift in the hospital it was a hell of a shift and I was so tired that I took a short cut on the way home every bone in my body ached my poor feet were killing me and there

Why Me?

was nothing more I wanted but to put them in a bowl of hot water and Epsom salts. If I had played it smart, I would never have taken the shortcut I had never taken it before that night as my father had warned us often enough that it wasn't safe, so many would say that I was asking for trouble. But nothing bad ever happens here, does it? I was only a mile from home when I came across mad Jack Hennessey sprawled along the road with blood pumping out from his head in truth I thought he was dead as there was so much blood on the ground, when I first called his name he didn't stir so I bend down to check to see if he was still breathing that was when he grabbed me by the hair and pulled me down to the ground when he started beat the crap out of me at first I thought he was confused and thought I was one of the lads he was fighting with earlier I tried to talk to him I begged him to stop and just when I taught he had heard me he looked at me for the first time and grunted oh how he loved fresh meat then the beating stopped and he raped me for what seemed like an eternity at some stage I must have passed out as my last memory was of him with hand around my throat telling me that if I ever told a soul about what had happened he would come back and finish the job and in a way I wished he did just that there and then. It was close to four o clock in the morning by the time I made it back to the house I was lucky in a way that I lived on my own I had time to clean my cut and have a long hot soak ever part of my body hurt beyond anything you could imagine I guess there was part of me that was in denial of what had happened. I didn't tell anyone because I was so afraid that no-one would believe me, this kind of thing doesn't happen around here, does it? I truly believed that everyone would say I deserved what I got as I shouldn't have taken the short cut. It was months later that I realized that I was pregnant, there was no way I could tell anyone now, my family would have disowned me, can you imagine how my holier than thou sister Lady

Why Me?

Campbell would react, if Mum and Dad knew it would kill them. I felt so ashamed and alone I had no-one to turn to so like a true ostrich I buried my head in the sand and tried to forget about that night and the pregnancy, you would think with me being a nurse that I would have known better. I can't say for sure what I was going to do once the baby was born that's why I was on my way to the lake, part of me wasn't thinking. The night Phil found me I was on my way to the lake to drown myself as I couldn't see any other way, my head was in such a spin. What I hadn't planned on was the baby coming three weeks earlier, normally the first one is late more often than not. Once the labour had started there was no way I could go through with my plan at that moment she became a person in her own right and I had no right to take her life away I was on way back to the house when Phil found me in the middle of the field curled up in a heap trying to keep the baby warm, she came far quicker than I could have believed possible, it must have been her way to save us both, I knew that I had lost way too much blood more than was considered normal if Phil hadn't jumped into action the way he did, neither of us would have survived, thank God he knew just what to do, all those years he spends delivering calves was what saved us both, to this day I have no idea how he managed to get us to your house as I was of no use to him. From the night that mad Jack attacked me I have lived in fear, afraid of my own shadows waiting for him to attack again and to think I used to feel sorry for him whenever he came into the hospital to have his cuts bandaged, I used to think if only someone could get through to him to give up the drink that he would have a much better life. Even now, I don't know which is worse than the thought of what happened or the fear that my deepest and darkest secret or an even better description would be a nightmare will come out, or how foolish I feel that I tried to get him to change his ways. I never want my

Why Me?

wonderful daughter to know how she was conceived as none of this was her fault, she should never know about her birth it would be too much for her to handle, she only needs to know that I loved her more than life itself she was loved beyond belief, not only by me but, by you guys also. Not once did I regret that she is here, she is my everything, she is beautiful in every way. she is everything that I could have ever wanted for a daughter she must never know the truth about her birth or her father and if you decide not to tell her anything about me I would be happy with that, but if you feel that she needs to know about me I have written her a letter as well. I trust you with my pride and joy in some way, it makes it easier for me to leave this world knowing she is in safe hands. By the time you read this, it will be too late for you to stop me, later tonight I will return to my favorite spot by the lake and slip into the next world, my final wish will be that my body will never be found please pray for my soul to reach the gates of heaven. I need you to understand that there is nothing that you could have said or done to prevent me from leaving this world, if it is not tonight then it would be tomorrow or the next night, so please forgive but the scars of the night are just too deep and raw and with each passing day it gets harder to accept what he did and the thoughts that he might do again is too much to bear. My sister must never find out about mad Jack as she would say it was my own fault that I would have brought this on myself somehow. If she was ever to find out about Evie she would make her pay for my mistake. Evie, need to be protected from her at all costs as I would be afraid she will want to take her and that would make me turn in my grave as she is far too judgmental and controlling, she would make the poor girl's life a misery, she would make her pay for my mistake. I have written her a letter to say goodbye it is short and sweet as we never had the sisterly relationship. Thank you for accepting me the way you have, your home is filled with so much love I

Why Me?

know Evie will be so happy.

Lots of love Tina

August 1975

The years rolled on and in holy Ireland is a given that I would go on to have more babies, six kids made into this world with three miscarriages and one stillborn was more than enough for any woman to cope with. My luck was in the night we met a lovely couple from the north of Ireland, they were here on holidays to escape the parades and the madness that comes with it. I wasn't a 100% sure what they were on about as we never had any trouble here with parades or the likes, I had often seen the news where they would be scenes of cars being burned out and people rioting on the street but all that was a far cry from quiet old Clifden. We became friends almost straight away the boys had so much in common and they enjoyed each other's company, we found that they would call in most evenings and it was on one such occasion that Mabel asked' 'Why do Catholics have such big families, did I always wanted a large family?'

'Jesus, are you off your rocker no I never wanted any if the truth is told.'

'Why, don't you do something about it then?'

Like what, I asked her? She roared with laughter and said have you

Why Me?

never hear of the pill or condoms. I was amazed as I had never heard of the likes and after a quick lesson on what was what and when she found out that this was not an option here, she agreed to send both to me for as long as I need them, I would not be able to breathe a word to a living soul or we would both in so much trouble. I was never so in debt to anyone before or since, she was an auld life saviour there would be no more kids for me that is for sure. We remained great friends for years and they would come down for their annual holidays right up until they were both killed by a bomb that had exploded while out doing their shopping minding their own business. I really missed Mabel and her letters, the summer was not quite the same since they died as we both looked forward to their visits we both lost two great friends. I know they were not Catholic but I would often light a candle for them on the rare occasions that I actually made inside a church door I always feel as if I would just burst into flames as God was more than aware of all of my failures.

15th August 1982

My world has ended, life is going to be unbearable without my dear Eddie my rock and my protector what in God's name am I going to do without him by my side, there is no way I can cope with these kids, their consent whining was sending me to spare I'm sure that I will murder them in their sleep one of these days. They are so inconsiderate with all their crying for their dad, seriously I miss him a lot more than they ever could, they seem to forget that they will grow up and move on with their lives and their precious dad will only be a distant memory. Sure everyone says that the kids will bounce back that they are resilient but I'm the one that will always be on my own remembering all the plans we had that we will never get to do now, it is true that I might not have loved him with all of my heart at the beginning but over the years I can safely say that I loved him more and more each day. Sure, who else would have put up with my drinking never mind the affairs, some of I don't really remember as I was so drunk at the time? He never once laid a finger on me and he never would in a million years, I know that a lot of the other husbands in the towns are brutes and spend their time beating the crap out of their wives and children for no reason at all after a few pints in the pub, my wonderful Eddie was as close to a saint as you could get. I loved him and never wanted to hurt him, I know that that might be hard to believe. These are the hardest days of my life, much harder than I ever expected. Now, that he is not here and never will be again I realise just how much I loved him and how tough on him I was, he never deserved any of the crap I put him through why he put up with me all these years I will never know. I regret not allowing him into my inner world, maybe if I had I would not have been so angry all of the time. Too late for all those thoughts, it will be best for me to have another drink to dull the pain.

17Th August 1982

Seeing Ruth at the funeral nearly drove me around the twist, I was surprised at myself that I was so calm and didn't make a show of myself. She had some balls to just waltz in the way she did after all these years, a brazen hussy.

It was four days later, when there was knock at the door, I could hear Molly say that I was having a lie down maybe it would be best if she could call back later, part of me just want to scream piss off and leave

Why Me?

me in peace, I was fed up of all the do gooders, only this time I didn't recognise the voice it sounded like an English accent I nearly fell out of the bed when Molly said it was Ruth, I was not prepared for the her, never the less I said she could come in but would have to give me a few minutes to make myself presentable as she needed to speak to me she could wait till I was ready, there was no way she was leaving here without a piece of my mind, just who the fuck did she think she was, I was fuming who does she think she is. She was going to get with both barrels if she thinks that she can stroll in here after the heartache she caused poor Eddie and I would feel sorry for her she has another thing coming, I flung the door to the sitting room open 'What the hell are you doing here are you insane I don't want to hear any of your sorry for my loss crap or any such nonsense you have some neck to come to my door, it is best if you leave as I have nothing to say to you.' Temper was rising with the thoughts of how she just strolled into the funeral home with such confidence it made my blood boil. I barely recognised her at first as it had been years since I had seen her, it gauds me at just how well she looked, I remember her been slightly heavier than she is now she had the maddest head of curly red hair that always looked un-controllable. She was looking much younger than her years, well-groomed and elegant and moved with grace, Eddie would have been in awe if he could see her now more than likely he would have had a heart attack.

When she walked into the funeral home, you could hear a pin drop as no one had heard from her in years, there were so many rumors floating around the place ranging from she had died to she ran away with some rich tourist. It is unusual in a small village like this that no one had any information on her, if anyone knew where she had gone it was the best-kept secret in the west. Over the years Eddie had often tried to find out anything he could about where she was as he was churned up over not knowing if she was alright. The veil of silence was quite remarkable as it never happens here.

'I'm Sorry, Evelyn but I owe you an explanation for showing up the way I did.'

'You Owe me nothing, it's not my heart that you broke you nearly killed the man, he was never the better of what you did, never.'

'Do you think I don't know that, before you judge me you should hear why I left? I loved Eddie more than I can explain he was my one true love, my biggest regret is never having the courage to tell him why.'

'Well, if you had loved him that much you sure have a funny way of showing it, I hope you are proud of yourself, if that's how you love someone I'd hate to see how you would treat someone you didn't like.

'No, I'm not proud of myself if you must know, I had no other choice it was the only way I could protect him.'

'Protect him, Protect him from what? Tell me, what was it you put in the coffin you had one hell of a cheek you had no right to there in the first place never mind putting anything in with him you had some cheek.'

For the first time in my life, I was lost for words as she took a seat across the table. I was barely audible when the words came flying out of my mouth, that she needed to get out of my house before I strangle her, I had no notion of listening to any sob story she was about to say. She had messed up and lost the best man in the country her loss was my gain.

'I understand that I'm the last person on earth you want to see now

Why Me?

and I'm sorry if me being at the funeral upset you in any way that was never my intention as I know only too well how difficult all of this is for you and the children, never the less I feel it is important for me to try and explain why I'm here and what had happened all those years ago she said.'

I was getting ready to kick her out by her scrawling ass out the door when Molly came into the room with the tea tray and before I had a chance to get the words out of my mouth.

Ruth had started to thank her as she pick up the pot and began to pour the tea into the two cups.

I roared at Molly, seriously how stupid could that girl get, what on earth was she doing making her tea. The girl has no cop on I will wring her neck later.

After Molly closed the door Ruth had started talking again saying that I had a beautiful family and that they were a credit to me. I couldn't get a word in edgeways and in the end, I stopped trying and let her continue. I was completely blown away by the whole bizarre situation I was so far out of my comfort zone that I didn't know what else to do but to listen, all of the fight I had inside just left me part of me, admired her confidence the way she walked into the room the other evening with her head held so high not once did she react to the whispering that echoed the room she never batted an eyelid it was easy to see his family loved her like a daughter, there was no point in denying it I was overcome with curiosity what had happened, what was in the envelope she put in the coffin.

'I'm sorry if me being here has upset you in any way as that was never my intention, but had to come and say goodbye to Eddie, there hasn't

Why Me?

been a day that has gone by that I haven't thought about him. You see I need to give him back his engagement ring even after all this time the envelope I put it in had a letter to tell him why I had to go, I had no choice in the matter as I was afraid of what would have happened if I stayed. I know it was cruel leaving the way I did but it was for his own good if he was to ever find out what happened he would have gone mad and there's no doubt would have done something stupid. The reason I left was because the night before after Eddie walked me home from the pub, mother asked me to go out and check that the shed doors were locked, I was on my way back to the house my arms full of turf for the morning when I came across a neighbour next door banging his bike up against our gate, I stupidly went over to see if he was ok, he went into a frenzy and leathered into me, he was calling all sort of names, he belted me black and blue he even managed to ripped my clothes off before I had a chance to push him away and tried to run as fast as my bruised body would allow me to I was afraid to say I was not quick enough and that he caught me before I made in back to the house he knocked me to the ground and raped me, I couldn't believe it, so close to my own front door how could he as he was walking away he threw a rock that ended up breaking my ribs, the only reason I got away from his he tripped over his trousers and I finally made to the door before he got up, I guess I was lucky that he was rotten with drink and unable to move otherwise there is no doubt in my mind that he would have killed me there and then, no question about it. I was terrified beyond belief, my mother found me on the kitchen floor in the early hours of the morning she almost fainted at the state of me, she spent the next few hours washing my cuts and put ointment on my bruises, she wrap my ribs in cloth she was blaming herself for asking me to go out , but it was something we had both often done in the past. We knew old fella was as nutty as a fruit cake and was no stranger to

Why Me?

fighting in the pubs, but we never in our wildest imaginations did we think that he was capable of anything like this, after drinking pots loads of tea and many tears we agreed that we couldn't go to the cops as Eddie would have killed him with his bare hands, before they had a chance to pick him up not that the fecker didn't deserve everything he got but my dearest Eddie did not, there was no way I could be responsible for him being behind bars because of me so we agreed for his own good he could never find out about any it, the only way we could achieve this was if I left as soon as possible. I was heartbroken I had lost everything that night but I would not let that brute ruin Eddie's life he had ruined mine and that was more than enough. So, my mother packed my bags, I would leave on the next bus before Eddie came home from work, he was never meant to have seen me on the bus that day as leaving him was the hardest thing I had ever done the pain from the bruises were nothing compared to the pain in my heart, I knew the bruises would heal but my heart never would. I was blessed that there were no locals on the bus so I sat in the back and cried all the way to Dublin, then I got on the boat and headed for London to my aunt eight months later, I gave birth to twins a boy and girl, Lucy and Adam, sadly they died shortly after they were born I just about got to hold them. I had them cremated so I could place their ashes in the Irish sea so they could be free to travel the world. I lost everything that night I was never the same again, I would have loved to have come home but I would never have been able to keep this hidden from Eddie. He would have seen straight through me and If Eddie knew any of this it would have killed him for sure it was hard leaving and even harder staying away as I knew just how hurt he was, I was broken and he was the only one that could have fixed me. When mother said he was on his way over with his brothers I moved to Scotland just in case our paths crossed, where I have been ever since. I never married or had any other children as there was no one that could ever complete me the way Eddie did. I was over the moon when I heard you two were getting married and heartbroken at the same time, when the children were born I cried for days and days as I knew Eddie always wanted to be a father and how amazing he would be. I was angry at the world for letting this happen and prayed that I would wake up in the morning to find out it was only a dream, but no can do. It was an impossible situation. Evelyn, I'm really sorry if I have upset you in any way but I felt it was only right that you knew why I was here. I knew I have no right to ask but I would hope that you keep what I have told you to yourself. I will be leaving the day after tomorrow but if there is anything I can do for you please let me know here is my address.

My blood was running cold as I asked her what was her neighbors name again, as the story reminded me of the letters I found at mum's, terror took over my whole body as it began to shake, as I begged Ruth to tell me his name she refused at first eventually she said it was Hennessey, that he was a complete head case and sure he nearly killed his own daughter. I suddenly was overcome as I fell to the floor my head was spinning in total chaos and confusion, how could this have happened again this sounds way too familiar why was he allowed to get away with it. In fairness to Ruth, she cradled me in her arms without saying a word for a long time until I was able to get up of the floor. I went over the press took out two glasses and a bottle of Eddie's poteen filled our glasses as I prepared to tell her about the letters, I have found in my mother's room not long after Molly was born. We need something strong for this one, Ruth eyes filled with tears as I told her what I knew about my mother many years before, she was outraged When she realized that she was not the first there were no words either of us could use to express the pain that ran through our bodies, with each word I spoke it was if she was reliving her own experience of the night and every night since, to say we were both in shock with the realization that he had done it more than once, we both wondered if he had done the same thing to anyone else but agreed that we would never know that for sure We swore to keep each other secrets on both fronts, we made a vow never to tell another soul. In was late into the night before Ruth left looking as if she had been on the tear for days. Eddie would have been in his element knowing that a strong bond was born the night between the two great loves of his life his two women. It was a strange feeling to have spoken about my mother out loud to another person it would be fair to say that there was some healing in it for both of us. By the end of the night, we had finished the bottle in addition to becoming great friends, we both were lucky to have loved Eddie for also being part of his life, only now we had a more sinister connection. How weird was that, I bet no-one could have predicted it. We both had shared a part of us that we had never shared with anyone else it was unlikely we ever would again, we laughed and I cried not really knowing what to make of the whole scenario. I felt so sorry for Ruth as she had gone through this on her own and was always going to be on her own, I had assumed that she would have got married but now I understood why she didn't, I knew I would never marry again we agreed that there would never be another Eddie in the world.

June 83

Today Molly and I had another row, I don't know how to make things better between us, I wish that I was not so hard on her I know how ridiculous it is to blame her for any of this, but every time I see her she sparks something inside of me and it has been like that since I

Why Me?

found Tina's letter, it doesn't help that I'm not sure if her father is Eddie or Stephen, I believe it was Stephen as the resemblance has always been so strong and with every day that passed she looks more and more like Tina, I had asked Stephen about her after I found the letters and he gave me some photo's he had found in the house, there's no way to know for sure but maybe Eddie was her dad after all and the reason she looked like Stephen grandmother had nothing to do with him and more to do with Tina. Deep down I'm afraid that she sees me for the fraud that I am as I know that she senses that I'm hiding something, she has to turn out to be the person I would have loved to be, she is the better version of me in every way, she is beautiful, clever, confident and has the natural ability to have everyone on her side. From the day she was born she had an air of I'm here, she was always so capable and independent that she didn't need me, she could do it on her own and in her own way, it was as if she was punishing me for my actions. Maybe that had something to do with the fact I was so unhappy about the pregnancy or that fact she was in the ICU for so long I hate to admit to even myself that I'm jealous of her. Jesus, what kind of mother does that make me and I don't feel the same towards the others. I know that no matter what life will throw at her, she will be able to come out the other side strong. There is no way she will ever be controlled by anyone, she is stronger enough to follow her dreams no matter what anyone says. She is her own person and she makes no apologies for it, as if she says to the world this is me like it or not I don't care. In all the years since she was born no one has ever said a bad word about her, quite the opposite, it's always she is a wonderful girl, you must be so proud of her, she is a credit to me.

I can see that she is completely devastated since her dad died and yet she stands with such composure, they had the most incredible bond the likes of it I had never seen before and I guess I don't understand it.

Why Me?

She was like his mini-me, which is bizarre as the chances of her being his is so small, even though he knew there was a chance she might not be his it didn't stop him from loving her, in fact, he loved her more because of it. I wished that I was a better person so I could be a better mother to her. She is so different from the others I have often wondered if she is from another planet. I take out my frustration on her, she is always my target and I'm not proud to say that I have tried to turn the others against her, but it never works. I know that I'm hurting her, but yet I can't stop.

After Eddie, died I know that she was hurting too they all were, they needed me and I was nowhere to be found and she has to step up to take on the role to provide for the others, I was trying my hardest to check out of this life, my only friend that could console me was a bottle of Jameson. She was the one that stopped the social workers from taking the young ones into care, I have no idea how she charmed them.

I was so angry at her for leaving, I could have strangled her with my bare hands if I had the strength I would have. After she left I hit an all-time low for a few months, there was not an hour in the day that I was sober, there was no hiding my drink, everyone and their dog knew I was a problem and that I was to be avoided at all costs, I was unpredictable and volatile and fueled with Jameson I was not afraid to use my fists so approach with caution even my drinking buds started to avoid me, I drank to escape the pain, the more I drank the more I needed to drink until no matter how much I drank it no longer dulled the pain, there was no way to escape it, it followed me everywhere. Then one morning I woke up in a ditch battered and bruised with no idea of how I got there, unable to move. I was alone I had no choice but to stay there until I had sobered up, I cried and cried my heart out, from the bottom of my soul. It was many hours later before I was able

Why Me?

to get myself up, It was there that I met my dark shadow face to face, by the time I crawled out I was just hallowed bones, I was ashamed of who I had become I had nothing, I was nothing, this was my turning point I couldn't go any lower so I had to stand up and try to rebuild myself and I knew that it would have to start with giving up my best friend the drink. It was the hardest thing I have ever done but I locked myself into my room removed myself from everyone. There were not going to be any more excuses I need to become a better version of myself, to do that I need to give myself time to heal from the inside before I could face the world. The first few weeks were the hardest, my days and nights were filled with the ghost of my past, at times I didn't think I would make it to the next hour never mind to tomorrow, I was more anxious, restless and irritable than normal and barely slept a wink all of these I was familiar with as they were part of my daily life, it was the headaches and the dizziness, vomiting and diarrohea were the hardest, followed by the tremors and the shakes, the Hallucinations were worse than the nightmares. I prayed to Eddie to give me the strength to carry on, I spoke to him as if he was standing in the room with me, I'm not sure if it was the hallucination or not but he was holding me in his arms for all of it, gently telling me that I could do this, that I was stronger than I knew, he gave me hope when I had none, he kept me strong I know if I say this out loud I would be locked up, then very slowly I started to feel a little better, he let me know that I was not on my own and that I would never be alone as I always had him by my side, he can me the confidence that I could change that I was better than this he gave me hope that it was possible to recover from this to be whole again he never once judged me not even now. He made see that bottling up all of my feelings was the reason why I drank so much. I know that I should have asked mum about Tina's letters, if I had done that then all of this could have been avoided. My biggest mistake was hiding my feelings, if only I had spoken to someone, I would have been happier. I wouldn't have been so alone or angry and full of self-doubt and hatred. I was the master in my own downfall, not anyone else. I promised him that if he could get me through this that I would forgive myself and take responsibility for my own actions and stop blaming everyone else for my feelings. I kept expecting everyone to understand how I was feeling without telling them, what I was going through, in truth I was expecting them to be able to read my mind especially those that were the closest to me. I would have to learn to let people in, to communicate better, to tell them how I was feeling and not bite their heads off when they tried to help. It was not a sign of weakness to ask for help it is a sign of strength, everyone needs help at some stage in their life, now I realise that you have to let them in. There are no mind readers in this world. I have so many regrets, I don't know where to begin but now I have the chance to change and I must take it and do something with my life.

Very slowly, I started to emerge stronger and more hopeful, it was some time before I could admit that I was very grateful that Molly left when she did, if she had stayed, I would still be blaming her for everything that was wrong in my life. I need to tell her I'm sorry for how I have treated her and let her know that this was all my own doing not hers. I pray that I will have the courage to tell her, if she doesn't forgive I wouldn't blame her. It would be nice to have a better relationship with her, perhaps time will heal us both. I can't say I would blame her if she wanted nothing to do with me, as I'm not sure I would give me a second chance if I was her, she has every right to be angry at me. It takes so much more energy to be mad at the world than it does to forgive.

Why Me?

December 87

Molly surprised me when she came home today, it was the first time we have seen or spoken since she left. I knew that she was unsure about staying here and at what kind of reception I would give her she was braver than I ever was. I was little afraid of seeing her as we had not parted on the best of terms and we have had no contact since. I delighted to see her she was even more beautiful than I remembered, how that was even possible I don't know, she left a young girl but standing in front of me now was a confident elegant woman. It was a weird feeling having her home, both of us not sure how each other was going to react, thankfully everyone was home so it covered up any awkward moments. It was lovely to hear them laughing and teasing each other, they had always got on so well, it was the best Christmas of my life, the only thing that could have made it even better was if Eddie was here with us. This was the happiest time in my life, I had never felt like this before, totally content. These were my amazing children how could I have not seen this before now I was such a fool; I couldn't see what was in front of me. Eddie would be so proud of them if he was here I know he is watching over us all, but I would give anything to have him here with us if only for today. I'm so thankful that Sara had invited her to the wedding as without the invite she would never have come home. Hopefully, before she goes back we will get a chance to have a chat to clear the air and to start to build a better relationship it would have to be now or I might never have the chance again to tell her that I loved her and was sorry for all the pain I caused. Sadly, we never got the chance there was always something to get in the way. Before, we knew it was time for her to leave. After she left I cried for the missed opportunity for all the years I had wasted I knew that I would never have the courage to tell her again the moment had passed.

Why Me?

June 88

Molly is coming home today I'm so nervous I couldn't sit still, I was like a cat on a hot tin roof I wanted everything to be perfect for her she was going to be here for two weeks. It was lovely to have her home it made me realise just how much I missed her when she was not here, she was always happy and so full of energy it was infectious we were getting on for the first time in our lives, we were not in each other throats and I could see clearly now that it was always me that had started it. Now that I had stopped hating her I could see why everyone liked her. I'm so proud of her.

When she told me that she was coming home to work for the Reid's I had mixed emotions, how would we get on when we would see each other every day. I was glad and apprehensive at the same time, if she felt the same, I don't know. I could kick myself at times as I still let the snide remarks slip in, it comes out of my mouth before I can stop it. on one hand, I'm so proud of her and the other hand resentful as it reminds me just how much I failed her and all of her success are down to her and have nothing got to do with me and that hurts me more than I imagine it hurt her. I'm in awe at how she has just got on with her life despite all the obstacles she makes it look so easy, no one can see just how hard it has been on me when they say look at her, how well she is doing I can't help the old feelings of being inadequate rising their ugly heads. I know that no one else thinks like this but I and I just need to get over myself but no matter how hard I try I keep falling back to old habits. It was easier when she was away as there was not a permanent reminder of just how crap of a mother I was. It is like I have this internal battle going on in my head that I can't stop. There are so many days recently that I nearly return to drinking.

Why Me?

Feb 91

When I got sick, I was so angry that I would have to have my kids looking after me again. I would have preferred to have a heart attack or to be killed in a car crash eaten by a lion anything but this. There is part of me that says it serves me right for being such a bitch that I deserved to die in the most excruciating pain known to man. What else could I expect, it was payback time our action will catch up to us sooner or later. Karma always comes back to bite you in the arse.

Why Me?

Chapter 25

I was flummoxed with what I had just read; it was if this was a screenplay for a movie rather than my mother's life. This kind of things does not happen to normal people! does it? You might hear on the news or in the paper but, never in a million years do you think it would ever happen to someone you know or you would be part of it. Reading about this in the paper does not prepare you in any way for how it affects the people there are no words to describe the effects and the emotion involved. It made for very hard reading, the tears burned my eyes as if they were on fire, the pain I had in my chest as if it was being crushed, I had never experienced anything like it before today. It was disturbing just reading the diaries I couldn't get my head around what these three women went through, the veil of silence that surrounds their lives. It was no wonder my mother was the way she was, how could she have been any other way. She was hurt so badly on so many different levels, if only she would have spoken truthfully to Gran or Dad I know they would have helped her and then she might not have isolated herself from everyone, I could understand why she had built so many walls around her it was the only way she could cope. She must have felt betrayed by gran and grandad, it looks as if from the moment she read those letters she hit the self-destruct button on a massive scale, and yet I wouldn't be surprised if she had always known what had happened to her mother on a subconscious level and that is why she had no self-confidence, the drink became her trusted friend this was so very sad, I wonder if

Why Me?

Dad knew something was amiss and if that was why he never left her, always defended her no matter what she had done. I can't imagine how hard it most have been on Mum to know that she was the result of such brutality, it easy to see how it would destroy anyone, I guess no-one every thinks about how it affects the child. I can understand why Granny would never want her to find out. I sat on the floor with the letters in my hands howling, I didn't recognize the sounds that were coming from my body I was rocking back and forwards from the pain that I felt on behalf of these three amazing strong women as well as for myself as I was part of the chain, I had never felt like this before. Once the tears started there was no stopping them, I had spent so many years not asking for help, trying to be strong refusing to show any emotion believing that tears were a sign of weakness, the doors had been opened and there was no way to close them now, I cried and cried for all those wasted years of not knowing my mother, for the woman she could have been or should have been. She was robbed of so much just as her own mum had been. It's hard to get your head around that you have been brought into this world in such a horrific way and knowing that you were the product of such an evil act would mess with anyone's head beyond belief. A baby should be the result of the love shared between two people not like this. It makes me sick to think of poor Tina Dillion what a nightmare, her whole life taken from her she was robbed from being a mother, my mother was robbed from the love of her mother and I was robbed of the love of a mother and as for poor Ruth who was robbed of everything in her life after that night.

Why Me?

Oh, Christ, that must mean that Mrs Campbell was mum's aunt which would make Stephen her cousin that must have been the biggest kick in the teeth. I bet the cranky Mrs Campbell must have guessed that something had happened and being unable to put the pieces together and that was why she hated mum the way she did, it would certainly explain why she was so cruel to her. All of this is heartbreaking; the Hennessey fella should have been shot, what a despicable excuse for a man. I was so angry at him for all he did to Tina , and my mum but also for robbing me of the loving mother and for robbing me of my childhood.

I couldn't help myself, I was talking to Mum as if she was here, mum why didn't you talk to gran she would have been able to fill in the blanks she would be able to help you come to terms with it, she loved you more than you knew, you should never have had to deal with this on your own such a cruel world we live in. If only you would have spoken to someone you could have had a happier life, you could have had the life you dream of as a child, none of this was your fault, you were not responsible. I was half expecting her to answer me and disappointed when she didn't. Reading these letters brought me much closer to her than ever before, it felt as if I finally understand. Mum, I forgive you for all the hurt that you caused me and please forgive me for all the times I gave you a hard time, for all the times I fought back I didn't understand why you disliked me I now understand that you did the best that you could and for that I'm thankful. It was a relief to know that she wanted to say she was sorry and that she loved me If I hadn't read these diaries with my own eyes, I wouldn't believe anyone that said she did. I felt closer to her now that she was gone than I ever did when she was here. It made me glad that I did look after her the best I could when she was sick, I hope I gave her some sort of peace.

I was all over the place since reading the diary, parts of me felt guilty for reading them and half relieved that I did. I couldn't concentrate on anything for longer than fifteen minutes, I was snappy and irritable with everyone at work everything seemed pointless. Not even Ronan could cheer me up bless him he was trying his best to be understanding, as he thought I was grieving for mum, he was in total shock when I told him about what I had read in diaries we spoke about how this was going to affect the others in the family, there was a part of me that didn't want them to read them but I knew deep down that they had to know the truth just as much as I did, the secret had already caused to much pain and hurt I would have to tell them there was no other choice as keeping the secret had already ruined three people's lives, but, how was I going to do it I don't know, I need to get my head around of all it first, I was so confused as I needed to process the fact that the man I loved, cherished may or may not be my birth father it was hard to get my head around it, the possibility had not even sunk in yet. The world as I knew it had fallen to pieces it was an impossible situation dammed if I don't and dammed if I do the truth will have to come out sooner rather than later or I will end up losing my marbles or an alcoholic like my mother. It hurt like hell the thoughts of Dad not being my birth Dad, every time I think about it there is a stab of pain

Why Me?

in my heart. He was the one who nursed me when I was sick, clean my bruised knees when I fell off my bike, who was there for every moment of my life, who read me stories at bedtime, teased me about my crazy hair. He loved me more than anyone else in this world and I loved him, he was my rock my world my everything. There is no way anyone could have done a better job than he did; there was no one else I could have ever wanted as my Dad. When he died I thought I would never be able to cope without him but somehow I'm here by the skin of my teeth most days. I wonder if he knew that Stephen could have been my dad, if he did he never showed it, I wrecked my brain trying to think of anything out of the ordinary that ever happened, the only thing I could think of was the night before he died he did say he loved me more I could ever imagine and that he could have not loved me more if he tried to and that I made him the happiest man in Ireland and that I would always be his little girl no matter how big I got. I didn't think anything of it at the time, looking back now knowing what I know I wonder if that was his way of telling me. The one thing I'm sure of is that he always loved me and made me feel special every day he will always be my real dad, being a sperm donor doesn't make you a Dad.

It all made sense now, the way Stephen was watching me at Mum's funeral I thought he acting strangely perhaps he was wondering if he should say something or not, or could I be reading more into it than there is. I guess I will have to decide at some stage if I want to go and see him or not, for now, that was not too high up on my agenda.

Chapter 26

My mind was still in stewing mode, the evening Amelia came to the door with a takeaway in one hand and a bottle of wine in the other. 'You didn't sound like yourself yesterday so Dermot came home early for a change so here I am. I hope I haven't called at a bad time, have I? Is Ronan still away?'

'Yes, he is in London for a few days. I'm delighted to see you, please come in. The smell of the food is making me hungry.'

I hadn't realized just how hungry I was until I started eating. We finished the bottle of wine in record time and opened another one, after having a few drinks too many I blurted out what was in mum's diary's, I gave her the short version she was as dumbfounded almost as much as I was, afterwards she couldn't speak for ages I was bewildered to her reaction, it was a bit over the top given the fact that she never really liked mum and they were not best of friends or anything. She was not making any sense, she kept saying she would have to tell her mum, and this would break her heart. She was getting very cross as she screamed all sorts calling old Jack every name under the sun. Did that man have no end to the misery he caused, even after all these years he is destroying people's lives, Mum is going to freak out? I still didn't understand so I poured us both a large brandy, as she called Elizabeth to come over as soon as she could as, this couldn't wait until tomorrow, the sooner she knew the

Why Me?

better, after she put the phone down she said that Jack was Elizabeths father and he was an evil man that this time he had out done himself. Elizabeth was at the door in no time at all, once she was inside we gave her the short version of what was in the diaries then we sat down and read the diaries together, it was painfully hearing her read them out loud, she was shaking uncontrollably as read them, the tears flowed from all of us as if there was no tomorrow. Elizabeth was normally so calm and in control, now she looked like a shadow of herself this was a lot to take in, needless to say we had lots more brandy to help us through it. When Elizabeth roared 'that bastard is still hurting people from the grave just as well he is already dead it saved me the trouble.' We nearly fell off the chair to hear her cursing.

I had heard some version of what had happened in her the past, but nothing like what Elizabeth was telling me now. It was heartbreaking. What I didn't understand how he was your father, as your name was Lynch and he was Hennessey. My name is Lynch Hennessey, just everyone always called me Lynch after my grandparents, no-one ever called my mother or me as Hennessey, I wonder if they knew about any of this and that was why I was known as Lynch.

How could one vile man destroy so many people's lives, what a horrible human being he was? 'Elizabeth said that she would love to get her hands on him as she wouldn't be able to stop herself from winging his neck.' I wonder if I would have been brave enough to stand up to him, I find it hard to remember anything about him, it is as if I wiped him from my mind a long time ago, to be honest I don't ever remember meeting his parents, I'm sure he had brothers and at least one sister but they never came to the house and we never went to their's, thinking about it I'm not too sure where he came from it couldn't have been from here or people would have been talking about them. We were at a loss to understand what would drive a man to be so horrendous to another human being not that there is any excuse to justify it but there must be a story behind it was he always a troubled child or did he wake up one morning a changed man. I guess we have more questions than answer's nevertheless I'm not sure if it would be a good thing to go digging into his past as there is no telling what it could turn up it might be pandora's box. Maybe all of his family are unhinged and need treatment, or he might have been a one off. We wondered how many more lives he had ruined the chances are that his family might have disowned him a long time ago and they might not want to hear his name I do know that none of them came to his funeral the chances are they were glad to see the back of him, there is no knowing what damage he has caused I guess we will never know and maybe that is for the best. For now, at least it will be better to let sleeping dogs lie as I'm not sure that I can absorb anymore information on his reign of terror, it makes my blood run cold to think that his blood flows through my body.

'Stop, that mum, you are nothing like him, not then and certainly not now and you never will be you're lucky as the Lynch in you out ranks any blood you have from him.'

Why Me?

With that Sara, ran into her mother arms and held her so tight she could barley breath. The tears flowed like a river from all of us, we looked a mess with our red faces and runny noses nothing glamorous about us now, any attempts to hold back the tears was well and truly wasted, the more we tried to pull ourself together the worse it got, there was nothing we could do about it but go with the flow.

By six in the morning, we could cry no more and were ravenous with the hunger so three drunken fools were attempting to cook breakfast. Let's just say we made such a mess, never the less we accomplished our goal and somehow managed it without burning the house down, the gods were definitely looking down on us as we were trying to soak up the booze we didn't give a second though to the charcoaled sausages. Suddenly Elizabeth dropped her food and nearly fell around laughing, 'Well, well she said behind every cloud there is a rainbow do you know what this means ladies? We looked at her as if she was completely crazy. How could any of this be good?

'No, listen,

'Ok, where is the rainbow then'

'Don't you get it. We both shook our heads and regretted it immediately as it was like fireworks going off in our heads.

'You're one of us now Molly, you're part of our family for real, I always knew you were special and we already felt like you're part of the family this is just the icing on the cake. I'm your Aunt. Now you can call me Aunty I've always

Why Me?

wanted to be an aunt and now I am, what a strange twist of fate. We laughed so much or as much as our heads would allow us, maybe we were always destined to find each other and I for one I am glad we did, we all were. We said a prayer for my mum, Tina and Ruth that the angels would wrap them in their arms to heal their wounds and bring them peace. It helped me just to know that they were together again looking down at us giving us their blessing. There had been far too much heartbreak it was all so sad, it must have been a nightmare for my mother carrying this horrific information around with her, it's a shame that she didn't speak to someone it could have helped her no end. None of these wonderful ladies should have had carried this burden in silence, just imagine the women they could have been if none of this had happened. We quickly agreed that we should all take the day off work to help our heads return to normal, we would have been useless to everyone, or as my Dad would say we would be as helpful as an astray on a bike. We decided that we should show the diaries to the rest of the family when we were all together for Christmas as it will be a lot to take on aboard. Stuart joined us as soon as he got back from Galway, equipped with more wine and food. We vegged out on the couch for the rest of the day eating crap and watching old movies, there was no hope that we were capable of doing anything even remotely productive. Thankfully Stuart took over cooking duties and kept us well fed and hydrated. We promised each other that there would be no more secrets as to many lives had been ruined by them.

Over the next few days Elizabeth started to wonder about

Why Me?

her father, she knew nothing about him or had met any family from his side. She had never realised how odd that was in a town where everybody nearly knew what you had for breakfast. Somebody would always know something or be talking about whoever. Maybe it was time to find out a little more about him she thought to herself, but did she really want to know what might crawl out from under the woodwork. Was she ready for it!

The End

Printed in Great Britain
by Amazon